The Fairytale Keeper

Andrea Cefalo

Library of Congress Cataloging-in-Publication Data Cefalo,Andrea

Scarlet Primrose Press/Andrea Cefalo

Summary: Adelaide's mother, Katrina, was the finest storyteller in all
of Airsbach, a borough in the great city of Cologne, but she left one
story untold, that of her daughter, that of Snow White. Snow White
was a pet name Adelaide's mother had given her. It was a name
Adelaide hated, until now. Now, she would give anything to hear
her mother say it once more.

A rampant fever claimed Adelaide's mother just like a thousand
others in Cologne where the people die without last rites and the
dead are dumped in a vast pit outside the city walls. In an effort to
save Katrina's soul, Adelaide's father obtains a secret funeral for his
wife by bribing the parish priest, Father Soren.

Soren commits an unforgivable atrocity, pushing Adelaide toward
vengeance. When Adelaide realizes that the corruption in Cologne
reaches far beyond Soren, the cost of settling scores quickly escalates.
Avenging the mother she lost may cost Adelaide everything she has
left: her father, her friends, her first love, and maybe even her life.

LCCN: 2012932754

ISBN: 0985167815
ISBN-13: 978-0985167813

Praise for The Fairytale Keeper

"A…resonant tale set late in the 13th century… with unexpected plot twists. An engaging story of revenge and redemption… An opener to a future series." - *Publisher's Weekly*

"Really great story. The author's style reminds me of many great historical fiction pieces that I've read. Strong emotion injected into almost every page." -*The Vine Review*

"…a unique twist on the Grimm's Fairy Tales. Part fairy tale retelling, part historical fiction…. The Fairy Tale Keeper is a story of corruption, devotion, and tough decisions." -*Copperfield Review*

Awards for The Fairytale Keeper

- Quarter-finalist in Amazon's 2013 Breakthrough Novel Contest

- Indie Book of the Day

- Finalist in Writing.com's "Hook Us" Competition

Reader Reviews

"The story that Cefalo weaves is intriguing and leaves you hanging on, wanting more." -*Hooked to Books Book Review Blog*

"…it doesn't feel like any retelling. Because it's not. *The Fairytale Keeper* is its own unique story…very entertaining, containing a strong female role, a sweet romance, and much more." -*Lulu The Bookworm Book Review Blog*

DEDICATION

To Ken

CONTENTS

Winter 1245

Fat snowflakes fall lazily to the ground. The streets of Cologne are dusted like sugared gingerbread. The row houses look like the newest gingerbread church confections I had just seen weeks ago at the Christmas market. I open the shutters. An icy wind blows through the window, through the thin wool of my tattered nightshift, through my fair skin, deep to the bone. I shiver violently and dive quickly under the blanket.

"Are you mad Adelaide?" Mother asks with a shiver. "Close the shutters or you'll catch cold."

"But Mama, look. It's snowing."

"Is it, now?" She smiles warmly. "First snow of the year."

I move over quickly. Mother sets down the candle by my bedside and slides in next to me. I press my frigid toes against her warm legs. We smile at each other and reach our palms out the window, side by side. Flakes fall and melt quickly against the heat of our palms. I look at her ruddy skin, wondering how mine is dreadfully fair. I pull my hand back into the room.

"You have such pretty skin, my little Snow White," Mama says, reassuringly, as she closes the shutters for the night. I recoil from the name I used to love. The cruel urchins of the market overheard Mother call me this once. Now they tease me for my pale skin and dark hair by shouting, "Snow White!" as they throw rocks or rotten fruit at me.

I slip deeper into the covers and rest my head on her soft lap. She runs her fingers through the tangles of my black hair though she never pulls. My limbs unhinge as I sink closer to a deep childlike sleep.

"Tell me my story. Tell me Snow White." I say, slipping deeper into the blankets, shifting until I am most comfortable.

"You always hate it when I tell your story, Adelaide." She sighs as her finger is caught on a tangle which she abandons for a neater section of my hair.

"That's because you haven't added to it since I was born. I am thirteen winters now. Surely there is more to tell." I say with a yawn.

"A baby in my eyes still." She coos, and I roll my eyes. "How can I know the story of your life when your life has barely begun?"

I huff in protest.

"I cannot write your story, Snow White. Only you can write your story."

"Then, tell me another story." I resign.

Two years later...

11 March, 1247, Afternoon

Once upon a time in the middle of winter, when the flakes of snow were falling like feathers from the sky, a queen sat at a window sewing, and the frame of the window was made of black ebony. And whilst she was sewing and looking out of the window at the snow, she pricked her finger with the needle, and three drops of blood fell upon the snow. And the red looked pretty upon the white snow, and she thought to herself, would that I had a child as white as snow, with lips as red as blood, and hair as black as the wood of the window frame.

…she had a little daughter, whose skin was as white as snow with lips as red as blood, and her hair was as black as ebony, and she was therefore called little Snow White. And fifteen winters after the child was born, the queen died.

-Snow White

1

۵۵و

I place my hand on the nose of the brown workhorse as Father and Johan remove her dead body from its carriage. He shakes his head and snorts, the steam of his breath floating into the cold March fog.

I am not supposed to be motherless. That happens to other children. Yet here I am, watching Mama being placed on a pyre. My legs shake as I approach her for the last time. I haven't slept in days.

A loosely-knit ivory shroud is tightly wound around her lifeless skin. Her once pink lips are violet and flattened. Mama is dead, I think. Seeing her again makes it all dreadfully real, and the grief robs me of breath.

I brush my fingers along the waves of her clay-colored hair and trace her high cheek bones, resting them on her cold, hard hands folded gently across the waist of the cream-colored tunic she was wearing when she died.

The bouquet of wild flowers I had plucked for the funeral is now wilting in my iron grip, and the leaves have browned. She is too good for wilted flowers, I think, and toss the bouquet to the ground. I return to Father's side where he stands with Mama's cousin, Galadriel.

The dead flowers begin to roll away with an icy gust of wind, but Father kneels quickly to collect them. He pushes them against my stomach and muffles a cough. Men do not cry in Cologne, at least not outside the walls of their homes, so he stares straight ahead stoically with his jaw tightly clenched.

Father Soren moves hurriedly through the funeral rites. His face twists with disgust and I imagine he fears contracting the great fever that has killed so many in Cologne. His callous eyes stare through us, devoid of compassion.

He speaks faster as the heavy clouds darken and the roar of thunder builds. I despise him and his church. In this, I know I am not alone. These vile men hide in their churches as the people of Cologne succumb to the fever without last rites. They are the ones who order the bodies of our family and friends to be dumped like refuse into an enormous pit far outside the city walls.

Yesterday, Father sent friends to find a priest who could serve Mama her last rites. St. Severin, St. Kunibert, St. Gereon... even the cathedral's priests refused us and stated that, as it was Sunday, they were busy preparing for Mass, but I know better. No priest would come to our home for fear of catching the fever. I pray Saint Peter shall pardon this missing sacrament and grant Mama entry to Heaven.

I hope these men all perish without their last rites. I hope they are placed on that horrid cart destined for the pit outside the city, their crooked bodies hanging from the edge of the cart with the poorest and most decayed victims, mouths agape, surrounded by flies.

Father says we are lucky to have a funeral at all. We are lucky that 1247 has been a fruitful year for us. We are lucky to live in a city where a cobbler can earn enough to bribe a priest into giving a funeral service. We are lucky Father comes from a long line of cobblers, and that the wealthiest families of Cologne purchase his shoes. We are lucky the fever hasn't stopped pilgrims from coming to Cologne and buying from our booth in the market.

But I do not feel lucky today.

Father Soren quickly bows his head in silence. Then, with a snap of his chubby fingers, he summons his dark-haired associate, Johan, to light the pyre. The straw below Mama ignites and flames lap at her like the devil's tongue. An anxious twitch possesses my leg. She cannot be dead, I think. She would never leave me.

I run to the pyre and pet her hair, but she does not wake. I kiss her cold hard face and beg her to rise, but she does not hear. I beg louder, choking on sobs.

Father Soren gasps with disgust.

"Stupid urchin!" He hisses. "She's infected herself now!" He backs farther from the smoking pyre and points a shaking finger toward me. "She'll give us all the fever."

I shake Mother's shoulders and cry for her to wake. My flowers fall and are swallowed by the growing flames as unbridled sobs burst from my throat. I embrace her body tightly, knowing now she shall not rise.

Smoke stings my lungs and fire smarts my skin like hundreds of tiny whips, but the burns are nothing compared to the wicked pains of grief that wring my stomach like a wet rag, that smite the breath from my lungs, and put a hardened lump at the back of my throat.

Father pries my arms loose and pulls me backward. I fall to the ground coughing. A rim of ambers glows along the hems of my chainse and surcote which I smother in the cold, soggy ground.

"Take your coins and go, coward," Father spits as he pitches a small bag to the ground by the growing flames in disgust.

Johan retrieves the bag before it catches fire.

"I should have had your wench placed on the cart and disposed of properly, Schumacher," the priest declares. He stares straight into Father's eyes and spits on Mama's corpse.

Father's eyes narrow, and his face flashes a violent scarlet as he charges Soren. Soren's buggy eyes widen with fright and shock, as he runs to the opposite side of the pyre. He shifts left and then right, trying to anticipate how Father might come for him. Johan stands with crossed arms at the head of the pyre.

"You wouldn't hit a priest, would you, Schumacher? It's a hanging offense." Soren warns, swallowing hard.

Father unsheathes his dagger. "I don't plan on hitting you."

Galadriel gasps. "No, Ansel, don't do this! Katrina wouldn't want you to hang."

Galadriel is right. Mama would not want this, but Father's rages rarely wane with reason. I have no doubt that he could kill the priest. He has a lean strength that increases three-fold when he's angered. I've seen him beat a thief nearly twice his girth in the market. It took nearly a half-dozen men to pull him off, but Johan is a Goliath with a broad sword at his hip.

"Johan!" Soren cries. "Will you not protect me?"

Johan bounces the bag of coins in his hand. "That depends on what your life is worth to you, Priest."

"Traitorous oaf! Our deal was already struck."

Father rounds the pyre, and Soren rushes behind Johan who smiles at his good fortune.

"You can have half the purse!" Soren squeals.

"If I let the shoemaker kill you, he'll let me keep them all." Johan observes.

"Done. The purse is yours."

"The purse is already mine, as I see it. What else can you offer?"

"A guilder."

"Two." Johan counters.

"Fine," Soren hisses. "Two guilders!"

"As I see it, Schumacher, the priest has paid a fine of two guilders for his wrongs and receives no pay for the funeral." Johan reasons.

"Ansel, please," Galadriel pleads once more. She approaches him slowly like he is a wild animal. She reaches for his sleeve, and her eyes widen as she attempts to calm Father with her striking gaze, but he looks past her to Soren.

A long moment passes, and I feel torn between siding with Galadriel and urging Father on. The rogue spat on my mother and deserves to be punished. I should like to see Father give him a thrashing he shan't soon forget. Father sighs and sheaths his dagger.

"Ready the carriage, Johan," Soren orders, turning away.

My hand rests on a cobblestone, and revenge tempts me. I pick it up, rise, and pitch the stone, aiming for the back of Soren's bald head. He yelps as it strikes his shoulder. He turns and narrows his eyes at me.

"You little witch!" He hisses, rubbing the injury.

He approaches the pyre and kicks a log from beneath it. The structure collapses. Mother's burning remains tumble to the ground. Soren races to the carriage and jumps aboard. Johan whips the horses, and they charge toward the city walls. Father races after them in vain.

I drop to my knees, wailing in anguish. I cry as the dark, moaning clouds pour down upon us, rain sizzling in the flames. Mama's charred remains extinguish under the cold deluge.

Father runs to me and falls to his knees. He turns me away from the defiled corpse. "Do not look," his voice cracks, and he embraces me tightly. He cries violently, angrily, as I sob into his shoulder. I had never heard my father cry like that before, and I hope I never have to hear it again.

∽ର≀ଛ

Father stands, and pulls me with him. He urges me forward, forcing my gaze on the long road ahead of us back to the city. "Night approaches."

6

"We cannot leave her here like this," I cry in protest, but Father does not reply and continues to push me forward. I know now he shall return to bury her.

"I hope you do not intend to do this alone." I say quietly. "There are wolves and thieves outside the gates at night." He does not answer. I fight the urge to beg him to reconsider, for I know my protests shall fall on deaf ears.

My crying ebbs and flows from violent bawling to whimpers. I cannot fathom ever being happy again after this day. The tears still pool and flow down my face which is raw from the water, the wind, and whips from the long black strands of my hair that cannot be tamed in this weather. My throat grows painful and tired and my cries slowly abate. My anguish is locked away, and I feel nothing, not even the sting of the cold March rain.

The sky slowly darkens from grey to black as we approach Severin's gate, which, like all the gates, is closed every night. Father knocks on the heavy wood. The window slides open and a one-eyed, old man appears from behind it. "State yer business," he says matter-of-factly. His long, wet, silver hair blows out from the window.

"Gregor, it's us," Father says.

"Ansel?" The man squints with his one good eye.

"Yes."

"I'm sorry about yer missus," Gregor says gently. He continues with his condolences as he jumps from his stand. I wonder if he knows we can no longer hear him. The chains crank as the massive gate rises, revealing Gregor, a sweet old man barely as tall as my shoulder.

He and my grandfather, whom I never met, were childhood friends. Plagued with rheumatism, Gregor was forced to give up masonry long ago. He now mans the gate for little pay. When Father noticed Gregor's toes poking out from beneath his shoes a fortnight ago, he made him a new pair without charge.

"Do the shoes fit well?" Father asks, looking down at his work. Gregor does not answer, but looks past Father to Galadriel, staring at her with a nearly religious captivation. It is the way men have stared at her since she arrived, as though they would either like to eat her whole or revere her for an eternity.

Even in her soaked, drab, grey tunic and cloak, Galadriel is beautiful. Her blonde hair shimmers even on a stormy day like this. She has skin as fair and clear as fresh cream. Her light blue eyes are wide, and I can imagine jongleurs composing songs in her name.

"Gregor? Are you all right?" I ask to snap him from his awkward stare.

"Oh, yes!" Gregor finally answers. "Oh! My feet are as warm an' dry as the Holy Land itself, Ansel!" Gregor's pointed nose passes his lips, bobbing up and down when he talks. He parades his footwear, and then looks up at Father with concern. "I'm really sorry 'bout Katrina, Ansel. She was a queen among women."

"She shall be missed," Father sighs, casting his gaze downward again. "Is there a carriage that can take them back? I would not want them to walk alone in the rain."

"Oh, yes. Of course, Ansel. Ivan! Get one of the carriages over 'ere and take these girls back to the cobbler's!" Gregor shouts at a tall, young, blonde man whose pale skin makes me look Arabian. "Shouldn't ya accompany the ladies back 'ome, Ansel? 'Tis a cold night ta be out."

"No, Gregor. I have business to attend to."

"Anythin' I can be a 'elp with?" Gregor asks with deep sincerity.

"Have you got any shovels?"

"Course, but what would ya be needing 'em for?"

"Our funeral did not go as planned. I need a pick, as well." Father coughs to cover the crack in his voice.

Ivan ambles over, pulling the horses and carriage behind him. He straightens at the sight of Galadriel and stares for several moments, though she does not seem to notice.

"It's not safe ta be outside 'a the gates after dark, Ansel. Oh, a drunkard was cut through outside the Weier gate on 'is way 'ome last week," Gregor says.

Father opens his mouth to argue, but Gregor continues, shrugging his shoulders. "But if it's a shovel and a pick ya want, we 'ave 'alf a dozen back in the stables. I could send Ivan with ya if ya like."

Ivan appears angered and shakes his head slowly and sternly. It is difficult to believe anyone of his impressive stature would be afraid of anything. He is taller than my father by a head.

"Thank you for getting them home and for the shovel."

"I wish I could do more. Are ya sure you shan't accept any 'elp?" Gregor asks.

"Yes," Father sighs as he walks toward the stables to get the shovel and pick.

Ivan opens the carriage door, but I am planted where I stand.

"I shall see you both soon." Father says.

My heart pounds and the air thins. If I go home without Father, I might never see him again. I cannot lose him, too. Not now. I imagine him being overcome by a large band of thieves or a pack of ravenous wolves. I must make him stay, even at the risk of scavengers getting to Mother before she can be buried.

"Go on, Adelaide," Father sighs, running his hands through his black hair. I shake my head, and he raises an eyebrow in warning.

I barrel into him and squeeze him hard. "Please, do not go," I cry into his wet cloak. "We can all go in the morning," I plead, looking into his pewter eyes.

"Get in the carriage, Adelaide," he replies somberly and pushes me backward. "I have fought much worse than vagabonds and wolves alone and survived."

Gregor hobbles to the stables and returns with a crossbow. Father straps it to his arm.

Father turns toward the gate, and I dive to the ground, squeezing his legs in an effort to keep him there. "Don't go!" I cry.

"Adelaide! That is enough!" he scolds and shakes me from his leg. "Get in the carriage!"

Father has made his choice, and there is nothing I can do to change it. I rise and stare at his face for a moment, trying to memorize it in case he never returns. I hug him tightly, sobbing again.

"I love you, Papa," I whimper into his cloak.

"And I love you," he whispers so quietly no one could possibly hear.

I look at his face once more, turn, and step into the carriage. He stands and watches as we ride away down Severin's Strasse. I do not even bother to keep my composure in front of Galadriel, giving in to tears and sobs, which, I fear, shall never end. I can feel her piteous stares. I am anguished with memories stirred by the places we pass on our way home and terribly worried for Father's safety.

11 March, 1247, Night

A rich man's wife became sick, and when she felt that her end was drawing near, she called her only daughter near to her bedside and said, "Dear child, remain pious and good, and then our dear God will always protect you." With this, she closed her eyes and died....

The girl went out to her mother's grave every day and wept, and she remained pious and good. When winter came, the snow spread a white cloth over the grave, and when the spring sun had removed it again, the man took himself another wife.

This wife brought two daughters into the house with her. They were beautiful, with fair faces, but had evil and dark hearts. Time soon grew very bad for the poor stepchild....

Now it happened that the King proclaimed a festival .... All the beautiful young girls in the land were invited, so that his son could select a bride for himself. When the two stepsisters heard that they too had been invited, they were in high spirits.

They called Cinderella saying, "We are going to the festival at the King's castle."

Cinderella, too, would have liked to go to the dance with them. She begged her stepmother to allow her to go.

"You, Cinderella?" she said. "You, all covered with dust and dirt, and you want to go to the festival? You have neither clothes nor shoes, and yet you want to dance...! It's no use. You are not coming with us...."

-Cinderella

৵৹৫

I stack the kindling and light the long extinguished fire. Little things cruelly remind me Mama is dead. I remember the way she stacked wood. Her eating knife sits alone on the mantle beside the lavender she loved to collect and dry. I pick up a bunch and smell it. It smells like her. Anguish settles like lead in my stomach and I feel I may start crying again, but I am too weary and my head throbs from all the crying I've done already. I put the lavender back and sit at the table across from Galadriel, looking away from the hearth and its painful reminders.

"Will I ever be happy again?" I ask hoarsely, barely breaking Galadriel's deep gaze into the fire.

"Yes," she says distractedly.

"It doesn't feel possible."

"It gets... 'better' is not the word for it," she rolls her eyes as they glimmer with tears. "It gets easier. I felt the same when my mother died, but I can remember her fondly now. I cannot do that yet with Ulrich and Lars." She sighs hopelessly and forces a smile.

"Oh." I feel guilty for bringing up the death of her infant son and husband who had died four months ago from fever. The thought of feeling this way for four months is not comforting. "Allow yourself to be sad, and when you cannot bear it a moment longer, find a way, any way, to occupy your thoughts. That helps," she says with a thick voice, nodding her head and folding her lips in as she avoids my gaze. "You shall forget for a while, almost too well sometimes. Every now and then, something reminds me of them, and I think I shall turn around to see them standing there. Then, I remember they are..." *Gone.* She swallows hard and tears roll down her cheeks. She takes in a deep breath and sighs.

"We don't have to speak of this."

She nods, her brow knit and eyes glassy with tears. She chokes back a sob, then, composes herself with a deep breath. She straightens and flicks tears from each cheek.

I think of Father. Is he burying her now, I wonder? Are there thieves watching him, waiting to strike him dead for his boots and cloak? Are wolves stalking him from beneath the hill? Is he fighting them off with a pick in one hand and a shovel in the other? I could have helped him. What if he is dying right now, all alone? I should have found a way to go with him. I could have gotten out of the carriage and run for Pantaleon's gate. The man at that gate does not know me. He would have let me out. Thoughts race through my mind, and I grip my temples in a vain attempt to silence my thoughts. But I cannot.

13

My thoughts only linger on Father for a moment. So many horrible images occupy my mind. I sit across from Galadriel, but I am not there at all. My thoughts travel to the past, to two nights ago. I am in my parents' bedroom, watching my mother fight for life.

Her purple lips gasped for breath. I knelt at her side, praying all night for God to save her. If I had only prayed harder, if only I had sinned less, surely He would have answered my prayers.

Father lost hope before I did. I thought she was too strong to die, too stubborn, but the fever claimed almost everyone it touched. Father knew this. I knew it too, but I thought Mama was different. I refused to believe it would kill her.

My heart broke each time I thought she was gone, but she came back to us dozens of times, fighting for breath. Eventually, I stopped praying for her to live, but prayed instead for God to end her suffering. Yet we continued to relive her death over and over throughout the night as friends tried to find a priest for her last rites. But no one would come.

Finally, Father whispered a few words into her ear. I do not know what he said, but he kissed her hands and cheeks, and she let herself die.

∾◉ℰ

I try to distract myself. Keep occupied, Galadriel says. I watch the flames grow and fall, from blinding white to an orange flicker. It sparks memories of the funeral pyre, but I shall not let that hurt me now. I try to relive Mama's funeral in my mind in a hundred different ways, somehow changing its tragic end.

∾◉ℰ

I stare down at Mama's shrouded body, my eyes cloudy with tears. I think I see something, but I know it cannot be so. She is dead. I watched her die, but did I see her left hand twitch? I shake my head in denial, yet hope it to be true. I wipe the tears from my eyes. I stare, possessed with hope, fixated on her hand, hoping to see another twitch so I can stop the funeral.

The priest quickly finishes his service and silence lingers. Time slows as Father Soren orders Johan to light the fire, pointing his chubby fingers at the stacks of wood and straw. My eyes widen with desperation and my legs shake.

"Move!" my thoughts beg, yearning for Mama to stir again. "Move!"

Still, she does not stir. Johan drops his torch to ignite the fire and my head throbs with indecision. Perhaps she hadn't moved at all, I think. Perhaps I have gone mad? The flames begin to grow. The tallest peaks lap at the bottom of the funeral pyre.

Her finger pulses again. I run and press my face against hers. I grab her cheeks and shake.

"Please! Wake up!" I shout, but she does not respond. Father runs for me. I turn around, guarding her. "Her finger moved! She is not dead!" I shout.

Father's feet anchor into the ground for a moment. His face displays a range of emotions. He shakes them from his head and runs for me again, ready to pull me from the pyre. As his arms wrap around me, ready to take me away... she moans.

His eyes widen, and he pushes me from the fire. He scoops her up and sets her gently on the ground. Everyone gathers around in awe, and Father Soren crosses himself. Father pulls a large knife from its holster, delicately slicing through the shroud. She moans again.

"Katrina!" Father gasps and hugs her limp, but alive, body to his chest. He rubs his face gently against hers and roughly kisses her cheeks and forehead. He quickly stands with her cradled in his arms—

A loud pop from the hearth fire snaps me out of my daydream.

Galadriel puts her head in her hands and cries. I rise and grab two mugs, filling them with ale.

She sighs as I set the mug before her.

"Thank you," she says between cries. "We usually only have wine at home. I have missed ale."

We drink in an uncomfortable silence.

"Did your mother ever tell you how Ulrich and I met?" Galadriel offers with a sniffle.

I sip the ale slowly to consider my answer. It irritates me that she brings up her dead husband again. It makes me wonder why she has come to my mother's, her cousin's, funeral if all she cares to think about is her own dead family. But perhaps a story will distract me.

"No. Mama never told me that story."

"Oh." She smiles and looks up.

"Ulrich was the third son of the Duke and Duchess of Lorraine. He was supposed to be a bishop or abbot or a cardinal."

I nearly choke on my ale. If Galadriel's husband was the son of a duke, that meant he was a nobleman, which makes Galadriel a noblewoman.

"So what does that make you?" I ask bluntly.

She knits her brow in confusion.

"Your husband…he was a duke or lord." I prompt.

"Ulrich was the Count of Bitsch." She replies.

"So that makes you—"

"Oh, a countess," she interrupts.

"Is this a jest?" I ask.

"No."

"Are you of noble birth?"

"No."

"I thought noblemen only married noblewomen."

She sighs in annoyance. "I assure you the tale is true. Do you want to hear it or not?"

I nod.

"Ulrich's siblings were taught by tutors at the castle until they were old enough to be sent to other courts. But not Ulrich. He had to be sent away." She lifts the mug to her mouth again and gulps heartily.

"Why?"

"Because his mother spoiled him terribly. He grew so wicked that people called him Ulrich the Devil, so the Duke sent him away to a monastery. The Duchess did not like that very well. I heard she had awful fits. The Dower Duchess of Lorraine is quite spoiled herself," Galadriel confesses, the corners of her eyes starting to relax from the drink.

"Will you pour me another mug, Adelaide? Mine is empty already." I fill her cup. "Where was I? I have lost myself," she says with a slight slur.

"You were telling me about—"

"I remember now," she interrupts. "Ulrich grew up at the monastery, but he never wanted to join the Church. When he was grown, he wrote the Duchess and begged to come home, so she sent for him in secret. The Duke was furious with her. They had no title for him, no land, no wife."

Galadriel takes a sip of her ale.

"The Duke was at war with his brother and hadn't a title to give to Ulrich. So they made up a title for him, the Count of Bitsch, hoping it would attract a maid whose father had a lot of coin or a big army.

But no one wanted to go to war just so their daughter could marry a third son with a made-up title," she pauses briefly.

"So the Duchess decided to hold a festival in Ulrich's honor so he could choose his bride. She invited every eligible maiden from Lorraine, but the girls could only attend if their fathers paid five guilders apiece to help pay for the war. I still have our family's invitation. It was pouring rain when it was delivered. I was sitting by the mantle, picking peas from the fireplace..."

"Picking peas from the fireplace?" I ask.

Galadriel nods.

"Why would you pick peas from the fireplace?"

Galadriel looks down. "When my mother died, my father remarried. He was a merchant and gone most of the year. My stepmother Gisla hated me and made me a slave in my own home. I do not know why she treated me so badly, for I never gave her reason.

"But my mother had always told me that if I was a good and pious girl, the Lord would provide for me. So I tended to Gisla's daughters and did the same household chores as our servants. Still, Gisla would throw my supper of peas into the soot of the fire. I would have to pick them from the ashes or go hungry."

"That is horrible!" I cry.

Galadriel shrugs, takes another gulp of ale, and continues. "I was sitting by the hearth when I heard the knock on the door. It was a dwarf. I had never seen a dwarf before, you know.

"He had the deepest voice and demanded to speak to the man of the house, but Father was off on his travels, as usual, so I called for Gisla. I watched as the half-man reached into a satchel on his back and pulled out a rolled piece of parchment tied with a little gold ribbon. He read the invitation then handed it to Gisla.

"The girls in the village had two months to ready themselves, and it was all anyone spoke of. The richest families raced to the tailor's, but our father traded in fine fabrics. Gisla had a letter sent so that he would bring Ebba and Dorthe, my stepsisters, beautiful dresses and jewels from his travels. Gisla told him not to get me a dress, saying I was an insolent girl and not ready for marriage even though I was nineteen, practically a spinster.

"I begged Gisla to let me go to the festival, but she just laughed at me. I'll never forget what she said. She told me that there was not enough water in the Rhine to wash the cinder soot from my face, and that it was better I did not go, for everyone would laugh at me. Still, I asked her every day until, one day, she agreed.

"She scraped several days of uneaten peas into the soot of the fireplace and told me that if I could fetch every last pea from the soot by morning, then I could go.

"I stayed up late into the night picking peas from the soot, but each time I thought I had gotten the last pea, I found another and then another. I don't remember falling asleep, but I must have for I remember waking the next morning to a rustling in the room. Three pigeons were foraging in the soot. At first I thought to chase them away, but then I noticed they were eating the peas. When the pigeons finished, I dug through the ashes looking for peas, but there were none left. The pigeons flew away, and I ran to follow them, wondering where they'd come from. I followed them through the city, past Saint Lucie's, all the way to hallowed ground where each pigeon landed on the tree just above my mother's grave."

"Really?" I ask in disbelief and she nods.

"I went back home just as the bells tolled six and waited for Gisla to awaken. When they came to break their fast, I begged them to check the hearth. Gisla searched and searched, but did not find a single pea. She was very angry, and Ebba and Dorthe just laughed at how foolish I would look going to the festival in my sooty chainse and surcote.

"That night, two days before the festival, Gisla came to me again. She told me I could wear one of my nice dresses, which she had taken from me, if I could pick all of the peas out of the ashes again. I was so very tired. I remember lying on the cold, hard ground by the hearth with a candle in hand, picking through the ashes while I fought to keep my eyes open.

"The church bells awoke me in the morning. There was a pigeon sitting on the window sill, but the hearth was filled with peas. I wanted to cry, but as my stepmother and sisters were still sleeping, I raced to pick out the rest. But they woke soon after and caught me digging through the ashes, delighted that I had failed.

"I ran from the house, crying. Mother had told me if I was pious and good that God would answer my prayers, but she was wrong. I was good, they were wicked, and yet they were the ones who got to go to the festival, not I. I kept thinking how unfair it all was.

"But when I arrived at my mother's grave, two doves were sitting in the tree, and a third landed between them. At first, I felt I'd gone mad or maybe I was dreaming, for hanging from the tree by my mother's grave was the most beautiful silk cotehardie I had ever seen. The sleeves were fitted to the wrist, and the fabric of the tippet cascaded to the bottom of the dress. The elbows and shoulders were trimmed in royal purple velvet and silver embroidery with little pearls. A velvet cloak trimmed in furs hung next to it. Inside the cloak were two pockets. One held a riband necklace with a large amethyst pendant and a pair of earrings. The other held ten guilders!"

I look at Galadriel with doubt, thinking she had had too much ale. "I thought you were going to tell me a true story."

"It is true!" she says. "I swear it on my own soul. It is true."

"Very well," I say, suspiciously.

"I grabbed it all, the dress, the cloak, the coins, and ran to the nearest inn. I paid them for the night. I ate, I bathed, and I plaited my hair so it would be perfectly waved in the morning.

"The next day a caravan of beautiful carriages came to the village to pick up all the girls. I paid the driver my five guilders and he let me into the carriage with the others.

"What did it look like? The castle, I mean," I ask, for, although I have heard jongleurs and minstrels tell of them at the market, I have never seen one with my own eyes.

"It was the most beautiful castle I have ever seen. The stone walls seemed to grow right out of the side of the mountain. Its towers rose higher than the clouds. The walls were tall and lined with tapestries," she said, making swift gestures with her hands to illustrate the height. "Chandeliers, bigger than carriage wheels and lit with dozens of candles, dangled from the ceiling. There were flowers everywhere, and the tables were covered with fruits and meats, breads, cheeses, and tarts.

"The great hall was filled with girls, more than a thousand, I would say. But when the trumpet sounded, the hall grew completely silent. The half-man who delivered the invitations now announced our challenge. We had to discover the Count's real name. The Duke, Duchess, and Count were announced as they walked to a long table at the other end of the hall.

"The girls charged like men on the battlefield, but not me. A good, pious girl gets her prayers answered, Mother had always said, and so I stayed in the back. I laughed with the jongleurs and tried to solve their riddles. I spoke with the cooks, and tried foods I had never tasted.

"Girls would pass by and say how handsome the Count was with his black hair and green eyes. They were disappointed not to have learned his name, but most decided to make merry anyway. The girls flirted with the minstrels and sang to their songs. They danced, and drank, and laughed. I ate the food with glee, happy to eat something besides peas.

"A dark-haired man stepped out from the kitchen carrying a platter of cheeses. He asked me my favorite dish, and I pointed to the elderberry tarts. He shook his head and took me to a silver platter of little stacked cakes. I'd never seen such beautifully decorated cakes, and each was small enough to fit into the palm of my hand." Galadriel draws a circle in her palm with a finger.

"He handed me a little white one with pink roses made of frosting and plum curd in the middle. I took a bite, and we smiled at each other. He had the most beautiful green eyes.

"I looked to the front of the hall and noticed that the Count's chair was empty. My mouth was full of cake when I realized who this man really was. I swallowed hard, but as I stepped forward to confront him, my foot slipped on spilled wine. I thought I would fall, but he caught me by the arm and pulled me up slowly." Galadriel sips again from her fourth cup of ale, her face speaking greater volumes than her words.

"I was so embarrassed, and he looked at me with such worry, so I did the most brazen thing. I asked his name!" She pauses to take another gulp of ale. I find myself on the edge of the bench, waiting for her to continue.

"And, then, he whispered it in my ear. Ulrich." She sighs. "One of the girls must have noticed and soon a swarm of them headed for us, so he ran off through the kitchen.

"Ulrich returned to his seat, but the festival was nearly over. The trumpet sounded, signaling the end, and all the maidens headed toward the hundred or so carriages that waited to take them back to their villages. I stayed behind until the trumpeter noticed I was the only maiden left in the great hall.

"He called after me harshly and ordered me to leave. Ulrich was walking toward us, and as I was about to say his name, I heard Ebba shout from the stairwell. I turned to see her pushing her way through the crowd, charging toward me.

"I felt the cold stare of a hundred girls upon me as I ran for the staircase on the opposite side of the castle. One of my shoes slipped from my foot, but I left it behind. I quickly found a carriage and returned to Metz, knowing I would have to go back to Gisla."

"Why did you run?" I ask.

"I thought Ebba would embarrass me in front of everyone. I thought she would tell them all that I was just a servant girl who picked her supper from the ashes."

Galadriel is now loose in speech and posture. Her expressions are dramatic, like a child's, as she tells her story. She stumbles as she rises from the table and meanders to the barrel to fill her mug. I wonder if Father shall be angry when he finds she's drunk us dry, but I say nothing. She sits and sips from her mug, the corners of her eyes softening further.

"How did Ulrich find you?" I ask.

"He found me at Gisla's. I had to go back. I hid my cloak and gown beneath the floorboards so Gisla would not take them from me. Ebba and Dorthe swore I was at the festival wearing a beautiful silk gown. Gisla thought the girls had gone mad, but she still punished me for running away.

"Three days later, the half-man came to our door with the shoe that had slipped from my foot, ordering us each to try it on. Gisla demanded a moment to give her daughters a chance to wash their feet.

Ebba, being the eldest, was to be the first to try on the shoe. Gisla knew the shoe would not fit. Even though Ebba had slight feet, her largest toe was long and fat, so Gisla grabbed a knife and ordered her to cut off her toe."

"No!" I gasp.

"She did! Ebba didn't want to do it. I suppose I could have cried out that the shoe was mine and asked the little man to place it on my foot, but I bit my tongue instead so I could watch them suffer like they'd made me suffer.

"Gisla tried to convince her that a toe was worthless, that she'd be rich and noble and have land if she could fit into that shoe, but Ebba cried. And while Ebba's head was in her hands, Gisla raised the knife and chopped off her toe.

"Ebba bit into her knuckle to keep from screaming. Blood squirted straight from the end of her foot, and her face went white. She fell back in a faint, and Dorthe caught her. Gisla wrapped the foot while Dorthe fetched the shoe.

"Dorthe jammed the shoe on Ebba's foot, which must have hurt terribly. She awoke screaming, and Dorthe put a hand over her mouth to silence her.

"Gisla's eyes were as wild as a madwoman's when she saw that the shoe fit. She forced Ebba to stand and told her to walk. Ebba limped, and Gisla slapped her and told her that if she couldn't walk like a lady then she had lost a toe for nothing.

"Ebba walked as best she could, and the half-man was fooled at first. But when he approached her to take back the shoe, she quickly pulled her foot away. Gisla argued that the shoe belonged to Ebba and it was hers to keep, but the half-man said it would be returned to her in time.

"He reached for the shoe again and discovered the trickery, for blood had begun to soak through the shoe. The half-man pulled it from Ebba's foot to reveal a bleeding wound where her toe should have been.

"He was very angry, but Gisla swore it was an old wound that had reopened, and so the half-man said if she was truly the owner of the shoe then she would know the Count's real name. Ebba guessed his name was Roger or Edward, and the half-man ordered Ebba and Gisla to be arrested.

"Gisla, as slippery as a snake, asked the man if it wasn't enough that Ebba had lost a toe due to her undying love for the handsome Count. He conceded and even granted Dorthe her chance to try on the shoe. Gisla took Dorthe to the back to try on the shoe, but her heel was too wide, so Gisla ordered her to slice off the edges of her foot.

"Dorthe refused, but Ebba held Dorthe down and placed a hand over her mouth to muffle the screams. Gisla grabbed the knife and shaved the skin off each side of her foot. Dorthe's eyes widened from the shock of the pain and screamed into Ebba's hand. Tears welled in her eyes. Blood flowed from the wounds, so Gisla wrapped the injury in linen. Gisla placed the shoe on Dorthe's foot and forced her to enter the hall.

"The half-man's eyebrow rose suspiciously. Dorthe stood so he could not take the shoe from her foot, but he asked why her ankle was wrapped in linen. But before Gisla could reply, Dorthe fainted. The shoe fell from her foot, and the wound was revealed.

"I ran toward the shoe and grabbed it. I placed it on my foot and, though I was in rags, I could see recognition wash over the half-man's face. 'The Count of Bitsch's name is Ulrich, and I am the maiden for whom he seeks. My father is a merchant, and I am his true daughter. These women make me a slave in my father's home as he travels and have deceived you with trickery,' I said.

"The half-man snapped his fingers, and two large guards entered the house again. He ordered the arrest of all three women, and asked me to gather my belongings and join him in the carriage. I packed my gown, shoe, cloak, and jewels. This left no doubt in the half-man's mind that he had found Ulrich's true bride.

"Gisla, Ebba, and Dorthe were forced to walk the entire route from Metz to the castle at Nancy. When the Duke heard of their treachery and cruelty, he stripped them of their freedom and made them serfs at another of his castles. He also ordered that Gisla be stripped of a toe and the skin of her heel.

"Ulrich and I were officially betrothed, and the half-man, whose ~~name was Derk, was sent on one last mission: to find my father. Derk~~ was successful and happy to be finished with his travels. Father arrived and when told of my harsh treatment, apologized and begged my forgiveness, which I gave immediately. He did not know of Gisla's callous nature.

"Ulrich and I were married the Tuesday next with my father in attendance. We set off for Bitsch the next day. By winter, I was with child, and, by fall, Lars had arrived. He was a happy child with my fair hair and his father's green eyes. By the next winter, this one past, it was all taken from me. My greatest loves perished." A tear streams down Galadriel's cheek.

"I'm sorry." I say, for I don't know of any words that could console such pain.

She nods and swallows hard.

"Did you ever find out who placed the dress at your mother's grave?"

"I used to think it was my mother's angel watching over me," Galadriel replies. "But where was she when I lost my husband and my baby? Where was God then? What was the reason in giving me that dress so that I could go to the festival; so Ulrich would marry me and give me a son, just to have them die months later?" Galadriel puts her head in her hands and sobs.

12 March, 1247, Early Morning

Galadriel's cries have stopped and she has fallen asleep, but not for long. She jerks her head from the table and glances frightfully around the room. She looks lost until our gazes meet.

"You should go to bed. It's late," she yawns.

"I'm not tired," I lie. "You can have my bed." She waits for my reassurance. "I shall sleep in Father's bed if I tire."

She groggily climbs the ladder to my room, and I am relieved to be alone. My back feels blistered from sitting by the fire for so long, and I move to the other side of the table where Galadriel had sat.

I watch the fire and wonder where Father is and when he shall return. The worry should consume me, but I feel nothing but weariness.

I rest my head on the table, and, just as my eyes close, I hear the tapping of footsteps. I wake with a start and scan the room for Father until I realize the footsteps are coming from above, their soft, slow beat quickly giving them away. It is Galadriel.

She yawns loudly and clumsily descends the ladder.

"Do you always keep insects by your bedside?" An eyebrow arches in disgust at the two fireflies dancing in the glass jar she holds at a distance.

I shrug.

"I shall get you a candle this week," she replies.

"Father has a candle in his room. Shall I fetch it for you?"

"No." She looks down at the jar, wrinkling her forehead. "I sleep best in the dark. I don't suppose you shall need these with a fire like that, but I prefer not to spend the night with them." She sets the jar on the table, turns, and stumbles back to bed.

"Ivo," I sigh, shaking my head and feeling a grin spread across my face. I lift the jar of lazy flies, each one sitting on opposite walls of the jar. I slowly lift the cap and watch as each firefly escapes and flits around the room until they find an exit through the hearth.

I am so sleepy, but tell myself I shall not go to bed, even though my head feels too heavy for my neck to support. My hands make a comfortable resting place. It is not long before my hands shake, weary from the weight of my head. The waves of the fire hypnotize me, and I surrender to the weight of exhaustion. I surrender to dreams.

⚬⊙⚬

Tink. Tink. Tink. Three fireflies smack forcefully against the sides of the jar. I will be late, I think. With jar in hand, I sneak down the ladder, down the steps, and out the door, taking Filzengraben. Tall shadows of row houses lean over me, making the night even darker. The road feels eerily empty until the glow of a night watchman's swaying lantern in the distance catches my eye. He takes Severin's Strasse heading toward the Priest's gate and his light is gone just as quickly as it had come.

I turn left onto Foller Strasse, at the first manor that makes up the vast de Belle's estate. I climb the vines on a low wall and jump into the de Belle fields where Ivo's family farms.

The glow from the jar lights my way through the deserted fields. The crunch of my feet through the stalks stresses the silence of the night. I fly through the small wheat field to the apple trees on the other side, searching for the tallest and most gnarly tree at the end of the meadow where we always meet.

The spark of a hundred fireflies radiates through the mist, and yet I am alone. I pace, frightened, hoping he will appear. The wind blows and macabre shadows dance. A chill crawls up my back, and I close my eyes tightly from fear.

I hide behind the tree and listen for footsteps, only to hear howls and whistles. It is only the wind and the roar of thunder in the distance. It is only the wind, I tell myself. It is only the wind.

SNAP. I stumble and grip the tree.

A breeze rushes violently down my body as something falls from the tree and lands inches from my feet. A frightened cry slips from my lips.

"What took you so long?" he asks, his grin wide, for he knows he has startled me. His voice is an echo.

I turn and shove him, "That's not funny, Ivo" I say angrily, my voice echoing after his.

"What? Did I scare you?" he teases and tosses his white blonde hair from his eyes. "Here, I brought you a jar," he says, but I push the jar away.

"I brought my own," I reply, waving the jar an inch from his face.

"My eyes must betray me. You actually remembered to bring your own jar." He feigns surprise.

The mist rises from the soggy ground as we make our way farther from the manor, deeper into the fields. We banter, jest, and boast as we normally do, but we both know Ivo shall be the victor of our hunt for fireflies. He's always the victor now that his legs and arms have grown so long. He's faster than me. He jumps higher than me.

"Did your parents hear you?" I whisper.

"No. Yours?"

"No," I say with a smirk.

I am normally an obedient daughter, but the thrill of sneaking out is too delicious to ignore. My parents shall sleep through the night and never know, I tell myself. Besides, I am safe here and doing nothing wrong.

"I'm glad you brought your own jar. Now I can fill up two of them," Ivo boasts, his wide lips curve, pinching his cheeks so tiny lines fan from the corners of his eyes.

"Ivo Bauer, you're such a braggart." I hiss and go to shove him. He recoils with a smile. "I think I know why the flies circle about you so," I tease.

"Is it because they are attracted to the smelly girl who's always following me about?" he replies. I roll my eyes and punch him in the arm. He grins and I notice a split in his lower lip. He turns on his heel and bolts toward a swarm of fireflies, laughing.

I follow as quickly as I can, but my feet turn to lead, sinking ankle deep into the sludge. I pull them out one at a time with a thick slurp. My arms flow sluggishly through the mist as though I am fighting my way through swamp water. I leap forward, determined to catch more fireflies than Ivo, yet catching nothing but air. The swarm moves as one, avoiding my clumsy attempts. The hum of their wings grows louder and seems to whisper to me.

You are weak, they say.

Weak…weak…weak, they hum, faster and louder, flying within reach and then circling me.

"I am not weak!" I growl.

They flit in a spiral and spell it out. *WEAK.* I put my hands to my ears and close my eyes until the buzz fades. I peel one eye open and then the other. Far across the muddy field, Ivo leaps into the air, capturing flies with his jar in large gulps. The bright glow from his vessel shines from across the mud-caked meadow.

A single fly escapes his grasp and flits toward me. I jump with all my strength and trap it. I peer into the jar and smirk ruthlessly, but it sneers fearlessly back at me, its teeth long and pointed like daggers.

You'll never save them, it giggles in a high-pitched voice, its large eyes glowing as brightly and eerily as its tail. *You can't even save yourself.* Its jaws open wide and snap down twice. I toss the jar to the ground and leap back. The jar glimmers as the little beast flies innocently.

Suddenly Ivo is at my side. "You've only caught one fly?" he laughs. "Are you giving up already?"

"I just don't feel like it anymore." I peer fearfully into the jar.

He collects the jars and twists the lids open. The flies scatter, flashing through the mist as the thunder grows louder.

I walk toward a tree and rest against it, staring at my empty jar, haunted by the fly's message.

Ivo follows, leaning next to me and I sigh.

"Ah, don't be cross," he laughs and nudges me with his elbow.

"No, that's not it," I say. He stands silently, waiting for me to continue. "Do you think I am weak?"

"When it comes to catching fireflies? Yes, you are terribly weak." He smiles widely. I shake my head and cannot help but smile back.

I nudge him in the ribs. "Be serious! Do you think I am weak?"

He smirks, looks down at the ground, and shuffles his feet a little as he thinks. He sighs and shakes the hair from his face.

"We all have weaknesses..." he says, staring straight forward. His fingertips brush the inside of my hand. "But it's the people, the things that we have weaknesses for that bring us the strength and courage to do what we must." His fingers wrap around my hand and my pulse quickens.

A crack of thunder causes me to jump and the sky dissolves in a heavy downpour, drenching us immediately. I cup my free hand and the rain pools inside it. Rain pours down Ivo's face and drips off his nose. I feel the same happening to my face. We look into each other's eyes and smile.

He drops his jar in the mud and slides his hand beneath the soaked tangles of my hair, gripping the nape of my neck. My heart races as his other hand slides to the small of my back and he pulls me in close. His warmth is a welcome contrast to the damp cold of our clothing. I gasp, and feel the heat of my breath reflect off his face. A warmth rushes to my cheeks, my belly...

We both are weak. I relax in his arms and reach for the sides of his face. For the briefest moment our eyes catch and then close.

A flash of light blinds me through my closed eyes, and a deafening crash shakes the earth. Lightning. I cower beneath him and feel myself scream.

❧

I awaken with a start, knocking over the empty jar. I grab my hot cheeks, still blushing from the dream. But it isn't just a dream. It all happened nine months ago. When there was no fever and Mama was alive.

My stomach tightens as I think upon the kiss that almost happened. I look around. Father is not yet back. It is still dark. The thought of bed crosses my mind, but my heavy head and eyelids convince me to stay where I am. It is the kind of dream I hope to continue. But not just to see Ivo. I want to see Mama again. I rest my head on my arms and sigh as I surrender to slumber.

❧

I hear the gong of church bells and realize it is the ringing of my ears. Ivo's lips move as I scream, but I do not hear him. His hands grip the sides of my face like a vice.

"I can't hear you!" I shout, unable to hear my own voice. I try to pry his hands from my head.

Staring at his lips, I realize he is asking me if I am all right. "I'm fine! Are you all right?" I shout.

His eyes dart across my face and he nods, mouthing the words: *I'm all right.* He releases my face and hugs me so tight I cry out in pain, but neither of us hears it. Our eyes meet again, and a wave of disappointment shadows his face. Our kiss shall not happen, at least not tonight. The ringing in my ears gives good reason not to have an uncomfortable conversation about it.

Lightning, I mouth.

He nods his head in response. His eyebrows rise as a wide grin spreads across his face. He shrugs, shakes his head, and laughs.

The ringing fades, but I still cannot hear. He points to the direction of Foller Strasse, and I nod in reply. In less than a moment, we are standing in the torrential rains a block from my home, the streets still empty.

I hope the lightning strike did not wake my parents. I hope they did not check on me. Perhaps Mama shall, but she is lenient. However, if she fears for my safety, then she shall certainly wake Father. He is not lenient. My stomach churns with fear of his punishment.

A figure stands outside our house, gazing into the distance. She floats in a diaphanous cream-colored chainse and surcote, untouched by the rain. The wind has died down, though her hair and the fabric of her clothes blow around her. By the grace of God, it is Mother who looks for me. I know I must hurry before she wakes Father.

A man runs across Filzengraben from Hay Market. It is Father, drenched and panic-stricken.

I utter a curse. Ivo looks confused so I point in Father's direction. A pang of guilt and fear strike me, for I have worried my parents and caused Father to hunt me down in the middle of the night through a storm. Such is the burden and blessing of being my parents' only surviving child.

Ivo shan't be punished or worried for. His father cares only that he is back by morning, ready to work.

I swallow my guilt like a lump of dry flour. My father has only struck me once in my life, and I deserved it then. I deserve a much harsher punishment for this, and, although half-resigned to it, I am afraid of it as well. At the least, a harsh punishment shall alleviate my guilt and the dry lump that accompanies it. My parents shall believe my lesson learned, which shall allow them a good night's slumber without worry for their insolent daughter.

Ivo slows to a jog and follows me through the rain-soaked street. He walks with me.

"No," I pant between breaths. My words echo again.

"No?" he shrugs.

"You are not walking me home. If Father sees you with me, he may say something to your father. There is no sense in us both being punished." Father will be more severe with me if he knows I was out at night with a boy, even if that boy is Ivo.

"Adelaide!" My mother's cry echoes through the storm. As our eyes meet, I can see her relief. She looks at Ivo and smiles knowingly at him. I run with a throbbing side and legs into her arms. She hugs me tightly, but she is cold, and her arms are as light as the linen of her dress.

"You are covered in mud!" she cries as she frantically looks me over for mortal wounds. "Are you all right?"

"She fell when the lightning struck," Ivo responds before I can. "I asked her to come catch fireflies with me, Frau. It's my fault."

Worry washes over Mother's face as she realizes how close the lightning had struck. She's always been so good at hiding her worry, so seeing it now makes me feel terribly guilty. Tears well in my eyes as I wrap my arms around her neck.

"Please, don't worry and don't be angry with Ivo, Mother. I chose to go. It is my fault, but I shall never do it again! I swear it."

Father rounds the corner of the house.

"You've found her?" His forehead wrinkles in confusion, and he stops in his tracks when he notices Ivo standing behind me. "Did Ivo find her?"

"No—" Ivo starts.

"Don't be so modest, Ivo," Mother quickly interrupts. "Addie told him she planned to catch fireflies tonight. He heard the lightning strike and got worried so he went to look for her."

I am shocked by her ability to lie so quickly. Even so, Father is too wise to fall for it, but loves her enough to allow her such little white lies.

"Thank you for bringing her home, Ivo," he states dryly. Ivo nods, his eyes shamefully turned to the ground. "We should get sleep and so should you. Send your father my regards. If you should be so kind to return my daughter twice, I shall send my regards to him myself," he threatens.

"Yes, Herr," Ivo replies. Father waves his hand to dismiss Ivo who turns and jogs along the street back to his home.

Mother throws a weightless arm around me, looking me over with a grin. "Let's get you inside and scrub that mud away until that pretty skin of yours is looking snow white again. I shall tell you how I prayed for a daughter with skin as white as snow, lips as red as blood, and hair as black as the sill of our windows."

Snow White is a name I do not enjoy. It is a term of endearment from my mother, but a phrase of torment used by the artisan and merchant children who mock me for my fair skin and black hair. I would never tell Mama, for it would hurt her to know, and while I have no love for the name, Snow White, I do have love for the way she speaks it.

ॐ

"Addie?" a soft whisper calls, but I do not recognize the voice.

"Addie? You should go to bed."

Galadriel shakes my shoulder, softly coaxing me out of my dream. I open my eyes reluctantly, but hesitate at my parents' bed, not wanting to sleep in it. But exhaustion and hopes of good dreams lure me, and I slip beneath the blankets on Father's side. I roll over and inhale deeply. The pillow still smells of her. Lavender, wheat, and a crisp breeze. I am careful not to disturb her side. I hope it shall smell like her forever.

I miss her. A tear rolls down my cheek as the numbness fades away and an odd array of emotions radiate through my empty chest; longing, joy, sadness... too many for one night. My face sinks into Father's pillow, which smells of ale and leather. I no longer resign to sleep. I welcome it.

12 March, 1247, Afternoon

I open a squinted eye. I am alone in a dark room in a large bed, cold from sweat. A biting chill blows in through the open window, and I pull the blankets over my head. I want to close the shutters, but I cannot convince myself to leave the warmth of the covers.

My head is pounding. I squeeze my temples, shifting tangles of hair from my face. I am exhausted, but too cold, too in pain, too restless to sleep.

For a moment, I resign to waking. For a moment, my memories of the past few days escape me. I am the girl I was before this horrible fever struck Cologne: a girl whose worst problem was just a bad headache and having to close the shutters though she's shivering. Then I wonder why I am in my parents' bed.

Memories come back in a flash and I sit up. Any peace or confusion I had moments before is gone, and grief twists itself like a drill through my chest.

I fall back onto the bed and roll over to Mama's side. The smell of lavender swims through the air, and agony spreads from the pit of my belly to form a lump in the back of my throat. I cover my head with my arms to escape the smell and the pain it brings. I cry for a few moments and fall asleep.

Worry plagues me, but not enough to wake me fully. I toss and turn, and then I sleep deeply and dream.

ഛ๑୧

Mama stands in front of the hearth cooking porridge and berries for breakfast. It was all a horrid dream, I think, as I reach out to touch her, but my hand passes through her arm to the smoke billowing around the pot.

"Where is your father?" she asks, handing me Father's bowl of porridge. I gasp. She is nothing but steely ashes. Flakes of her skin glide like snowflakes to the floor, revealing bones beneath.

"I...I do not know where he is." I stammer and step away.

"Take this to him." she says coolly and coughs a cloud of black smoke.

I open my mouth to tell her that I do not know where he is. How can I take him his porridge if I do not know where he is? But fear robs me of voice. Mama's cloudy, lifeless eyes look back at me, and she cocks her head as if she wonders why I am looking at her strangely, why I do not follow her orders, why I am frozen and speechless.

I take another step back and she steps toward me. Mama opens her mouth to speak, but stops, distracted by the ashes flaking from her half-skeletal hand. Her eyes widen with fear, with shock, and she coughs roughly. The black smoke billows from her mouth and she chokes. She gasps, and a coughing spell consumes her, flames shoot from her mouth. She falls at my feet and crawls toward me. I am frozen. She grabs my dress and pulls.

Finally I am able to leap back, but the floor vanishes. I am falling from a great height, but just as I am about to hit the ground, I awaken.

ᴄᴏ⒬

I sit up in bed and cry out. I look to Mama's empty groove in the bed next to me and my stomach twists. I'll never run to her when I have a bad dream ever again.

"Adelaide…" moans Galadriel. "Are you all right?" She walks in, gripping the walls. Her usually porcelain skin is sallow.

"I am fine. Has Father returned? Have you seen him?" I ask.

"No." She says, inching closer. Sweat beads across her forehead. "Perhaps he is at the market."

"You are unwell."

"It's nothing to worry about. It's not the fever. I am well enough," she says.

"No, Galadriel, you look…unwell. You should rest."

She sits on the end of the bed and a crisp wind blows across her skin. I can smell the ale in her sweat. I don't want her sitting on Mama's side of the bed, even if she is only on the end.

She pulls a small loaf of bread from a pocket in her dress and sets it on the bed, her nose shriveling up as though the smell of it shall make her retch.

"I thought we had no bread," I say as I fumble with the loaf. If it weren't for my rumbling stomach, I would leave the whole loaf to Father. Food has had no taste since Mama had taken sick. I chew a bite and my mouth fills with the taste of moist, mealy sawdust. We

41

haven't any bread in a week with all that has happened. I should salivate over it, savor it, but it is tasteless.

"Your neighbor, Igor, brought it this morning."

"Igor?"

"A tall, blonde boy," she says, shakily. "He asked after you."

"Oh." She means Ivo, but I do not bother with correcting her.

Galadriel turns forward and stares out the window once more. There is a long silence. I worry Father is not in his shop below, for I hear nothing, so I excuse myself to check for him, finding him absent. I return to my parents' bedroom, disappointed and worried.

"Is he there?" Galadriel asks.

"No."

"Surely he is at the market purchasing leather or selling his wares then," she says with clear doubt.

I chew on my lip as I try to think of a way to leave without her knowledge. I know she'll not let me go to Hay Market, even with the excuse of purchasing food or leather for Father. She would insist on accompanying me, even in her condition, and slow me down.

"Did you sleep well?" I ask half-heartedly.

"Yes... well enough." She struggles to get the words past her lips.

"You don't look like you did," I say, knowing I have been rude. "Perhaps, you should rest some more." If she would just go back to sleep, I could leave and look for Father without her interfering.

She says nothing, sitting silently for a long time. I lean toward the edge of the bed to peak at her face. Her pasty skin has turned a gruesome shade of green. Her eyes squint and lips fold with discomfort. A wiry strand of blonde hair falls into her line of vision and many others poke out of yesterday's perfect plait. But even like this, she is remarkably beautiful.

She starts to rock back and forth and the sweat beads across her pallid forehead. I can see she needs to retch. I feel guilty for what I am about to do. I really do. Mama used to do this to Father all the time, for he had the liquor sweats every Sunday before Mass. It seems mean, but is a cruel kindness in the end, and it shall get rid of her so I can go find Father.

"I wish we had some eggs to cook. Father used to purchase them on Fridays and Mama cooked them Saturday mornings, boiling them in hot water. It's been weeks since I've had them," I say.

"Uh..." A sickly sigh squeezes through her lips. I lean across the bed again. The green in her face deepens, so I continue.

"Mother cooked them too long. I like them soft so you must soak up the yolks with your bread or lick it out of the bowl." Just speaking of egg yolks made Father retch every time.

The ferocious roar of Galadriel's stomach startles me, and I am afraid she might retch all over the bed, but she does not. She doesn't retch at all, so I must think of something more disgusting.

"Father would always grow sick of the eggs though and sometimes he'd want a chicken. There was a man who'd butcher them at the market fresh for us in trade for a pair of turn shoes. Have you ever watched a chicken run around without its head?"

Galadriel's stomach howls. She turns to look at me, but I stare at the ceiling and avoid her gaze.

"It turned my stomach to watch, but it was worse to clean it out. The smell was horrid, like old chamber pots. I couldn't even eat the poor thing after that. But Father never minded, he'd have wrestled me to the ground for the heart, not that I wanted it. He would slurp it right up and squish it between his teeth."

Galadriel gags monstrously. I shield my face with the blankets in case she turns my way to vomit. Thankfully, she jumps to her feet and runs to the window. She retches once out the window and then runs down the stairs and out the door.

I cover my ears so I don't have to hear the splashes and coughs, which make my own stomach turn. Every few moments, I ease my grip to see if she is finished, but it seems she'll vomit for eternity. I feel a little guilty for making her sick, but, from what I know about Galadriel, she would have suffered all day to avoid the embarrassment of what she just did.

The sounds of her vomiting stop, so I rise from the bed. I grab a mug and dip it into the water basin. I walk down the stairs and through Father's shop, carefully checking the floor for anything I might not want to step in. I slowly open the door, but am too afraid to look. I stick my arm out the door, shoving the mug in her direction. I gag over the smell and have to run back inside, placing a piece of leather over my nose.

"I'm sorry you're unwell," I call out the door.

"I should be sorry," she calls back, then swishes the water in her mouth and spits it onto the ground. "I'm supposed to be caring for you."

"You should rest," I say as she enters the room, no longer green, but wickedly pale and dripping with sweat. Several strands of hair dangle from her head now, and I feel for her. Had our roles been switched, I would be mortified, but I need for her to go to sleep so I can leave without her sending someone after me.

"I feel a little better now," she sighs and I give her a doubtful look.

"Do not stay up for my sake. I plan on sleeping until Father returns," I lie.

"Oh."

"Take my bed again," I urge.

"Are you sure?"

I nod.

I watch Galadriel ascend the ladder to my room before I crawl back under the covers of my parents' bed. Hopefully, she falls asleep quickly so I can leave without her noticing. I trace the patterns of the wood ceiling with my eyes, count the slats, and look for hidden images within the grain. But with Galadriel gone, and no other significant distractions available, my mind wanders back to worry.

I wonder how long Father has been gone, and I start to think. The bells had struck eight as our carriage stopped at the house last night. The trip to the hill takes an hour by foot.

I have never dug a grave before and haven't the slightest idea how long it takes. Two hours, I suppose. So that is an hour to walk there, two hours to dig, two hours to bury and pray, then an hour to walk back. Six hours.

So he should have returned by... two this morning! That cannot be right. I count again and arrive at the same time. Oh God, what time is it now? I know it is past seven, for the sun is up. What does it matter what the time is now, I think. I know he is late by six hours at least!

Fear quickens my heart. He could be at the market, I try to convince myself. I envision packs of wolves and bands of thieves again stalking Father through the mist. I see him shivering with blue lips in his drenched clothing, freezing and alone in the cold of night. I curse myself for letting him go. I should have followed him. Why didn't I follow him?

Surely half of an hour has passed since we returned to our beds, and Galadriel is either asleep or close to it.

I dip the ends of a rag into the water basin and quickly scrub my face. I sloppily braid my tangled hair, toss my surcote on over my chainse, grab my cloak and... *DONG!* I jump. The bells toll. I hang my head out of the window and count each ring. Twelve chimes pass, and my heart sinks as I realize Father has been gone for sixteen hours.

I run on my tiptoes into the living quarters and over to the ladder to the loft. I assume Galadriel is asleep for not a sound comes from above. I sneak quietly back to the hearth and scrawl a quick note on the table using the end of a charred stick. I hope Galadriel is able to read.

I am at Hay Market looking for Father. Do not worry. I shall return soon. ~Adelaide

Perhaps, Erik, Ivo's Father, knows where my Father is. If not, two sets of eyes are better than one, so I decide to ask Ivo and perhaps his younger brother Levi to aid me in my search. But would they be home or outside the gates in the fields?

I pull the cloak high over my head and look down as I move quickly through Filzengraben, hoping not to be recognized. It is less crowded than I expect. I suppose most of the villagers are working in the fields, selling their wares at the market, or making purchases there. I turn onto Foller Strasse, which is empty as usual for this time of day, passing a number of row houses as I head toward Ivo's home. Biting my lip, I knock on his door and wait. No one answers so I race past the houses to the stone wall surrounding the DeBelle Manor and climb the thick vines that encompass it like a raven's claw on its prey. With the exception of a few serfs, the DeBelle Manor field is empty. I drop from the wall and sigh. I had hoped to find Ivo quickly, though I knew that was not likely.

The farmers spread manure and plough the fields this time each year, so it is most likely they are far outside the city wall. I take a small alley onto Severin's Strasse. Its narrowness makes the row house seem so much taller than they are, and I hate the feeling of being so closed in, but I'm onto the wide road of Severin's Strasse soon enough. I pass St. Catherine's church and then St. Severin's. I pout as I make my way to Severin's gate, for I know Erik is less likely to let me borrow Ivo for the day if heavy work must be done.

The gate is open, as is usually the case for midmorning, and the daytime guard does not give me a second look for he's flirting with a pretty young woman who looks quite bored with him. Once beyond the gate, I lift my cloak and skirts and run between the fields in search of Ivo or anyone who might know where he is. In my haste, I miss the sight of a cobblestone which catches my toe, and sends me tumbling to the dirt. My left arm breaks my fall and catches on a sharp rock which slices a large gash in my forearm. A child's laughter echoes from nearby. His mother slaps the back of his head and the boy is back to work, but not before a dozen serfs turn their attention to me. My cheeks flush hotly in embarrassment, but their pause gives me time to ask of Ivo's whereabouts. They point south.

I watch the blood drip down my hand with indifference for the wound does not hurt. I wonder if I am overcome with worry or numbness, but it does not matter so I keep running. I see Erik's red hair blazing like a beacon in the sun. Thank God I only had to cross three furlongs to find them. Greta steers a plough as Levi whips the oxen, while Erik steers the other and Ivo whips. I am afraid to request Ivo for the afternoon. Plowing is grueling, and his absence shall make the day even more difficult.

I fold my cloak over my dripping wound and bloodstained hand, and hike through the lumps of dirt and manure. My legs tremble as they adjust to the slower pace. Levi turns, distracted by a butterfly and sees me. He drops the whip and runs toward me, crashing into me so hard I nearly land in the mire. He squeezes me around the waist and squints up into my face for the sun is directly above us. I wrap my uninjured hand around him and try to smile.

"I'm sorry about your Mama, Addie" he says with a pout.

I brush the hair from his dark brown eyes. "Thank you," I say and he hugs me tighter.

"You'll squeeze the life out of me, Levi," I gasp, chiding. He smiles brightly.

"Well I don't want to do that!" he yells. "Look, Father is letting me whip the oxen this year!"

"Really? I can hardly believe how grown you are," I say and he smiles again before racing back to his whip.

Erik drops his plow and heads toward me. Sweat beads across his pink forehead and the large muscles in his arms bulge under his sodden ivory tunic. Empathy has softened the normal severity of his face which, on any other day, would make me too nervous to speak.

Greta follows, her face also sweaty and softened. Dark blonde hairs stick to her forehead. The muck comes halfway up to her knees. Some might bless her for being so short or mistakenly judge her sweet by the looks of her, but they would be wrong. Greta is every bit as tough as Erik.

Ivo walks between his parents, jaw clenched and eyes down. He is sad like me because we are great friends and when one friend suffers so does the other. My numbness flees, tears form, my arm throbs, and I swallow the desire to run to him and cry. Levi runs between them all, whip in hand.

Their faces are down, with the exception of Levi, and no one speaks. The silence makes me uncomfortable and I wonder if I should say something.

"Your mother was a good woman," Greta says. They nod collectively, staring at the ground, hands folded before them. "I shall continue to pray for her soul, but I do not doubt the Lord has called her home and that she sings with the angels."

"Thank you," I reply. They look up.

"How fares your Father?" asks Erik.

"I do not know," I choke and swallow. Two fat tears slip down my cheeks. "I haven't seen him since the funeral. I thought, perhaps...that, perhaps... Have you seen him?" I stammer as I try to hold back sobs.

Erik looks at me, his eyebrow raises in disbelief. He gives Greta a stern look. She and Levi return to her plough without another word. Erik pulls Ivo aside and they whisper for a few moments. Ivo steps back angrily as his father speaks. He shakes his head in disbelief and his hands ball up into fists. His father grabs him by the shoulders and Ivo softens, casting his eyes downward again and nodding his head reluctantly. They turn to look at me, neither of them smiling.

Erik returns to his plough, and Levi stands between his parents, whipping his father's oxen and then his mother's. Ivo walks toward me, and we embrace strongly. He sweeps the hair from my face as I cry into his shoulder, soaking his mustard-colored cyclas. He rubs my back as it rolls with sobs but he does not tell me all will be well or that my mother is in a better place. He says nothing at all.

"Something... horrible... has happened," I utter between sobs.

Ivo growls. His hands ball into fists. "Father Soren... son-of-a-hog-shivver. He certainly looks half-pig. That rogue."

"Ivo!" His vulgarity is so fluent it shocks me despite my own feelings of resentment.

"He defiled your Mother and made you walk a mile in the cold rain. He left you outside the gates at night! A girl was slit from ear-to-ear outside of the Brook gate only weeks ago." The thought of a woman murdered so close to where Father went last night wrings my stomach.

"How do you know all this?"

"One of the dyers. She found her floating in the stream."

"No! How do you know what happened at the funeral?"

"Father just told me."

"How does he know?" I yank him by his cyclas, and he faces me. He gives me a sideways glance and tries to pull away, but I pull him harder.

"Your Father told him last night."

"When? Do you know where he is?"

"I don't know where he is now, but I know he was at the Gilded Gopher last night."

"When? What time?"

"I don't know."

I am so angry I could spit! Father let me worry all night and day for him while he was drinking himself into a stupor at the Gilded Gopher.

The Gilded Gopher, I think angrily, its name is a jest. From what I overheard Mama say of it, it is far from being gilded. It is a filthy pit that serves cheap ale and the company of fallen women. And, though it is a vile place, its members are all carefully selected. All members must agree before inviting a new man in, and only the most trustworthy are allowed. Membership is seen as a privilege.

"We have to ask Erik where the Gilded Gopher is. Father might still be there or maybe someone there knows where he is now." I stress.

Ivo stares at the ground and scrunches his lips to the side, a nervous habit.

"What is it?" I ask.

"I know where the Gilded Gopher is—"

"You do? Let's go." I say and yank him by the sleeve, but he pulls back.

"I can't take you there."

"Ivo, I know the rules, but this is different. I am not an angry wife going to drag her drunkard husband out by his ear. My father is missing! We must find him." I plead.

Ivo huffs. "My Father'll have my hide for this."

"Then take me as far as you can, and you can go fetch him or find out where he is," I say coolly. "Wait…since when do you know where the Gilded Gopher is?" It angers me to think of my Ivo inside the walls of the Gilded Gopher.

"They voted me in a month ago." He says, and we turn to walk toward the city wall.

Severin's gate approaches. I lift the hood of my cloak in an effort to hide my face for I do not want anyone to recognize me and offer their pity. The cloth from my cloak has stuck to the gash, and as I lift my arms it pulls at the wound.

"Are you cold?" Ivo asks, wrapping his arm around my shoulder trying to warm me.

"I am fine." I say, but he rubs up and down against my wounded arm anyway. I want to pull away from him and tell him he cannot just wrap his arm around me like I am some fallen woman at the Gopher, but it feels nice to have him close, so I say nothing. I pray he does not notice the blood that has soaked through the cloak and try to make me go home.

His hand strokes my wound and we flinch simultaneously. Holding his hand up in front of his face, he sees his bloodstained fingers. He grabs my hand, spinning me around to face him and pushes the sleeve of my cloak up to my shoulder roughly to reveal the gash.

"What is this? What happened?" he yells. I rip my hand from his and shove the sleeve back down.

"It looks worse than it is. I fell on my way through the fields."

"It needs to be bandaged."

"After we go to the Gilded Gopher. We can stop at my house, and I shall bandage it there."

He reaches for my arm again, and I pull away. He huffs and shakes his head in annoyance at my stubbornness. We walk the rest of the way in silence. The road is quiet. I had assumed the Gilded Gopher would be closer to Hay Market or on Harlot's Alley, but we near Pantaleon's Parish. The walk gives me pause to think of what I shall say to Father when I finally find him.

I should like to scream at him for letting me worry. Then, I think, what if Father is not there? I feel guilty for wanting to yell at him. I say a quick prayer, and tell the Lord I shall be forever grateful if He returns Father to me.

My legs start to quiver beneath me, and I grab Ivo's shoulder to keep from falling.

"I stumbled," I lie. I am weary from hunger, I convince myself, and we keep walking.

My head swims, and I stumble toward the city wall in case I need to grasp it for support. A small red stream winds its way down my middle finger, trickling slowly to the ground. My wound has reopened. Heat drains from my face as everything spirals. My legs shake violently, and I reach for the wall, sliding down it to the ground.

I hear my name, and I see a face. Ivo. My cheek stings as he slaps me.

"Addie! Wake up, Addie! Oh, thank God," he shouts and then huffs. "You are worse than the oxen. You know that?" he scolds.

"What are you doing? Stop hitting me," I mumble in a trance. My eyelids bounce heavily, and I desperately fight the urge to sleep. Ivo rips the strings that tie my cloak and throws it aside. He stands and rips off his cyclas, standing before me in only his tunic which is slightly translucent with the sun behind him and riddled with holes. I notice a large golden bruise through a hole in his sleeve and another on his stomach which I can see through the tunic. He kneels and pulls a knife from his boot. He cuts away at the bottom of his tunic.

"I must tie this around your wound, Addie. It has to be tight to stop the bleeding." He shoves my blood-soaked sleeve past my shoulder and ties the fabric painfully tight around my gash. I cry out as the knot pinches my skin. He sighs and checks the wound which still bleeds. "Not tight enough."

He rebinds it. I feel him yank it tightly with all his strength. The world goes black.

∞

People are yelling, one belligerently.

"What is wrong with you boy? Erik'll hear of this! His no-good son bringing a respectable girl here…" gripes an unfamiliar voice.

"Ay! I'ma respectable woman, you stupid 'oreson!" a rough-voiced woman roars as she slaps the complainant with a loud *thwap*.

"What are you doing? Oh, no. Get her off the bar!"

"She's Ansel's daughter," Ivo protests. "She collapsed near Pantaleon's gate. Would you have me leave her in the street?"

"Let 'er stay, Paul," the woman orders, gruffly.

"Egh!" the man sighs, forfeiting the argument.

"God's teeth, Ivo? What happened?" a deep voice shouts in a slur. I recognize Father's voice immediately. The relief of knowing he is here and safe makes it easy to breathe again.

"She fell, looking for *you*," Ivo barks. "Take a look at her arm."

"Mind your tone boy," Father warns.

"Ivo, shut it or get the hell out," Paul grunts. "Ansel had a rough night."

"I can tell by the smell of him," Ivo snaps.

SWOOSH! A cold rush hits my face. I gasp and awake, soaked from head to toe with icy water. I look around in a considerable daze and nearly fall off the bar.

"See, she's a'ight. Now ya can stop yer fightin' and get the 'ell out. If ya don' ,I got plenty a' more cold water fer ya's. Ansel, ya look like ya could use some," the raspy voice calls. I look to my left, and Paul's wife, Sal, limps back to the kitchen with the empty bucket in hand.

"Alright, alright, Sal," retorts my father with his hands up as he stumbles backward from Paul who stands between him and Ivo as though the two are going to fight. Though I doubt my Father can stand, much less land a punch.

"It's a small gash. She's probly jus' 'ungry. 'Ere, eat some meat on yer way 'ome." Sal returns with a chicken leg and slice of bread, slamming it onto the bar in front of me. I flinch. She grins, her crooked teeth hanging out of her face like thatch from a rooftop. I thank her. I eat ferociously and feel my strength return. Ivo reaches for my good arm, but I pass him and jump into Father's arms, kissing him on the cheek.

"'Ay, Ansel! Can yer girl keep a secret or do I need t' knock 'er out? I don' wan' the 'ole city knowin' 'bout this place." Sal peaks around the corner of the backroom, waving a rolling pin. Father looks down, wraps his arm around me, and I nod my head. "Good," Sal says.

"You scared me," I say.

"It is late, I suppose," Father says light-heartedly.

"It's well past noon!" I cry, but Father says nothing. He's not the type of man to give apologies lightly, so he changes the topic.

"I think the pup wants a piece of the wolf!" Father laughs, wrapping his other arm around Ivo and slapping his chest. Ivo grimaces. "See, she's all right. She worries too much, like her...." he coughs, unable to bring himself to speak of Mama. His wife.

"You could have told her where you'd be," Ivo reprimands.

"Is it a surprise to either of you that you found me here?" he retorts and kisses the top of my head. Father is always his most affectionate and jovial self after a few drinks.

Before we leave, I look around and realize I am probably the only virtuous woman besides Sal to see the Gilded Gopher. There truly is nothing gilded about it. The stench of sweaty men and stale ale fills the windowless pub. Stained wooden tables and benches are packed into tight rows. Candles provide the only light.

We climb the stairs, and a woman passes us holding her tattered dress as if to hide her bosom. Dark circles encompass her dead eyes. She limps, though she appears to be healthy. My eyes avert to the wood of the stairs.

I knew such business took place here. She has sold herself, and I wonder what happened to make her so desperate. Daylight blinds me for a moment at the top of the stairs. A child lies on a pile of hay by the fire in the corner of the room. Perhaps this woman's husband died of fever, and she has a child to feed. Perhaps she was the concubine of a burgher who promised he'd marry her, but never intended to do so. I promise myself I shall never turn to such an abase business, but surely this woman had promised herself the same at some point in her life.

I bet this girl's parents had hopes for her once, however meager. I wonder if her parents deny her now, shamed by her profession. Better that they died before she made the bed she now lies in. I shall never put myself in such a position. I shall never give myself to a man before wedlock.

We walk silently. Ivo's narrowed eyes stare into the distance pensively. He has become hard to read. He used to be so much like little Levi, so jovial and always wearing his heart on his sleeve. But the fever has worn on those of us old enough to understand it, and especially those of us who have lost a family member or friend. Perhaps he is angry with me for being stubborn or with Father for letting me worry so. We make it to my house and Father heads straight for his workshop.

Ivo turns to head back to the fields. I reach for his arm.

"Wait," I plead.

"I need to get back to the fields," he replies shortly.

"I hate it when you're angry." I reach clumsily for his hand.

"He should have come back to tell you where he was." He reaches out for my other hand. I wrap my fingers around it and smile, looking into his eyes in the hopes he shall let his anger go.

"Did you get the firefly?" he asks.

"I did, and the bread."

He nods. "I saw it outside my window and in the middle of March!"

I shake my head and smile.

"Do you think we shall catch more of them this summer?" he asks with a grin.

"Are you sure you'd not rather spend your nights at the Gopher?" I ask with a hint of sarcasm.

He laughs as though the idea is preposterous. "I'm sure."

"Then we can catch fireflies all night long. I owe Father a good scare."

I'm glad to know that he's not fond of the Gilded Gopher and the base entertainment it holds. He turns and heads back to the fields. I want to ask him about his bruises, but there seems no good way to ask. I return home to an angry Galadriel and a Father who is passed out at his workbench.

12 March, 1247, Late Afternoon

Galadriel scowls at me, but thankfully keeps her anger silent. We try to coax Father to bed, but he refuses to rise from the table. Perhaps he knows what I had learned earlier, that lying in his bed next to the empty groove where Mama once slept is a cruel reminder she shall never return to us. Even with eyes shut tightly, her lavender scent still wafts through the room.

Galadriel climbs the ladder back to the loft and into my bed. Her skin is still grey, and I am sure she has been sick a few more times, for she stinks of vomit. I am alone and think for a moment about helping Ivo's family with their tilling, but know that I, inexperienced in such tasks, shall only hinder their progress.

My stomach howls, and I push at my belly with both hands in an effort to silence it. We have no food, and I know I must go to the market so we'll have something to eat, though I doubt anyone shall rise for supper.

My cloak is still wrapped around my shoulders, and I pull the hood up around my face, though it is far too warm on this spring afternoon to do so. I descend the stairs to Father's shop. He's slumped over the table, snoring in that odd way he does, folding his lips on the inhale and blowing out with long, slow "foo".

I bend and whisper in his ear to ask permission to get food, but he is too deeply asleep to hear. I nudge his shoulder gently and then roughly, but he does not wake. I reach gently for the purse attached to his hip, untie it, and attach it to my belt. I ensure the purse is near my good arm and remove all silver from it just in case there are thieves about.

I walk down Filzengraben, which has more people on it than earlier in the day. Hay Market is crowded and bustling, although I do not know why I expect it to be any different. I have always had to push my way through crowds here.

I hope no one recognizes me and offers their condolences. But with crowds like this, the vendors shall be keeping their eyes peeled for beggars whose hungry bellies sometimes cause them to have sticky fingers. Today is Tuesday, and Mama and I usually went to market on Monday mornings so I doubt anyone would expect me anyway.

I make my way toward Salz Alley, weaving through the crowd toward the bakers' stands, carefully avoiding our usual baker, Matthew, for I know he shall ask where my mother is if he does not already know of her death. The idea of crying in the midst of Hay Market's crowds terrifies me, and I tug on the brim of my hood to hide my face even more.

Keeping my head down to shield my face from view, I set my pfennig on the table, and the anonymous baker hands me three crusty loaves of bread. I find the dairy stalls and buy a pound of

Danish cheese. We still have oats at home, but we are low on spices and out of dried fruits. It matters not to me as food seems tasteless now, but perhaps Father or Galadriel would like them in their porridge.

I buy a pound of raisins and almonds in the spice market, but decide we have enough spices for one day. Spices are expensive, and I probably shouldn't purchase any more until we sell a week's worth of shoes. Besides, my sack is getting too heavy for my injured arm. We need something to drink, though, so I pick up some inexpensive wine and hurry home.

The house is silent. I carry the sack up the stairs and put the food in its place. I cut a slice of bread and cheese for Father and me. I eat and then water down the wine, pouring two mugs. I set Father's food and wine before him. He no longer snores, though his eyes dart back and forth beneath the lids. I untie the purse from my belt and attach it back onto his. He doesn't even stir, and I doubt he shall eat what I have set before him.

Next to him lies a wax tablet Mama had used to keep track of his accounts. I gently slide my finger across the words and numbers. We did not know many women who could read and write, but Mama was the only surviving daughter of a steward, and she learned to read and write by standing over the shoulder of her father, and later even aided him in his work. Her mother had died during breech childbirth, and the baby soon followed her to Heaven. Mama was only a toddler then.

I pick up the first tablet and read the list of orders. There are at least a dozen. I sigh. Not only should this order be done, we should also have a surplus of turn shoes to be sold at the market to the pilgrims who have already started to fill the streets and churches of Cologne. This is where we make the most coin.

There is only one finished pair of shoes on the table, minus the straps, and several others in different stages of completion: a red pair with only the sole, several tan pairs, and one pair in the new royal purple with only the heels completed. I pick through the scraps in the baskets. We need leather. I look at the list again.

Wilthelm Aducht had placed an order over a week ago for nearly twenty summer pairs. He wants five pairs of ankle boots for himself in tan, dark brown, blue, red, and purple, and a dozen pairs for his wife Elizabeth, and his daughter Matthild. Instead of straps, he has requested decorative clasps with his family's crest to be attached to buckles on each shoe. These were to be delivered by the gold and silversmiths yesterday. I look for the clasps, but do not see them. I hope the smiths are behind and that we won't be blamed if the shoes are a few days late.

There are other orders here and there; one for a baker, one for each member of a carpenter's family... What worries me most is that as soon as the Aduchts are seen in their extravagant new shoes, the other patricians and burghers shall place orders in an effort to appear even wealthier. Truthfully, it is a wonderful problem to have.

Father snores again. I unwind the purse from his belt loop, return the silver coins, and head back to Hay Market.

12 March, 1247, Evening

There was once a shoemaker who worked very hard and was very honest, but still he could not earn enough to live upon. At last all he had in the world was gone, save for just leather enough to make one pair of shoes.

Then he cut his leather out, all ready to make up the next day, meaning to rise early in the morning to his work. His conscience was clear and his heart light amidst all his troubles, so he went peaceably to bed, left all his cares to Heaven, and soon fell asleep. In the morning after he had said his prayers, he sat himself down to his work; when, to his great wonder, there stood the shoes already made, upon the table. The good man knew not what to say or think at such an odd thing happening. He looked at the workmanship; there was not one false stitch in the whole job. All was so neat and true that it was quite a masterpiece.

-The Elves and the Shoemaker

৩৩৩

"I need a yard each of red, royal purple, blue—"

"Adelaide? Is that you, Adelaide?" Michael, our tanner, turns around.

I look up from beneath my cloak and nod.

"I didn't expect to see you. My sympathies for your mother."

"Thank you," I say quickly through a tight throat, blinking back a stray tear. I look down so no one notices and dig through the purse pretending to count the coins.

"And a yard each of gold and violet. Then I need five yards of tan and five yards of dark brown. How much is that?"

"Six silver groschens." I know I owe a few pfennigs more, but I accept his generosity, for arguing would only bring attention to his discount and anger the guild members. He cuts and folds the leather into a pile and ties it off with twine so I can carry it easily. I hand him the coins and he places the leather on the table.

"A good day to you, Herr," I say and turn to leave.

"Give your Father my regards," he calls after me.

"Thank you, I shall." I turn and nod my head, then pull the hood tighter and walk back to Filzengraben and into Father's shop. I fear I shall wake him if I work at his table, so I take the materials to the table by the hearth. I am grateful for its emptiness and for Galadriel's extended slumber. It is five o'clock, and the sun will set in two hours. I hope two candles and a roaring fire shall be enough light for my eyes.

I spread the tools out along the table to my right. Needles, knives, awls, the overstitch wheel, and boar bristles. At first, I think to place the variety of lasts, foot castings, on the bench across the table, but, upon careful consideration, I realize the heat of the fire could damage them. I untie the twine and grab the five yards of tan. I roll it out across the table and drape a section slightly larger than a foot over the edge and cut it with the knife. I do this four more times and stack the sections on top of one another. I lay the scraps on the bench next to me, for I shall need these to build around the last in order to have well-measured sides of the shoe.

I check the awl's sharpness by digging into the wax. Although fairly sharp, I sharpen more for ease of use.

I fetch a last the size of Wilthelm Aducht's foot and trace the bottom using the awl. I do the same with a last that matches Elizabeth's foot and one that matches Matthild's. I press the scraps onto each side of the lasts to create the shape for each side and the top of the boot, lay them next to the sole patterns, add length for the sides of the boot, and scratch the perimeter with my awl, creating a finished pattern for each Aducht foot. I cut these patterns out with my knife, careful to keep the blade straight. But the blade has dulled and I have to sharpen it. Luckily, the Aducht's have symmetrical feet, so I can flip the patterns over to make shoes for their left feet. I use the Aducht patterns again, for they have requested two pairs of tan shoes each.

I use a variety of last sizes to cut twenty pairs of shoes that Father shall sell at the market. My injured arm is quite sore from this work and night has fallen well before I finish.

I light the candles, and, thankfully, the room is lit well enough for me to continue to work. I cut the dark brown leather using the patterns I've already made, then soak the tan patterns and use the dark brown patterns of the Aducht's feet to finish cutting the colored leather for the rest of their shoes. I remove the tan leather from the soak and wrap it around the lasts, then bind the leather with the flax thread so it forms nicely.

I run the overstitch across the edges to ensure an even stitching pattern. I warm the beeswax and draw the flax thread across the top, coating it well. I use the awl to poke holes where I intend to stitch. Using split stitches, I close the uppers, attaching the heel stiffener and joining the top of the boot to the sole using boar bristle and wax-coated boar's thread. Using split stitches, I close the rest of the boot and turn it inside out. My work is careful, but quick, as I hope to finish Father's orders.

When the sun rises, I take the supplies and the fifteen tan turn shoes I have made down to Father's workshop. I set them gently on the table around him and place all the supplies where they were. I climb the stairs and have no choice but to retire to my parents' bed. I fall face down into the mattress, neglecting the blankets. I am asleep before I even have time to notice Mama's lavender scent or her empty divot in the mattress beside me. For the first time in five days, I enjoy a deep, dreamless sleep.

ঔৣ

I awaken to the fragrance of cinnamon. Voices in quiet conversation come from the main room. My stomach rumbles and I whine, not wanting to rise from the bed. Exhaustion wins, and I fall asleep again.

The church bells wake me, and I wonder about the time. I don't know how many bells chime before I fully awaken. My stomach roars, and I can no longer ignore it. I rise, rub the sleep from my eyes, and stretch my tired arms, neck, and back. I look to where Mama once slept, and it makes me sad, but it is no new revelation today. I knew when I awoke Mama would not be here. It saddens me in an exhausted way, making my limbs heavy and my stomach ache, even though I am dreadfully hungry for the cinnamon-spiced porridge I can still smell coming from the hearth.

I turn away from her pillow and feel something hard and cold roll away and off the edge of the bed. *CRASH!* A hundred shimmering shards of glass sprawl across the floor. Ivo's jar. My lips curl into a smile as I think of him climbing into my bedroom to leave me a single firefly only a night ago.

Galadriel rushes into the room with worry on her face.

"Oh!" She gasps, placing her fingers to her lips at the sight of the broken glass. She looks shocked. I think she believes I had purposely thrown the glass in a fit.

"I must have kicked that over. I was so tired last night. I don't remember putting it there," I say.

"Oh," she sighs with relief. Turning on her heels, she slides out of the room and returns moments later with the broom and pan to gather up the broken glass. As soon as I notice it in her hands, I run over to take it and clean the mess myself. She pushes the broom and pan away from me.

"I made the mess. I'll clean it." But she does not listen and continues to clean the mess. "Thank you," I say.

I walk to the shutters and open them. The sun is high in the sky toward the west. It is past noon. Galadriel is gone by the time I turn around. I meander to the bench in the living quarters across from the hearth and sit across from her. She smiles.

"You seem well today," I say with a yawn.

"I feel much better."

"Did you go to the market yesterday?" Galadriel asks. "I found bread, cheese, raisins, and almonds, and your father found yards and yards of leather."

"I had to. We hadn't enough food."

"I wish you had awoken me so I could have accompanied you. The market is no place for a girl to make purchases alone. I hear it is riddled with thieves," she chides gently. It irritates me that Galadriel, barely a woman herself, would give me motherly advice, and I find myself fighting the urge to roll my eyes. She rises and heads to the hearth, scoops a heaped spoonful of porridge into a bowl, sets it before me, and hands me a spoon. "Besides, I'd rather like to see this famous market of Cologne."

"I know the market well enough to go there alone. Besides, you wouldn't have enjoyed it in your condition," I say. "I'm glad you rested. You look better today."

She gives me a sideways glance and nods. I dig into the porridge and lift the spoon into the air. Steam rises off the thick oats and a nutty cinnamon fragrance drifts through the air. My mouth waters and my stomach rumbles. I blow on the spoon to cool the porridge until the steam subsides, and I place it to my lips. The porridge is perfectly cooked, but lacks something of Mama's. The thought must be drawn on my face as I try to figure out what is missing.

"Not as good as your Mother's I suppose," Galadriel says. "No one can ever cook quite like one's Mother."

"It's fine." I am actually surprised that someone who has probably not cooked for herself in two years has made porridge so well and so similarly to Mama's. It must have been a recipe passed down.

The porridge cools, and I quickly finish the bowl and the mug of spiced wine before me. My stomach calms and I feel tired again.

"What time is it?" I ask Galadriel.

She looks up for a moment to think. "I believe it is half past two."

"I would take you to the market, but I am so tired."

"Then it would please me for you to rest and keep your health. We have enough bread and cheese to sup on tonight when your father returns," Galadriel says in that formal way she speaks at times.

"Where is he?"

"He is at the market selling the shoes he found this morning and fetching brooches for the patrician's shoes."

I nod and retire to my bed, falling asleep quickly once again.

❧

I wake to the chatter of voices in the main room and rise. Father and Galadriel sit at the table across from one another, dining on bread, cheese, wine, nuts, and an assortment of dried fruits.

"She awakens," Father bellows. I can tell he has had many glasses of undiluted wine for his cheeks are rosy, and he is merry.

"A miracle has befallen us, daughter."

I tilt my head to the side in wonder of what he speaks and sit beside him. I nibble on bread and cheese and pour myself a glass of good, strong wine.

He places his arm around me. "I awoke to a room filled with shoes and supplies for all of my orders. And before me lay a plate of cheese and bread and a glass of spiced wine."

"A miracle for sure," I say, reluctant to admit my role in the miracle, for I know I am not to go to the market alone. Nevertheless, I am certain he is aware that I did.

"I must admit, Father..." I pause for dramatic effect. He stares at me, waiting for a confession. "And please do not think me mad..."

He nods.

"... But I heard the most peculiar thing last night."

"What, pray, did you hear last night, daughter?" He goads.

"It was a strange high-pitched singing of many voices, coming from your workshop."

"Why, that is very peculiar!" he says jokingly, and I continue.

"So I climbed down the stairs and spied something miraculous indeed. A dozen tiny men, elves I think, were making shoes."

"Elves! By God, it is a miracle. "

I cross myself in jest and Father does the same.

"They did however charge for their services," Father continues, feigning disappointment. "Very inexpensive, though. It only cost me the price of the leather for fifteen pairs of shoes, but they cut out dozens more. Even the Aducht shoes were cut."

"They worked quickly and reasonably," I conclude.

"I checked the quality of the shoes and they were masterfully done. These mysterious elves cut and stitch just like you, dear daughter."

"Then they are master artisans for sure," I reply, and he laughs. It feels good to hear laughter again.

13 March, 1247

My fingers shuffle around the crust of my bread as we sup. I have wanted to ask Father if we could have another funeral for Mother, but I'm afraid to say anything. He hasn't mentioned the burial at all. What if something had gone wrong when Father returned to bury her? Perhaps wolves had taken her, or the ground was too hard, and he couldn't bury her at all. If such things had happened, I wouldn't want to remind him of them, and I wouldn't want to know of them. I split the crust and dip it in the stew to sop up the remaining broth. My mouth opens a dozen times throughout supper as I try to find a good way to ask.

"Out with it," Father orders.

I give him a confused look.

"You keep opening your mouth to speak, so speak."

Galadriel dips small ends of her bread into her stew and nibbles delicately while Father lifts the bowl to his lips to drink up the rest of his broth.

"I thought we could have our own funeral for Mother," I finally say.

"I think we should," Galadriel says. "What do you think, Ansel?"

Galadriel's agreement pleases me at first, but the way she coaxes Father is too much like the way a wife would coax a husband, and suddenly my suspicion of her tastes like poison. She turns her back to look for Father's expression as he rises to fill his bowl with more stew. My eyes narrow, and I shake the assumption from my head.

Father returns to the table and hunches over his bowl. He digs the spoon into his stew and begins to eat. I am unable to see his eyes, to read his thoughts. My question hangs in the air, and I almost want to take it back. I have upset him for sure. Perhaps, the burial had gone very wrong. My stomach twists, and I have to swallow the broth hard, for the lump in my throat has swollen again.

"Friday morning," Father says. It is all he says.

Galadriel offers to give me my bed that night, but I refuse out of fear she shall sleep in my parents' bed and ruin Mama's side. I fear that somehow she and Father might share the bed. I should know my father better than that. It is a wicked thought, but the more I try to ban it from my mind, the more present it is.

So she offers to share my bed with me and I agree. Perhaps Father shall return to his own bed tonight if he knows I shall not be in it.

14 March, 1247

The poor girl thought, "I can no longer stay here. I will go and look for my brothers."

And when night came she ran away and went straight into the woods. She walked the whole night long without stopping, and the next day as well, until she was too tired to walk anymore.

The sun was about to go down when she heard a rushing sound and saw six swans fly in.... The swans blew on one another, and blew all their feathers off. Then their swan-skins came off just like shirts. The girl looked at them and recognized her brothers. She was happy ....The brothers were no less happy to see their little sister, but their happiness did not last long.

"You cannot stay here," they said to her.

"Can't you protect me?" asked the little sister.

"No," they answered. "We can take off our swan-skins for only a quarter hour each evening. Only during that time do we have our human forms. After that we are again transformed into swans."

Crying, the little sister said, "Can you not be redeemed?"

"Alas, no," they answered. "The conditions are too difficult. You would not be allowed to speak or to laugh for six years, and in that time you would have to sew together six little shirts from asters for us. And if a single word were to come from your mouth, all your work would be lost."

After the brothers had said this, the quarter hour was over, and they flew out the window again as swans.

Nevertheless, the girl firmly resolved to redeem her brothers, even if it should cost her her life.

-The Six Swans

❧

Galadriel rises, but is still half asleep. My neck is strained from sharing the bed, and I can sleep no more. I convince her to sleep longer and promise we'll go to the market when she rises.

I make the porridge and take a bowl to Father, who is still awake in his workshop. The Aducht shoes are all finished. The shoes are finely crafted, and he had even added gold and silver embroidery to each of the ladies' shoes and lined the seams of Wilthelm's shoes with the same threading. I'm sure the only man with nicer shoes in Cologne would be the Archbishop himself.

Father leaves for the Aducht's to deliver their shoes and collect the rest of his payment. I quickly lace the last few unfinished shoes that he shall sell at the market.

The market is busiest in the morning. Waiting for Father to return would cost us a few coins and being gone from the market for nearly a week has surely cost us many. Praise God the Aduchts had placed such a large order to see us through without relying on Father's now meager savings.

I suppose I could just take his cart and set up the stand myself, but it is nine o'clock now. The streets shall be busy. Vagabonds could easily overwhelm me and steal our wares, disappearing into the crowds before any one of the thieves could be caught. Such things have happened before, even though the people of Cologne do not take kindly to thieves. Still, it is better to miss a few sales than to have all of our shoes stolen.

Galadriel wakes shortly after me, dresses, and breaks her fast as we wait for Father to return.

After helping Father set up his booth at the market, I take Galadriel for her tour. It is busy, but I have seen mornings with crowds packed shoulder-to-shoulder like herded sheep. We reach the potters first and an elderly woman with rheumatism begs by their stands. Galadriel drops a pfennig in the old woman's palm before I can warn her, and not a moment passes before we are surround by beggars. Galadriel gives them each a pfennig, and they are quickly on their way. An embarrassed blush rises to my cheeks. Giving a pfennig away at the market was a foreigner's error. It is a good thing we don't care to make purchases from the potters, for they would take us for fools and charge us triple the fair price.

"Well, I don't think I shall do that again!" she cries.

"The beggars shall tell their friends of your generosity, and thieves will think it easy to take your purse. You may want to pull up your hood so you're not recognized and clench your purse so it's not taken," I say. She blushes from embarrassment and takes my advice.

The blacksmiths and carpenters sell a myriad of tools, many of which I have no clue how to use. We pass the armorers quickly, for neither of us has a chance at knighthood, though I do wave to Michael, the armorer who Ivo apprentices with late at night. A flute player dances around the fabric sellers' and tailors' stands, following one burgher wife after another in hopes of pocketing a groschen or a guilder.

Galadriel stops to look at the gowns, but the tailor pays her no attention, for he is unaware of her wealth and status. After a few moments, we receive dirty glances and continue through the market. The fruit and vegetable stands are filled with jams, jellies, and all manner of pickled items. The vendors' shouts ring over the hum of the crowd. Some boast that their kraut has cured many sufferers of the great fever. A few desperate people toss coins to these merchants and rush back through the crowd with their pickles, probably returning to dying loved ones. I am sad for them and angry at the vendors who make a dirty pfennig off the desperate.

"May he catch the fever himself," I mumble.

"Hmm?" Galadriel replies, examining some currant preserves.

"That man over there selling each jar of pickles for three pfennigs, claiming it to be the cure to the great fever!"

"Appalling," Galadriel says. "Are you sure it does not work?"

"He has been selling his pickles for years. I am sure if they were a cure, every man in Cologne would sing the praises of his precious pickles! The man sells false hope and tasteless pickles," I spit.

A crowd has formed between the spice stands and the meat market. The typical chatter is broken by "oohs" and applause. Galadriel pushes her way through, pulling me along behind her. One brightly-colored jongleur is doing a handstand on the shoulders of a burly black-skinned man. I have never seen a man with such dark skin before, and I am sure the audience is just as much there to see the man as they are to see the show. His muscles bulge beneath his skin like meat from a sausage casing.

The black-skinned man tosses balls up to his slender friend who juggles them up and down using only his feet. The man below holds out his hands, encouraging applause. For a moment, the man on top falters and it appears he shall fall. Cries ring out, but as soon as the panic rises it is tempered with the jongleur's recovery. He flips his way down, bowing to the crowd on one knee. Applause roars through the market. The sky seems to be raining pfennigs, which both men race to collect. A few burgher children run toward the dark-skinned man now that the show is over to stare at him in awe. The man bends down and entertains them with a few coin tricks. The mothers move in to scoop up their curious young and put on their own show by giving the jongleurs a groschen each.

"It has been so long since I have seen such curiosities," Galadriel smiles. "I like this market of yours."

We pass the meat stands without a look, but Galadriel stops at one of the cheese stands, buying a slice for each of us and a pound for later. I smell the sweet fresh bread, cakes, and other confections from the bakers' stands. I love confections, and I am still hungry, so I purchase a yeast cake for each of us. Next, we pass the grain stands holding flour, oats, barley, and rye. The fish market approaches, and though many consider fish to be smelly and slimy creatures, I like the taste and prefer it to meat. Galadriel covers her nose as we pass, so I doubt she has a similar hankering for sea fare.

We walk past St. Martin's Church, and the cathedral, all the way to the flower market. A crowd of children surround a poorly-crafted stick cage.

"Shoo! If ya haven' paid yer pfennig, ya don' getta look! Go on with ya!" A man shouts, shaking his large stick at the filthy little urchins who scatter and disappear into the crowd. Their giggles ring through the hum. I raise my head to see what the fuss is about. A bear, perhaps? I had seen one once before at the market, but such a shoddy cage could never hold a bear. We approach, and a young man no older than nineteen paces back and forth in the cage speaking nonsense.

"A pfennig! A pfennig! See a demon in the flesh! Only a pfennig! A man possessed by the devil himself!"

Galadriel grabs my sleeve and drags me toward the cage. I look to her face wondering why on God's earth she would pay for such a thing. Her eyes narrow in hatred and her cheeks are red.

"This man is no more possessed by the devil than you or I!" she spits. The man looks her up and down for a moment, ogling her, which only seems to upset her more.

"Aye, Fraulein, he is! See f' yaself. Only a pfennig." A younger man approaches with a large stick, standing between us and the man in the cage.

"How would you like to be locked in a cage? Even a pig has a larger pen. This man belongs in an asylum," she says.

"Aye, Frau, perhaps with yer help, we could pay his, my son's, way in'a bedlam." The man feigns sadness.

"You take me for a fool! Did he spring forth from your loins at ten? You are thirty winters at the oldest, and your 'son's' only ten years your junior! You should be ashamed of yourself, exploiting a sick man for coins."

A crowd begins to form around us, and the young man with the stick grabs Galadriel by the arm. "He's our man an' we'll do what we wan' with him! Pay the pfennig or piss off!"

Galadriel's mouth drops. A countess would not be accustomed to his roughness.

"How much for him?" Galadriel whispers. The young man laughs.

"I said piss off." He shoves her and she stumbles backward.

"I'll give you a guilder for him," Galadriel offers in whisper.

"Three," he counters.

"Two and you shall take him to..." she looks to me for the name of the nearest asylum.

"St. Pantaleon's."

"Make what you shall off him today, but by three this afternoon, you shall deliver him safely to me at St. Pantaleon's. I shall be there with another guilder to ensure his arrival."

The man nods and Galadriel hands him a guilder.

I want to ask why she does this. It is one thing to give a pfennig to a beggar or two, but to part with two guilders for a single man? That is unheard of. I hadn't even thought of what St. Pantaleon's would expect for a donation from her. Curiosity gets the better of me.

"Why did you do that?"

"It is a long story that I do not wish to tell here."

I nod, and though I wish to pry, I hold my tongue.

Galadriel's cheeks redden with emotion.

"I have one purchase left to make and we shall return home," I say.

We walk through the carts and stands of the many flower vendors. I see an old woman with rheumatism of the hands with a few buckets surrounding her as she sits on the ground. I purchase a blend of her buttery daffodils and crisp white tulips. Galadriel and I meander back through the performers, beggars, burgher's wives, servants, and vendors, but not before a short stop at the meat market where

Galadriel purchases sweetmeats for supper. At the lumber market, I purchase two leftover cuts of wood, before we turn back toward Filzengraben and home. It is a silent walk.

♨

I should be working on shoes, but I find myself working on something else. I fashion a cross using the pieces of wood from the lumber market and tie it tight with the wax-covered flax thread, but the mismatched planks are knotted and chipped. I wonder how to improve upon this unsightly memorial as I unwind the thread and bite my lip. I dig through the scraps of leather and settle on dark green, her favorite color. I quickly stitch her name using the gilded thread and upholster each section of the wood with the dark leather, fashioning the cross again using the flax thread. Her Christian name is on the left side and her surname on the right in gold. I place the tulips and daffodils in a mug and set them by the window. Tomorrow we shall have a beautiful funeral for her. Such a beautiful funeral that, perhaps, I shall someday forget about the former.

I walk upstairs to fill the mug with water so that the daffodils and tulips keep until the morning next. Galadriel sits at the table, staring distantly.

"Are you alright?" I ask.

She looks at me and a tear runs down her cheek. I do not know what I should do, so I sit across from her in case she wants someone to listen.

"I… I had a sister once, but I barely remember her now," she says through a thick voice. "My mother had a husband before my father, but he died and so she remarried. My sister, Elizabeth, was twelve winters my elder."

79

I don't know what to say, so I say nothing. She sniffles and continues.

"She was... different to most people, but she wasn't bad. She wasn't a witch!" she cries.

"Even when I was little, I knew she was different. In the winter, there was no raising her from bed. When she wasn't crying or angry, her face was a dark void like there was no soul to her at all. But spring would come and her spirits would rise. She would become too busy to be still and she was happy at first, but as I grew older it was the summers that became dangerous to her. She stopped sleeping and she would ask us if we heard or saw things that were not there. When fall arrived she would calm down and return to her bed for the winter for her time of woe. Each summer was worse than the last. She not only heard voices, she started to speak to them. By the end of the summer, she was crying, screaming, begging for them to leave her alone. We had to hide her in the house and tell our neighbors she suffered a fever in order to keep her secret. She stopped eating and sleeping. Her already slight frame withered. I don't know how she survived."

"Is that why you saved that man today?" I ask, and she nods.

"She could not help it. She was a good girl, you know. She really was," Galadriel says, and I nod in agreement.

"Fall came, and we knew her sadness would come with it. She calmed down and stopped talking to the voices that plagued her so. We let her help the tailor as she had done for many springs and summers, but we did not know that the voices had returned. She spent less and less time with the tailor and roamed around town telling the most ridiculous stories. It was the end of October before Mother found out--when she heard rumors of witchcraft being spread throughout the town.

"I went in search of Elizabeth and found her by the pond, feeding six swans and sewing together six small shirts.

"'That witch has turned them into swans,' she'd say. She thought my mother was a witch and that we had six brothers who Mother had turned into swans so Father wouldn't be able to see them anymore. She said Mother had sewn those cursed shirts and that she planned to kill us next.

"She was mad. I know it. She thought if she could make them shirts of aster, she could break the spell and turn the swans back into her brothers. But we'd never had any brothers. I know it hurt my mother that Elizabeth thought her a witch, but she took it so gracefully. She had nothing but pity for her stepdaughter, God bless her.

"'I tried to get Elizabeth to come home. I even pretended to believe her stories and told her to tell our Father of the spell, but she refused, believing Mother would kill her.

"The story got wilder and wilder. She said that the swans told her she couldn't laugh or smile for six years, so Elizabeth stopped talking altogether. It broke my heart to watch. Mother tried to come to her, to convince Elizabeth to come home, but she looked at her with such fear. I begged Mother and Father to find an asylum where she could be cared for, but they refused.

"They said Elizabeth was harmless and that she wasn't a bother to anyone. Elizabeth never spoke to us again. She whispered only to her swans. She sat at the pond all day, sewing the little shirts for the six swans. Every day, Mother had me take her lunch and ensure she wore her cloak on cold days, but it didn't take long before people whispered about Elizabeth and her strange behavior.

"She really was harmless. Sometimes little children would come to the pond and help her feed the swans. As the children grew, Elizabeth lost her whimsical appeal to them, and the same children who had helped her, began to laugh and call her names. I doubt Elizabeth ever noticed it, for she never looked hurt. It hurt me though, and I reprimanded the malicious little imps, but I couldn't watch Elizabeth all day, and they teased her more and more.

"Around his tenth spring, one of these wicked beasts thought to humor himself by throwing rocks at the swans. The little bastard nearly killed one of them. Elizabeth thought these swans were her brothers. Imagine if someone tried to kill your brother. What would you do?

"The children ran to get help, but they were too late. When I got to her, Elizabeth still had her hands around the boy's throat though he was lifeless, his face frozen in terror.

"I tried to pull her from the boy. I tried to pry her hands from his throat, but she was so strong. I begged her to let go. I told her the boy was dead. I told her he couldn't hurt our brothers anymore, but she wouldn't let go.

"The shouts of a small mob were close, so I quickly closed the boy's eyes. A group of men arrived first and, thank God, they pulled Elizabeth off the boy so his mother didn't have to see Elizabeth strangling her dead son. Then the boy's mother arrived and fell at his side, wailing in grief.

"The men dragged Elizabeth away. For a moment, I feared they'd hang her on the spot, and, now, I wish they had.

"Elizabeth was arrested and accused of witchcraft. Mother, Father, and I begged to have her committed to an asylum where she could be cared for and could never hurt anyone else, but it was useless.

"She was sentenced to be... to be..." Galadriel gasps and puts her hands to her quivering lips. "They ordered that she be burned at the stake." She places her head in her hand and cries. I rise and grab the wine, pouring two full-strength glasses for us. She drinks and composes herself.

"On the day she was set to die, we prayed over her and hugged her tightly. We found a priest from another town to perform her last rites. He had a brother of his own who had been committed to the asylum. God bless him for his understanding. I still pray every day for Elizabeth that she is with God and at peace.

"I brought Elizabeth the shirts that she had worked on so hard, but she pushed them back at me, and I knew what she wanted me to do.

"She was set on the pyre, and thank God the wood was dry and stacked high. I placed my hands on her feet until the fire was lit. Just before Mother pulled me away, she spoke.

"'Have our brothers returned to us?' she asked me.

"I lied and told her they had. It made her so happy.

"Long after she'd expired and the town retired to bed, I went back to collect a small amount of her ashes. The town refused to bury her in hallowed ground, so we did that ourselves. As we rose, up the hill to the spot, I noticed a white cloud below the pyre. The six swans lay below Elizabeth, even the injured one, sleeping beneath her ashes. They stayed through the night."

"That is the saddest thing I think I have ever heard," I say.

Galadriel nods. "I still wonder how it all might have ended so differently for Elizabeth had we placed her in an asylum. It is what we should have done."

"You didn't know what was going to happen," I reassure her. "You've honored her today by saving that man in the cage."

We dine on cheese and bread at the noon bells. After the third mug of wine, I am warmed and mellow. I feel great pity for Galadriel who has lost a husband, a son, a sister, and a mother. She has little kin but us. And even we are but distant relations, barely more than strangers.

I excuse myself from the table to work and make more men's shoes for the Saturday market. As I get back into practice, I work more quickly, but get little done by the two o'clock bell. Galadriel descends the stairs in a red velvet gown with bands of gold embroidery around the wrists, upper arms, and trim. At her hips rests a matching belt. A deep brown cloak cascades past her shoulders and down her back, clipped at her collar with a morse. The cloak is so light; its only purpose must be a simple accompaniment to the gown that is extravagant enough on its own. Having an elaborate cloak seems frivolous to me, as does the gown. A red velvet ribbon with gold embroidery circles the front of her crown and is then intertwined with a plait that finishes the back. One large braid flows down her back, specks of the opulent ribbon's ruby and gold peeking through.

"We are going to an asylum, and yet I feel underdressed," I exclaim.

"Having a title may help my cause. Tell me I look better than a simple burgher's wife headed to market."

I nod, though her words sting. *A simple burgher's wife.* Almost every girl in Cologne could only hope to elevate herself to such status. Not me, though. I am happy to be an artisan. But at one time, it was what Galadriel could have hoped for herself, and yet she spits the words out as though they are flies on her tongue. I cannot help but wonder what I am. Am I less than a fly? The dung of a fly perhaps?

"I think we shall pretend you are one of my ladies, but we shall have to clean you up a bit and quickly at that. You can wear a gown of mine."

I do her a favor by escorting her to St. Pantaleon's, and she has the gall to not only insult my station, but she also expects me to wait on her! I am insulted, but I accept out of pity for her and for the man in the cage. This is but a game we shall play to help an unfortunate man.

Galadriel leaves me with the water, and I scrub myself quickly. She enters with the dress. It is the color of emeralds and made of fine linen with a finely fashioned leather belt. I put it on, and Galadriel brushes my hair roughly before braiding it.

"We shall have to find a mirror on the way back, but we haven't time for that now," she says.

ംഇ

We hear the Hay Market still buzzing loudly with activity though we are a block away. We head east on Filzengraben, walking past manors and fields, but mostly row houses like my own. The streets are as congested as one might expect. Carts come and go. Beggars, monks, and nuns mix in the throng as people rush from one place to another. We pass through the gate at Rotgerberbach and veer onto St. Pantaleon's Strasse.

Upon entering the grounds of the church, neither of us knows where to go, so a monk takes us to the monastery connected to the asylum. Galadriel asks him the name of the abbot and if she can speak with the him about donations she would like to make. He leaves us in the large hall and hurries away, but returns shortly after to escort us to the abbot.

"Abbot Thaddeus, I presume," Galadriel says sweetly.

"I am," the abbot replies coolly. "I hear that you wish to speak with me about a donation." He is composing a letter of some form and does not even stop to look at us. I laugh to myself about all the time Galadriel took to ready herself, for it seems to matter little.

"I do. However, I wish to ask a favor in return," she confesses.

"As donors usually do," the abbot returns. He drops his pen and looks up, his eyes narrow as he measures Galadriel up for a moment, but his face softens like most men's seem to do when their eyes fall upon Galadriel's face. "What is it you want?"

"There is a sick man being tormented in a cage at Hay Market. I purchased him from his captors in hopes that you would take him into your care with the appropriate donation."

"That is very charitable of you. What is this man to you?" he asks. His voice is laced with fatherly suspicion.

"He is a child of God to me. Is that not enough?" Galadriel replies smoothly.

"So are all the beggars, and lepers, and thieves. Shall you give them all a plot of land to sow?"

"I wish I could. I can only hope that my charity inspires charity in others," she says, and I admire her quick wit.

The abbot purses his lips in defeat. "How much did you pay for this man?"

"Upon his delivery, I shall pay his captors three guilders."

"Donate what God inspires you to, and we shall take him into our care."

"Your charity is greatly appreciated, Abbot." Galadriel hands him a velvet bag of coins. "I asked the men to meet me at the church. May we wait for them there?"

"Yes, and I shall send a few brothers to accompany you for your own safety."

Four monks escort us to the church which, though I have lived in Cologne all my life, I have never set foot inside.

Galadriel stands patiently at the entrance, but I predict the men won't be prompt -- if they come at all. They may simply take Galadriel's guilder and their captive and leave Cologne today. I decide to explore as she waits.

The nave is long, and the ceilings are tall and flat. Banded arches surround the nave, and there are aisles on either side. Through the arches to my left, there is an elaborately adorned shrine to Saint Maurinus, the martyred abbot. To my right, lies a shrine to Saint Albinus, an abbot and bishop who performed miracles and ransomed slaves. Perhaps it is St. Albinus who was working through Galadriel earlier, inspiring her to free the man in the cage. I had forgotten that his shrine is here.

I walk down the aisle between the pews, bow before the crucifix, and cross myself. To the right is Saint Pantaleon's Altar. Saint Pantaleon was a Greek doctor and saint. His peers grew jealous of him when he came into wealth and exposed his faith. The emperor Maximian favored him, though, and tried to convert Pantaleon. He refused, so Maximian ordered his execution, but Christ appeared many times, and Pantaleon could not be burned, boiled, racked, ravaged by wild animals, nor beheaded. It was not until Pantaleon wanted to die that the executioner could behead him.

Oddly, though, it is Saint Pantaleon's Altar that is adorned with brightly painted murals of the life of the Virgin Mary. I suddenly think of Mama, who told me the stories of so many saints, and kneel to pray for her.

I am nearly finished with my prayers when I hear the echo of voices through the nave. I cross myself quickly, rise, and hurry down the aisle toward Galadriel. The men have honored their word and brought the sick man after all. Galadriel hands the men their coins, and the monks take the man to the asylum. Galadriel follows to ensure his safety and insists on seeing the asylum. The monks oblige and we enter. There are many beds and many sick men. Monks patrol the aisles and care for the sick with kindness. Some of the sick are ghosts of men with empty eyes while others appear to be normal, and I wonder why they are here. We learn the sick man's name is Peter. He is shown to his bed and sits for a moment before getting up to pace the aisles. Understandably, he is still agitated. The cage and the captors were his home for God knows how long. It shall take him time to get used to this place. Galadriel waits for him to settle, but I tell her we can check on him the following afternoon, which satisfies her enough to leave. The church bells strike five before we are halfway home, and I suspect Father is worried about us. I should have stopped to tell him where we were going, not that he would extend us the same courtesy had our roles been switched.

❧

Returning home, I hear Father pounding at something before we even open the door. We enter the workshop; he looks up, and stares at me in Galadriel's fine clothing. He stands and bows before me as if I were the countess. His cheeks are rosy, and I can smell the ale on his breath, although I would not have needed to as he is a kind, silly man when he drinks. I curtsy clumsily and tell him about Galadriel's dress. He jumps from his stool, wraps one arm around my waist and grabs my hand with the other. We dance clumsily around the room as he slurs a tavern song. I laugh, and Galadriel watches us. Father stops and bows to her before starting our dance again.

He is the only man I know who doesn't measure her with his stare, and this pleases me, for I know he only has eyes for Mama. Galadriel climbs the stairs, changes her clothes, and prepares the sweetmeats for dinner. I pull a stool next to Father so I can help with the shoes and notice he has propped up the cross I made for Mama in the corner, displaying it like an altar piece. While constructing it, I had been worried he might be angry with me for working on it instead of shoes, using the expensive colored leather, but he isn't. I can see he is proud of it and has set it aside so as not to ruin it while he works. We work together with smiles on our faces until Galadriel calls us for dinner. We eat well and drink until our bellies are warm. Galadriel and I share a bed again, and for the first time since Mama's passing, Father sleeps in his bed.

15 March, 1247

Father wakes us before sunrise. I scrub the grime from my face and shiver as I throw off my night shift. I hurry into my hose, chainse, and surcote and slip on my boots. Rather than break my fast, I race down to the workshop. The daffodils and tulips are still fresh, and I gather them together, drying the stems with my surcote. I wrap the stems with green leather and bind the bouquet to the cross.

Mama has been buried like a Christian and had a funeral. Now she'll have my cross to adorn her grave and our kind words to send her into the next life. I pray this is enough for God. Saint Pantaleon was not buried in hallowed ground, given last rites, or funeral rites, yet there is no doubt he is in Heaven. I know Mama wasn't a saint or a martyr, but she was a good woman. That should be enough for God. If I were God, it would be enough for me, but if I were God, this world would be a very different place.

Father calls, and I take the stairs two at a time with Mama's cross in one hand and bunches of my skirt in the other. I grab a crust and gulp some watered-down wine while Father waits with as much patience as he can muster.

"Let's go," he says.

"My cloak!" I exclaim and head for the ladder to my room.

"It is around your shoulders," Father huffs.

"Oh."

A carriage awaits, and we descend the stairs to it. Thankfully, Galadriel has paid the fee so we won't have to walk the hour in the cold. The rooftops are covered with frost and the breath of the horses steams in the morning chill. The sun rises before us and soon the fields shall be busy with the bustle of tilling and sowing.

We set off toward the rising sun before turning onto Severin's Strasse and out the gate. There are farmers in the fields already at work. We ride past the hill where Mama's first funeral took place, and I am glad we don't pass it directly. Eight chimes of the many church bells ring in the distance, and I realize we have ridden for a little more than an hour.

"This is it," Father calls to the driver, and we stop. Galadriel speaks with the driver who moves off, halting his carriage a little further down the road. His horse tears up hunks of grass with its strong jaw.

The rounded mound of earth is fresh and undisturbed. My stomach knots.

She's dead. She's really dead.

Sometimes it still feels like a dream that I shall awaken from, but not now, not when I am standing before her grave. Now, it is all very real. How could God do this to us? How could he send a fever and kill all these people? How could he let Mama die? Were we not good enough Christians? She especially, who dragged Father drunk to Mass every Sunday.

I cry as much out of anger as out of sadness and hug Father. He wraps his arm around my back and squeezes me tightly. I cannot speak without sobbing. I doubt any of us can, and so we are silent.

I look up at Father whose eyes are red and glassy. He must be haunted by having to bury her the way he did only a few nights ago. I cannot imagine having such a memory, and I am reminded of the world's cruelty. I thought God was supposed to smite wicked men like Soren, but it seems to me only the good people of Cologne suffer. I look at the cross I've made, and it is nothing more than a marker to me now. I squeeze Father one more time, and place the cross at the head of Mother's grave.

I kneel in the frosted grass beside her grave and brush the dirt back and forth lightly with my fingers the same way I did when I ran my fingers through her soft hair as a child. I arrange the stones so they are neat, and I move to the end of the grave to kneel before the cross and pray for her in the hope someone in Heaven is listening.

Galadriel gasps. "Who is that?"

"It looks like a Benedictine," Father replies.

I turn and look. A monk is cresting the hill toward us, Bible in hand.

"Brother and sisters in Christ, my name is Brother John, and I am sent by a friend to give Katrina Schumacher a Christian funeral. Am I too late?" he asks.

"Galadriel, did you do this?" Father asks.

"No, I only purchased the carriage."

"Greta, Frau Bauer, spoke to me of the misfortune at your first funeral and asked me to come and give your wife a proper funeral."

I am overwhelmed with their kindness. I doubt I shall ever think an ill thought against Greta again.

Father nods, and I know he is grateful, but he'll not speak for he'll not cry in front of another man. "We'd like that very much," Galadriel says for him.

A silence follows, broken by the crunching of grass. Through the mist of dispersing frost appear Greta, Erik, Ivo, and Levi. Paul and Sal follow with the members of the cobbler's guild and the men, who, I assume, patron the Gilded Gopher. Michael, our tanner, and Matthew, our baker, arrive, followed by the other artisans whom we make purchases from. Several members of our church arrive and those who live around us on Filzengraben come to pay their respects as well. Last to crest the hill is Michael, the armorer who Ivo apprentices with. We surround Mama's grave, and Brother John gives her the funeral she deserves.

Ivo comes to offer his own condolences again and hugs me.

"I can't believe your mother did this for us," I say as he stands back and shrugs. "Well, if we can't rely on God, at least we can rely on friends."

"What do you mean?" he says.

"I'm just angry," I huff and pause for a moment. "It's not fair. How is it that Soren lives and Mama does not?"

Ivo is silent for a moment. "Well, if I were God, I'd much rather have your mother in Heaven with me than that pig-shivving whoreson, Soren," he says. Levi runs up between us and chides Ivo for saying bad words.

"Then God's being quite selfish," I retort, even though his comment makes me feel a bit better. "Soren could at least be punished for what he did to us."

"Who's getting punished?" Levi asks.

"No one," Ivo and I say, our voices overlapping.

"Is it that priest everyone keeps cursing? Perhaps God is thinking of a really good punishment for him, Addie. I know I'm in big trouble when Mama says she has to think about it," Levi says before he runs off again.

Ivo and I cannot help but smile at Levi's innocent wisdom. Perhaps God is thinking up a good punishment for Soren right now. I pray it is so.

৵৹৻

By noon, more than a hundred people have come. They share their woes of losing loved ones and friends, and we soon discover that only a few of the victims of the fever had been served last rites. Barely any were given a proper burial. The villagers speak of their anger toward our heartless church and also of vengeance.

My memories of the first funeral shall never go away, but I now I have a new memory -- a better memory that brings me peace. This is the kind of funeral every good person should get. If the church will not make it so, then at least we know the people of Airsbach shall.

17 March, 1247

It is cold enough to see my breath again. I squirm cautiously from the bed, careful not to wake Galadriel. The chill slithers down my spine, and I shiver. I snatch my cloak from the floor and swiftly wrap it around my shoulders. I rush to the window that looks upon Filzengraben to see if the people of our borough, Airsbach, would keep their promise.

"SCRAWH!" Father's snoring startles me. I hang my head over the edge of the loft and pain shoots through my neck. It is strained again from sharing my little bed with Galadriel who takes up too much space and most of the blankets.

What a pitiful sight, I think. Father's spent the night hunched over the table again. He hasn't gone back to his bed since the second funeral.

I wonder if I should wake him and try to get him to his bed. I tiptoe down the ladder and toward him. Shadows ring his eyes, and I wonder what time he came home last night. He smells of ale, but it is a Sunday morning. He always partakes in too much drink on Saturday nights.

It is probably best to let him sleep. I pull the hood of his cloak gently over his head to keep the sun from his eyes and wrap my own cloak around his shoulders. Surely last night's liquor still warms his blood, but I don't want him to catch cold. I want to hug him and breathe in the ale-smell that reminds me of our normal Sundays. My shivering hands pause above his shoulders as I worry that I'll wake him, but he sleeps like the dead when he's drunk so I wrap my arms around his waist, rest on his back, and take in a deep breath.

I start the hearth fire, and then tiptoe up the ladder. The cold pricks at my skin, and I rush to Galadriel's trunk, wrapping myself in one of her riding cloaks. "I share my bed, so the least she can do is share a cloak," I think as I toss it over my shoulders.

I open the shutters to my window again, and sit on the edge of the bed looking down on Filzengraben. I could not wipe the grin from my face if I tried. Sunday mornings are typically a somber parade, but no one walks to church yet.

I stay perched at the window and stare until the church bells chime eight, but no one is out except for a few drunkards and beggars. One might think every last person in Airsbach had disappeared overnight, but I know better. The men at Mama's funeral agreed not to attend St. Laurentius today, and, perhaps, never again. The message spread Saturday to those who did not come to the funeral, and it appears that no one, at least no one who lives on Filzengraben, has gone. Now Soren shall know how much we hate him. My cheeks burn from grinning for so long.

I imagine Father Soren sitting in a room behind the chapel waiting, angry because his altar boys are late. He sits slouched in a fine chair with a hand squishing his fat face, the other hand tapping his desk, waiting impatiently for someone, anyone, to show up and tell him what is happening, to explain where everyone is. But as the hours pass, it is not just the altar boys who do not show. The church is almost empty. When realization finally arrives that no one is showing up, his fist slams down on the table. Gripping the table for support, he stands and shakes his fist in childish rage. His hideous roar echoes throughout the building. He grips his chest and gasps for air, then falls to the floor and dies.

A satisfied sigh escapes from my lips.

I feel a little less angry with God today for He punishes Soren with humiliation. Soren deserves much, much worse than this, of course, but perhaps more punishment is to come for him. I should be at Mass today singing God's praises, for He has answered my prayers, so I thank him in my prayers this morning. I imagine we shall attend the cathedral from now on, and I will pray especially hard next week.

The blankets rustle as Galadriel stirs. I find I am secretly growing more displeased with her presence each day. I want to be alone to mourn. I want to work without interruption or the need to entertain her. I want to sleep alone in my bed. I cannot help but fear that Galadriel is trying to weasel her way into our lives in a desperate attempt to replace my mother.

She runs errands, cooks, and cleans just like a mother, just like a wife. It is kind of her, and I try to convince myself it is completely innocent, but I cannot purge my suspicions. I hope I am wrong about her, but something tells me I am not, and I just wish she would go home.

"Good morning," Galadriel whispers in her bell-like voice.

"Morning." My whisper is not as gracious. "Sleep well?"

"Very well," she yawns and stretches. "It is kind of you to share your bed, you know. I hope I do not disturb your sleep." Her polite response is irksome. If she were rude, I'd feel less guilty for wanting her to leave.

"Not at all," I lie.

Galadriel sheds her night shift and dresses in a drab chainse and surcote. She descends the ladder, and I listen as she starts the porridge.

"URH!" Father's groan roars through the house. I hurry to look over the edge of the loft. His head shoots up from the table, knocking my cloak and his to the floor. Sweat drips from his head, and his chainse is soaked through. The fire has warmed the house quickly, and I suppose he didn't need a second cloak around his shoulders after all.

Father squints and his eyes dart around the room, confused. For a moment, I know he has forgotten why he sleeps at the table. His face shows his thoughts: Did he upset Mama? Did he get home so late that he did not dare sneak into their bed?

I wonder what his face shall look like when his memory drifts back past last night. The color quickly drains from his face, and I know he remembers why he has slept at the table. Not because he was afraid Mama would be angry with him, but because she is dead, and it pains him to sleep in his own bed. I imagine he must feel quite guilty for all those nights he'd spent at the Gilded Gopher. All those nights he worried her. All those nights he could have spent beside her. I hate to see my father pained, but his guilt is well earned.

"Good morning," Galadriel says sweetly with a smile. Mama would have shot him a dirty look, and her "good morning" would drip with sarcasm. Father groans and puts his head in his hands.

"Morning," he grunts tersely. Galadriel continues to smile obediently. I can see in her eyes that his crossness hurts her. She turns back to the pot and continues stirring.

Father looks up and sees me peering at them from the edge of my loft. I snap up quickly, toss Galadriel's cloak to the floor, remove my night shift, and dress quickly before joining them by the hearth fire.

I rest my cheek on the back of Father's head and hug him tightly. "Does your back not wrench from sleeping that way?" I ask.

"It's nothing a little ale can't fix." He groans and stands to stretch, his bones popping like wet wood on a fire. He grabs a mug and fills it with beer from the barrel. I walk over to the window and open the shutter to see if anyone is in the street, but it is still empty.

"Have my bed," I offer.

"I've slept long enough. Close the shutter. You'll let the chill in." He rubs the stubble on his face as he stumbles toward the window. "What are you staring at?" He steadies himself with his drinking arm anchored on the wall.

"An empty street," I reply with a smile.

An eyebrow arches in surprise. "Church hasn't let out yet?" He leans over me. With one hand on the window sill, he looks into the street and his eyes narrow. He looks down at me for a moment and wraps his arm around my shoulder.

"It looks as though Father Soren hadn't a reason to start Mass today," I smirk.

"No one went?" he asks with surprise.

"Filzengraben has been empty since sunrise," I say excitedly.

Grinning, he slaps the window sill and laughs. He sips his ale and stares out the window for a while. He glances down at me, and my smirk seems to make his grin curl closer to his cheeks. But it quickly twists back to his pensive scowl, and he lurches back to the table. "What is wrong with him?" I wonder. "How can he not appreciate this? Oh well, his sulking shan't ruin my morning." I try to pay him no mind, but I cannot. Wondering what upsets him rains upon my happiness at Soren's humiliation.

Galadriel watches Father, too. Her porcelain forehead crinkles with worry as she stirs the burning porridge. Even her worried face is pretty, though. She curses as she realizes her porridge is charred, and apologizes. She squeezes out a smile as she plops several heaping spoonfuls into small bowls for each of us.

Father reluctantly swallows one spoonful after another. He masks his disgust well, but Galadriel takes a bite and grimaces at the taste.

"I ruined it." She says.

"It's fine." Father says.

"No, it's not. A whole pot of porridge, and it's ruined. I doubt we could feed it to pigs." She says angrily and drops her spoon in her bowl. "I'll throw this out and make another pot." She sighs and reaches for our bowls to take them away, but Father grips his with both hands.

"We don't throw good food away." He says.

Galadriel's face whitens, and she releases our bowls. She sits in her seat, and her face reddens with embarrassment.

We eat our food in silence, and it amazes me that Father can eat this slop with a stomach soured by last night's liquor. I can barely stomach it, but it is better than an empty belly, so I eat just enough to keep from having hunger pangs.

"Can I visit Ivo?" I ask.

"Have you finished eating already?" Father asks, and I nod. "I'm full." I lie.

"Give me your bowl. Go, then. Be back by supper," Father says.

I nod and kiss him on the cheek. I grab my cloak from the floor and run out the door.

ৰঞ্ছ

I sneak over to the window by Ivo's mat, hoping he is sleeping late this morning so I can startle him. I peel back the wooden shutter, and there is a yelp. Greta stands up from her sweeping. She stares back at me with a raised eyebrow and a fist on her hip. There are daggers in her eyes as she waits for an explanation. It'll just make her angrier if I lie. I feel the warmth of blush in my cheeks which only adds to the embarrassment.

"Is Ivo here?" I ask and smile impishly. She is not amused.

Ivo's mouth is wide as he is about to shove a spoon of porridge into his mouth. His eyes meet mine, and his brow knits with confusion. Greta's eyes grow larger, angrier by the moment.

"Ivo!" Greta squawks. Ivo and Levi startle at her scream, and the blackbirds flutter from the roof. Ivo rushes to her side. Erik is asleep on their straw mat in the corner and doesn't even stir.

"Yes, Mother?" he asks calmly, looking down to hide a smirk.

"This girl's confused the door with the window. Show her where the door is and how to knock on it."

"Yes, Mother," he chortles and my cheeks burn.

He goes to the table and scoops the rest of his porridge into his mouth quickly, then runs to kiss his mother, throws a cloak over his shoulder, and is out the front door in a flash.

Greta slams the shutters in my face, and I shrink into my cloak as I step back from the window. I meet Ivo at the door.

"This is a door," he says, speaking slowly to me like I am a simpleton. "To get our attention, you must ball up your fist and tap on it like this. Do you understand?"

"Yes," I grumble.

"Are you sure?" He cocks his head and smirks at my embarrassment.

"Yes," I snap, and punch him in the arm. "What's crawled up her hose?" I ask.

"Not you. Something else has set her off," he says. "I can't believe you thought I was going to be in bed at noon." He chuckles.

"It's not yet noon."

"Close enough," he says matter-of-factly, walking quickly.

"I bet I got up earlier than you did this morning." Unable to keep up with his pace, I grab his arm, cuing him to slow down.

"The rooster woke me up this morning. Actually the rooster woke up my father, and his boot woke me when he threw it at my head," he laughs.

"Well, then we woke up at nearly the same time," I quip, finally catching my breath.

A growl from my stomach interrupts the short silence, and Ivo looks at me strangely.

"I'm hungry," I say.

"Don't they feed you?"

"I'd rather eat mud than Galadriel's cooking," I declare with my lip curled in disgust. "She burned the porridge terribly today."

"Well, mud is in great supply," he teases. "There you go." He points to the ground. I slap his hand playfully and give him a look. "You think my mother's cooking is much better?" he laughs, casually tossing his hair out of his eyes.

"I'm quite sure your breakfast wasn't charred to cinders!"

"No, but I wasn't eating breakfast. I was eating dinner," he teases and I roll my eyes.

I follow him, wishing I had a full belly, but the market is not open Sundays. "I am so hungry," I whine, before I realize we are about to pass St. Laurentius. Getting snatched and questioned by Father Soren's guard is not how I want to spend my afternoon.

"Not that way!" I grab his arm and pull him back.

He points ahead. "I thought we could go out Kunibert's gate and climb trees."

I grab his arm and pull him the other way.

"What?" he asks.

"Just come with me," I sigh. "Do you think you could sneak me out something to eat?" I ask with my best fake pout.

He shakes his head. "Mother's on the warpath, remember?"

"What's she so mad about, anyway?"

Ivo shrugs. "So where are we going?" He makes it a full, four, gigantic, Ivo-sized paces ahead of me before he realizes I'm lagging behind. He turns and shrugs his shoulders.

"It's a… surprise," I reply, out of breath.

"We can stop by your place to get food."

"Then Father could change his mind and make me work on shoes all day."

He shrugs.

"I'll be fine," I sigh, just as we are about to pass the alley off Foller Strasse. I see Levi from the corner of my eye cross the alley while some other farm boys follow him at a run. Ivo and I take the narrow alley to see what he is up to.

"Levi!" I call, and he comes running.

"Hi, Addie! Want to help us catch the chicken? We'll get a pfennig if we do!" He hugs me, and I look down Foller Strasse to see a chicken running in zigzags with a half dozen farm boys at its heels.

"No," I smile, then kneel and whisper in his ear. "I'll give you two pfennigs if you get me some bread and cheese."

"Really?" he shouts.

"Yes, but it's a secret so don't tell your mother who it's for."

He nods, but looks a little uncomfortable at the thought of lying to his mother.

"Here's an extra pfennig. Give it to her and tell her you love her very much," I say.

Levi smiles widely and runs for the house. Ivo catches the chicken and hands it to the smallest boy. The rest whine while the little one runs to the manor yards for his pfennig. Levi returns with my bread and cheese.

"Who caught the chicken?" Levi cries.

"Matthias," Ivo replies.

"Oh," Levi says with a shrug just like his big brother. He runs off to join his friends who are now playing a game called "Chase the Chicken" in which one of them pretends to be a chicken while the others try to catch him.

I offer half the bread and cheese to Ivo, but he shakes his head. Good, I think, as I eat the whole thing in three bites. We make our way back down the narrow alley and onto to the wide thoroughfare of Severin's Strasse, making small talk about how my arm is feeling and predicting what had set his mother off this morning. It is a short walk from his house to the tree-lined city wall. I find the tallest tree and hope we aren't in the middle of our climb when the church bells strike noon.

"You climb first," I order.

"Why?" He asks. I think if I stay silent for long enough, he shall just start climbing, but he doesn't.

"Come on. Just go," I grumble, pushing him forward.

"Fine…" he shrugs, shaking the hair from his eyes as he grabs a limb. But rather than climb, he looks to me one more time. "Is this a trick?"

"No! If you don't hurry, we're going to miss it!" He turns and hoists himself onto the branch. Before I am even onto the lowest branch, he has climbed three. The muscles and veins in his arms swell, though he never struggles with the climb. I am much slower, for my wounded arm hurts. He pauses on a limb ten feet above me, turns, and swings down from the branch he's on, shaking his head with a gloat.

"It's my arm."

"Sure it is."

I eventually reach a place in the tree where we can see all the way to St. Laurentius and all the streets that wind around it. I motion for Ivo to come down a few branches. Before I am even seated comfortably, he is sitting on an opposing branch, watching me nervously.

"Scared of heights?" I quip.

"I'm scared you'll fall, and I'll have to explain it to your father." His foot twitches nervously. "I'm coming over there. Scoot forward."

Gripping the trunk, he slides over to my branch and sits behind me. He wraps an arm around my waist and pulls me close so my back rests against his chest. I gasp, startled from the pull and from being so close to him.

"What are we looking at?" he asks nonchalantly, as though being this close is ordinary for us.

"Well…" I forget. I lose myself in the warmth of his chest on my back and his arm around my waist, but I recover quickly enough. "Actually, we are listening for something."

The timing could not have been more perfect. The first dongs of the dozen church bells echo through the city. Although I've anticipated them, they startle me, and Ivo grips me tightly.

The bells chime noon, and there should be a flock of Christians filing out of St. Laurentius, slowly making their way back to their homes in Airsbach for dinner. Only a few parishioners walk through the doors.

Ivo rests his chin on my shoulder as we stare out over the city. The slow steady flow of his breath tickles my neck, raising goose bumps on my arms. Luckily, they are covered by my sleeves, so he does not notice.

I expect him to gasp or curse or react in some way, but he does not even seem to notice that no one has attended Mass at St. Laurentius, that Soren has been humiliated, and, soon, all of Cologne will hear about it.

"Don't you see?" I turn to look at his face.

"See what?" he asks in a daze.

"Look at the streets of Airsbach! At St. Laurentius!"

"God's teeth! It's Sunday," he laughs. Parishioners from the other churches of Cologne fill the surrounding streets, but only a handful of people come out of St. Laurentius. They look very confused.

"No one went to Mass this morning," I laugh.

"Good."

The few confused parishioners who'd attended St. Laurentius disperse and make their ways home. My eyes stay on the doors of the church like a cat would keep his eyes on an unsuspecting mouse. I want Soren to walk through those doors and into the empty street. I want to see the embarrassment, the anger, the bewilderment on his fat, ugly face, but he doesn't come out. It doesn't surprise me. It doesn't even disappoint me. Soren is a coward, and I am sure he shall spend the rest of the day sulking like a spoiled little boy.

For the rest of this lazy afternoon, we sit and watch the streets of Cologne. Ivo rests his chin on my shoulder. Though I know it's forward of me, I lay my head back on his shoulder so our crowns are touching. Time passes quickly, I imagine, as it always does when one is happy.

ഛൠ

The church bells chime three times more, and I know supper nears, but I don't want to go home. I've had time to think of what worried Father this morning, and I think I know what it is.

Perhaps, this is not over. Father Soren isn't a gracious man. He isn't likely to learn his lesson and beg his parishioners' forgiveness. He won't learn to treat the people of Cologne better. He shall want to find a way to make us fear him, obey him. He'll find a way to punish us. And what makes it worse is we do not know how, nor when, nor to whom this punishment shall come. Why hadn't I thought of this?

"Ivo, what do you think he'll do?" I ask, knowing he will understand what I am talking about. He always does.

"I don't know," he sighs, his breath blowing a strand of my hair out of place.

"My father looked worried this morning."

"Your Father? Really?" His head pulls back with shock.

"Does your father… did he look worried?" I ask.

"I haven't seen him much today." He leans back against the tree and pulls me with him. I lean my head on his shoulder again.

"Are you worried?" I ask.

"Nah, there's only one of him and hundreds of us." He rests his chin on top of my head.

"Do you think that is why your mother is angry? Maybe she's just worried we shall all be punished?"

"Nah, I think she's mad because you were trying to sneak into my bed," he chuckles.

"That's not what I was trying to do!"

"You should have seen your face when she caught you," he laughs.

"Mine! You should have seen yours." I push forward and turn to sneer at him, but lose my balance. I tip and nearly fall. His eyes widen with fright, and he catches me. My heart pounds from the shock. He climbs around the front of me and pushes me back up against the trunk of the tree.

"There, now you cannot fall," he says. I nod and look down because I am embarrassed by my clumsiness. I shift with discomfort. Our faces are so close.

His whole face relaxes as he looks down briefly, then back up, as if he were looking directly through me. "I'm going to kiss you."

"Right now?" I laugh.

He looks down. "Yes. Now." He laughs.

I giggle nervously. He slides closer, slipping his hand around the small of my back. Our cheeks nearly touch, and I freeze. My heart quickens, and I look into his eyes permissively. He shifts his head, and I close my eyes.

THUMP! THUMP! THUMP!

My eyes shoot open, and we turn toward the city. Ivo sighs and his head drops. Airsbach is filling with guards carrying heavy sacks filled with rolls of parchment.

THUMP! THUMP! THUMP!

The guards weave their way from St. Catherine's Strasse, Witschen Alley, and Filzengraben onto the smaller alleys that make up our parish. They are nailing something to all the doors. The sound of hammers smacking nails echoes through the city, ruining the quiet I had so appreciated. People open their doors and rip off the notices, struggling to decipher them as few of them are able to read.

At best, the parchments are a warning. At worst, I assume they are an issuance of punishment.

But the guards pass the boundaries of Airsbach and head into the other boroughs of Cologne whose inhabitants had attended church. We saw them exiting the churches at noon, so why are notices being nailed to their doors? Now, I do not know what to think, but the guards march soberly, and I know the news cannot be good.

Ivo rests his head on my shoulder again. I reach up and brush the hair out of his face.

"I'll walk you home," he sighs.

17 March, 1247, Evening

I pull the hood of my cloak up as we walk down Severin's Strasse on the way home. I worry a little that we might be troubled by the guards, but it is an uneventful walk.

Ivo pauses at my door, and I know it shall be strange when we say goodbye. I wonder if he'd be brazen enough to try to kiss me here, but I doubt that. He'd have to be mad to kiss me at the door of my father's house. We stop at my door, and I look down, waiting for him to say something funny to break the strange silence between us, but he doesn't. He turns awkwardly, without a word, and heads for his home.

"Wait," I say, and he turns. "Don't go...yet. Let's find out what the letters say before you head home alone. If it's not safe, then Father can walk with you."

His mouth opens to argue, but he shrugs his shoulders instead.

We run up the stairs, and Father sits at the table with the torn piece of parchment. Galadriel leans over his shoulders. Both of their eyes dart back and forth across the parchment trying to decipher it. I know Father cannot read, and from Galadriel's silence, I assume she cannot either.

Father turns and looks relieved to see me. "Ivo should head home before Erik goes out looking for him."

Ivo steps backward, and I grab him by the arm. "Can't he stay until I read the letter? Then he can tell his father what it says."

Father nods.

"She can read?" Galadriel says.

"Yes, I can read," I reply, annoyed she directed her question at Father and not me.

Father passes me the letter, and I read it once silently.

"What does it say, Addie?" Ivo asks, so I read it out loud.

◈

Any person not attending Sunday Mass has mortally sinned, abandoning Christ and his own soul. To believe or act otherwise is heresy. By order of our Supreme Chancellor, His Highness, the Archbishop of Cologne, all heretics shall be punished. According to Holy Law, only the gravely ill and the lame are permitted to abstain from Sunday Mass.

◈

No one says a word. None of us have learned church doctrine. What we know of sin, we know from what we are told at Mass, and Soren gives every Mass. Is it a mortal sin to miss Mass? I'm sure Father Soren would like us all to think so. Besides, I doubt the Archbishop even wrote this, for he is in Rome where he usually is, unless, of course, he arrived without the normal festivities, which is even more doubtful. And even if he were here, he hasn't made sure that those who die get last rites or funerals, so it is clear he cares not in the least for our souls. I doubt this is about our souls at all. This is about Soren squashing a rebellion within his own church.

Still, the threat of being punished as a heretic is something to fear. I'm sure Galadriel is quite afraid, having watched her sister burn at the stake, albeit for witchcraft. Heretics are treated the same. They are burned alive so all can see what it is like to burn for eternity in the flames of Hell. Galadriel's eyes are wide, and I imagine she is thinking of Elizabeth right now.

Father's brow is furrowed. His clenched fist, on the table. He seems to be as far away as Galadriel. I know he is angry, but is he afraid? Ivo said that there were too many of us for one man to punish. Could one man, even one as powerful as the Archbishop, burn an entire borough of people?

This has become a dangerous game, but it is Soren's fault! Why are we to be punished for his wrongdoings?

"So that's all. Soren just goes unpunished for what he did?" I huff.

Everyone looks at me sadly, not an answer among them. I expect at least one person to have my passion, my anger. I throw the parchment to the ground.

"His whole congregation abandoned him, Adelaide. His parishioners are forced to attend church or face death. He is the fool of Cologne," Galadriel says.

"It's not enough," I sulk.

"Can it ever be enough? Can he ever be punished enough to right what he did?" she reasons.

"I want to see him punished over and over again, until he begs for death, and burns for eternity in hellfire," I spit.

"Even if it means your friends are burned at the stake? Is that what your mother would want?" Galadriel adds. She is only a few years older than me, yet speaks to me like a child, like she is my mother. It angers me so.

"How would you know what she would want? You hardly knew her."

"Adelaide, enough!" Father orders. "It is over."

"What about another meeting?" I ask. "It doesn't say anything about us not being able to meet in this notice. Let's see how the rest of Airsbach feels about this. If no one wants to go back to Soren, what's he going to do? He cannot kill us all."

"Such things have been done before," Father says. "You have not seen what men are capable of."

"Fine. You all can give up, but I'm never going back to Soren's church!" I affirm. "Never!"

"You don't have to," Ivo says.

Father turns, looking daggers at Ivo.

"The letter says you have to go to church, but it doesn't say which church."

I pick up the parchment and read it over again. "He's right."

"I don't know." Father sighs.

"Why not? We'll be following the order. We should hold a meeting and see what the people of Airsbach think," I suggest proudly.

"And if spies are sent?" Father reasons.

"Good. Let them see we aren't defeated."

Father shakes his head. "No. You're not thinking, Adelaide."

Ivo nods his head. "Soren'll just have another letter sent the day he discovers our plan and devise some way to punish us if we don't go to his church."

Father nods in agreement. "Never tell your enemy your plan of attack, Adelaide. Remember that."

I nod, a little embarrassed and angered at being corrected.

"We tell only those we trust. No one in the guard, no friends of the guard, no kin of the guard," Ivo adds. "And, for now, we let on like we plan to go back. It'd be best to go to the cathedral. It shows our support for the Archbishop, and he has more power than Soren."

Father shrugs, purses his lips, and finally nods, seemingly impressed with Ivo. There is a long silence as Father's forehead wrinkles with thought. We stand almost strategically around the room, like pieces on a game board, except for Galadriel who sits at the table. Father walks toward Galadriel and places his hands gently on her shoulders. Why is he touching her? She blushes and looks down smiling lightly. Is this why she acts like a mother to me? Does she want to take Mama's place and be Father's wife as I've suspected before? How foolish I was to doubt my suspicions! She wants my Father! I know, now, this is why she has not left.

I'm boiling with anger. I want to jump across the table and claw out her pretty blue eyes so she can never look upon Father again!

The glare on my face must be quite scary, but neither of them looks up to notice. Ivo has, though. He comes closer so he can nudge me with his elbow, and looks to me with raised eyebrows. *"Are you all right?"* he mouths. My eyes dart back to Father's hands on Galadriel's shoulders. Ivo looks at them and looks back at me. His brow knits with confusion. He can be so slow at times. I shake my head and huff in frustration. Father opens his mouth to speak to Galadriel, but it seems he does not know how to say what he needs to. Is he going to ask her to stay or tell her he loves her? If so, I think I shall have to claw both their eyes out.

"Galadriel, you should go home. It's not safe here anymore," Father suggests, still staring at the ground. I have to bite my lip to keep from cheering out loud.

"And I was wondering if ... you would take Addie with you... just for a little while."

"What? No! I'm not leaving," I yell.

Father's face reddens, and he points an angry finger at me. "You will do as you are told!"

I jump. My heart pounds with surprise, and no one utters a word. The room is painfully silent, and I feel like a child at market whose mother spanks her in front of the crowd. My face reddens with embarrassment. I fear the stares of those around me, so I look to the floor.

There is a loud knock at the door. "Ansel... you home?" a deep, gruff voice shouts.

"Yeah," my father calls. "Go let him in, Addie."

"You seen my boy?"

"Yeah, he's here."

Erik's scowl is angrier than usual, and I worry Ivo shall be in trouble. "It's my fault Ivo's here, Herr. I begged him to walk me home," I explain, running after him as he climbs the stairs.

"I doubt you had to beg," Erik chortles, shoves his letter into my stomach, and sits at the table. "Be a good girl, and read that."

I do as I am told and peek above the parchment to gauge his response.

Erik shrugs it off. "We going to drink?"

"Fetch us some ale," Father orders, and I oblige quickly. Perhaps, if he sees that I am an obedient girl, he shall change his mind about making me leave Cologne with Galadriel.

I've only poured ale for Erik and Father before the door bangs again.

"Who is it?" Father calls impatiently.

"Otto," a booming voice replies.

"Let him in, Addie."

A large brown eye peaks through the hole the guard put in our door. One might expect a great stature to match Otto's booming voice, but he is only as tall as me and just as slight.

"You can read, can't you?" he asks, and I nod. I show him up the stairs as he waves the parchment angrily. "Those arses put a hole in my door!"

He sits down and slaps the parchment on the table. I wonder if I should keep pouring ale or read the parchment when there is another knock on the door. Father groans.

∞∞

My voice has weakened over the course of several hours as I repeat the words on the parchment over and over to the people of Airsbach. Ivo only lets our closest friends enter the house, but the second floor is filled, as is most of Father's workshop.

Soren, or whoever had those parchments delivered, is terribly stupid to have nailed them to our doors when so few of us can even read. It has only forced us to meet and discuss his demands. A bad move on his part, which perfectly illustrates how disconnected his church has become from its parishioners.

A crowd files down the stairs, and I hear laughter. "To the Gopher!" someone yells.

"To the Gopher!" the crowd cheers as everyone leaves the house. Father passes me without a word, and I suppose I am to stay here alone because Galadriel is among those heading to the tavern. I am shocked she's allowed to go.

Father sees Ivo ahead of me and grabs him by the arm. "Your father says you're comin', boy. Wait, wait. Take Addie to your place first," Father slurs, and Ivo nods.

Ivo and I are soon alone, standing in front of the open door to my empty house. I have a wicked thought, a delicious thought. Greta doesn't know that we should be at her house, and the drunkards at the Gilded Gopher won't miss Ivo. I look at the open door, then at Ivo, who smiles back at me and shakes his head.

17 March, 1247, Night

Ambers and pinks roast the sky, causing the row houses, trees, and church spires in the distance to blacken more and more as the sun sets. Ivo stares pensively at the ground as we walk, his blonde hair bouncing with each long stride. I follow his wide paces as quickly as I can. The brilliance of the sunset illuminates the silhouette of his lean back and arms through his translucent tunic. I tilt my head, watching the ebb and flow of his long muscles as he walks. I feel myself enjoying the sight of him in a way that I have never allowed myself to before. My lips curve into a smile as I watch him. He turns and catches my stare. Embarrassment burns my face, but he smiles and reaches for my hand, which I gladly give. We make the short trip from my house to his hand-in-hand.

He wouldn't join me in my house alone. I suppose that was the noble thing to do. That's Ivo. Noble. Like one of the knights out of

Mama's tales, if knights could be poor farmers. I don't see the harm in a moment alone. All I wanted was a kiss without interruption, at least I tell myself that is all I wanted. Things are so different, now, in Cologne with the fever and the unrest. Tomorrow is less a given than it ever was, and it makes me bold. I may as well say what I want to say, and do as I want to do, for who knows if I shall see tomorrow.

"You're quiet," I say. "Are you all right?"

"Yeah," he mumbles distractedly. He looks up and tosses his hair, uncovering dark blue eyes. He opens his mouth to explain, then thinks better of it and closes it again.

The walk to his house is short. To my great relief, he asks me to wait outside for a moment. I am sure Greta is still displeased with me, and shan't be happy that I am staying with them tonight. And if I know Greta, she won't hesitate in telling me so.

"Where have you been all afternoon? Where's your father? He better not be getting into any more trouble," Greta complains.

The sweet scent of pea porridge wafts through the evening air, perfectly cooked. My mouth waters, and my stomach rumbles.

"The men are meeting at the Gilded Gopher," I hear Ivo tell her.

"Hmph, they'd better be figuring a way out of this mess. Sara told me the Archbishop has ordered everyone back to church."

"Yeah."

"Come here," Greta pleads.

"Mother..." Ivo protests.

"I was worried about you, my son," she complains. Ivo's footsteps shuffle across the floor, and Greta sighs. I can hear her kiss him on the cheek a half-dozen times.

"I'm all right," Ivo sighs.

"Hmph, you're lucky," she replies, clapping something off of her hands.

"Did you still want me to go into the manor and pull the weeds from the beds...?" Ivo asks, changing the subject.

"Mmm hmm," she replies. "After that, you're in for the rest of the night."

"Father wants me to meet him at the Gopher and... Ansel wants Addie to stay here." I assume Greta gives him a dirty look because he breaks into defense. "I swear it. Ask him in the morning."

Greta sighs, "Ivo, I don't want either of you walking around tonight."

"Yes, Mother," he replies quickly.

"...But if your father orders it, you had better go."

A father's orders always trump a mother's.

The door swings open, and Ivo grabs my hand. We storm through the house and out the back door into the DeBelle Manor yards where we are to pull weeds from the garden beds. I am weary with hunger. Ivo sighs with frustration at my turtle-like pace. Before I can even bend to pluck one small dandelion, Ivo's thrown two piles of weeds behind him. I'm still bothered by his rejection, and I cannot hold my tongue a moment longer.

"Why did you say no?" I ask, tugging hard on a stubborn weed.

"What?" Ivo rises and knits his brow.

"Why didn't you come into the house with me?" I ask, shaking my hands to remove the mud.

He returns to the weeding, saying nothing.

"Are you afraid or are you too noble?" I accuse.

"I think the second is the better of the two options," Ivo grunts as he tosses another handful of weeds behind him, "so let's say that I am too noble."

"Why?" I ask.

"Why?" He repeats in confusion.

"Why must you be so noble?"

"Why must you be so stubborn? Why must the sky be blue and the grass green?" He jests, playing at seriousness. "These questions are for the philosophers and the theologians, not us."

"Be serious." I sigh, and I know he shall do just the opposite.

He kneels before me, one knee sinking into the mire, and reaches for my fingers with his mud-covered hand. "Because I, Sir Nobleheart, value your virtue, Lady Chastity.

I roll my eyes. "You weren't going to get my virtue," I huff, ripping my fingers from his grip and flinging the mud into the gardens.

He claps the mud from his hands, and rises swiftly, narrowing the gap between us in two paces. He approaches too quickly, and I step away from him fearfully. He grabs me by the wrists and pulls me close. "Why did you invite me in?" He whispers into my ear. The warm wind of his breath against my neck causes a ripple of goose bumps to rise across my flesh like waves on a pond crested by a pebble. My stomach tightens, and then roars embarrassingly loudly. I feel the burn of blush rise upon my cheeks, and Ivo releases me.

"Hungry, Milady?" he inquires, with a tip of his head.

I avert my eyes for a moment and nod.

"Well, Mother'll be almost done making supper," he says with a cough as though nothing of importance has transpired between us.

I kneel beside him and yank on a massive weed. It snaps at the bottom, and I fall back into the dirt. Ivo offers me a hand, and I rise. He bends in front of me, sticking his fingers into the dirt like a trowel and uproots the weed I had worked so hard on.

The clanging of a wooden spoon on metal rings through the cooling air. Ivo looks up and brushes the dirt off his hands. "Supper's ready."

◈

Four bowls are clumsily set across the table. Levi's large eyes and tiny nose perch behind his bowl as his fingers dance anxiously in place. Ivo sits a foot taller next to his little brother.

"How is Addie getting home?" Greta inquires as she spoons porridge into Ivo's bowl, her eyes darting between us.

"I guess her father'll get her in the morning," Ivo replies around a mouthful of food.

"So she's to stay the night?"

"I think so, unless they leave the Gopher early," Ivo replies, and Greta purses her lips with dissatisfaction.

"Well, if she's staying the night, she'll get your bed, boys, and you'll be in with me."

Levi's eyes light up and he flashes a smile full of green porridge. "We get to sleep in Mother's bed!" he cheers. Ivo chuckles at his brother and shakes his head.

◈

Levi has heavy eyelids before he even finishes his supper, and Greta looks weary, too. They must go to sleep early every night, for they rise at dawn during the week to head for the fields. I have to admit, I'm tired, too, but I'm anxious to make my way to the Gilded Gopher. I want to know what they discuss. I want to know what shall happen next Sunday. We make our way to bed, and I pity Ivo who doesn't look the least bit sleepy. It is so boring to lay sleepless in bed. I wonder why he doesn't just leave for the Gopher as his father ordered.

A loud snort wakes me, and I nearly jump from Ivo's bed. It takes me a moment to remember where I am, and as soon as I do, I am cursing myself for falling asleep. If it is past two in the morning, the men at the Gilded Gopher shall be beyond drunk and beyond important discussions. The bed is so warm. It calls me to lie back down. *You are probably too late, better just to get a good night's rest.*

I shake the thoughts from my head and throw on my cloak. I must go to the tavern. It is the only way I shall hear the truth.

∫∫

I walk along the houses and the wall quietly so I am not noticed. The full moon lights the streets. The brilliance shall make me easy to spot if I am not careful to stay among the shadows and hide the fog of my shallow breaths. Cologne is a cold, blue world on this cold March night. The sky, a bright indigo dotted with innumerable stars. The trees, a near-black navy. The buildings, a shade in between. It is quiet and beautiful, but I am not used to the silence, and it scares me.

...Swish-swash-swish...

"What was that?" I think. Fear overwhelms me for a moment. Someone follows me. My heart beats violently against the bones in my chest, and I press myself into the shadows between two row houses, looking around for some evil, wanton man who plans to rob me, or worse.

...Swish-Swash-Swish...

I whip around quickly, my eyes darting in all directions. Fear has me frozen in place as I watch for my attacker. I slide to the ground, feeling around desperately for any kind of weapon. I'm blinded by the heavy fog of my rapid breath. I envision a vagabond, stalking lowly in the shadows, waiting to pounce.

...SWISH-SWASH-SWISH...

123

It's getting closer. I shriek inside my head. Frantically, my hands sweep through the dirt searching for anything I can use to defend myself. My fingers stumble across a smooth, hard surface. A cobblestone. I wrap my fingers around it and pull it from the dirt. Thank God, it is as big as a fist. I hope it's enough to save me.

The shuffle is loud, only a few paces away. Still low to the ground, I spin around quickly, but it's too late. I feel the breeze as my attacker pounces. Long, bony fingers muffle my screams. A strong arm ensnares me, but I fight, and we both fall to the ground. The stone slips from my grasp and rolls a few feet away. I squirm toward it, but he has me by the legs and is working his way to my waist. The cobble is just within my grasp. Just one more inch, and I'll have it. With a grunt, I fight his pull with all my strength and grab it, clutching it firmly. I sit up quick and swing it down onto the side of his face. A second before I hear the crack, my attacker speaks in a desperate, familiar whisper.

"It's me."

"Ivo!" I cry, slithering backward through the dirt. "Ivo?"

He moans, and I hear him spit something out. A tooth lands next to my foot. "I woke up and you were gone." He groans again.

"Oh, my God! I'm so sorry!" He sits back cradling his cheek, and I lunge toward him. "Let me see."

I peel his hand from his face and press my cold fingers lightly to his cheek, tracing his red and swollen jaw line. He stares through me coldly. His hair shines silver in the moonlight, and his pale skin is creamy white. Even hunched over with a missing molar and a quickly swelling face, he looks angelic. I cock my head to the side and stare at him with pity. I contemplate pressing the cold cobblestone to his face to cool the burn, but that would probably make him angrier.

"I didn't know…" I explain apologetically.

"Well, I'd hope not," he replies bitterly.

"You should have said it was you before—" I begin, but his scowl silences me mid-sentence.

"Before you hit me with the rock. I didn't know you had a rock," he says slowly and thickly.

"I'm sorry."

He nods as though he accepts my apology, stands, and brushes himself off. I stare up at him remorsefully, and he smirks with the good side of his face. He extends his hand and pulls me up. My hand stays in the niche of his arm as we creep through the streets of Cologne to the Gilded Gopher. I make a hundred apologies as we make our way there.

He is about to knock on the door, but I pull him back. "How do I get in?"

He furrows his brow in thought. His eyes widen for a moment, and then he shakes his head. I can tell he has an idea, but doesn't want to share it.

"I'll walk you back." He suggests, his voice sounding thick from his injured jaw. "This is no place for girls. I'll tell you everything in the morning. I promise."

"I'm not leaving."

"Addie…" He urges.

"I'm not leaving, so either help me in, or I'll find my own way."

"Fine," he huffs, and shakes his head at my stubbornness. "Take out your braid, and cover your face with your hair."

He helps me shake my hair into my face. It is the first time he has ever run his fingers through my hair.

"You still look like you," he scowls. "Here. Wear my cloak over yours." I look up at him through my hair with the two cloaks on.

"Keep your eyes on the ground," he orders. "And don't smile. Hunch your back." He reaches down and smears dirt across my face. "Try to look...ugly," he says, and I smile because it means, even though I am hunched over and covered in cloaks and dirt, he still thinks I'm pretty.

"That's not ugly, Addie." I squint an eye and scowl. Ivo takes two handfuls of dirt and rubs them through my hair and upon my outer cloak.

"It's quite dark in there. I doubt anyone shall recognize me."

"No, but we want you to be ugly and dirty so no one shall try to buy you."

I nod as I realize the only way for me to get into the Gilded Gopher is if I pretend to be one of their harlots.

"What if a man asks me anyway?" I ask.

He's silent for a moment.

"Say no, and if he persists, then get me."

"I'll just try to be as ugly, and mean, and invisible as I can," I say.

"Good."

I knock on the door, just as Ivo has told me to do. He stands around the corner and shall knock once I have entered, or come to my aid if I need it.

A large man opens the door, and I don't say anything, hoping he'll let me in, but he stands in my way.

"What do you want?" he barks.

"What do you think?" I snap in a hoarse voice. He steps aside. I add a limp for good measure. I descend the stairs into the tavern, purchase ale, and find a seat in the far corner. I look around for familiar faces. Upon Ivo's entry, the men ring out a cheer, and I can see Erik, but not Father.

Dozens of conversations hum throughout the tavern ranging from boisterous laughter to devious whispers to heated arguments.

My eyes adjust to the flickering candles, and strange silhouettes become familiar faces. I listen intently to several conversations, overhearing many things I shouldn't hear, things I do not want to know.

Otto brags to Gregor about his many affairs. He says he courted Sal many years ago before Paul married her, and that he sometimes used to wish he'd married her, but, seeing how ugly she's gotten, and that she has not birthed a single son, he's glad he didn't.

Otto isn't any happier with his present wife though, and says he should have never married her either since the barren witch never gave him a child who lived past two winters. Then, he describes his poor wife's appearance unkindly. I have to put my hands in my lap to keep from throwing my mug at his head, and I bite my tongue to keep from accusing him of being a dirty braggart, undeserving of a wife or sons.

The boasting continues, and Otto must not recognize the discomfort in Gregor's face, for he continues with his tales. Otto says he courts Ivan's sister, Ilsa, who he says has the face of a horse.

Otto describes the affair vividly to Gregor, Severin's gatekeeper, who works with Ivan. At first, poor Gregor is stunned into silence by Otto's disgusting boasts, then he tries unsuccessfully to change the subject each time Otto takes a drink.

I realize these two aren't likely to discuss serious matters, so I find another seat. There must be someone here who discusses the Archbishop's demands.

For over an hour, I hear nothing but confessions from a bunch of drunkards. It makes me wish I had stayed in bed. I nearly give up hope until I hear Elias, the only sober man in the house, discussing important matters.

"That's heresy," slurs a drunkard whose voice I do not recognize.

"How do you know it's heresy?" Elias replies.

"A priest said so," the drunkard slurs back.

"And how do you know he speaks the truth?" Elias asks as the drunkard guzzles his ale.

"I don't know." the drunkard stumbles.

"That's right. You don't know because it's all in Latin," Elias speaks with childlike enthusiasm. "But I have a Bible in German!" he whispers with even more excitement.

"*Pfffftt*," the drunkard scoffs as though it were more likely that Elias had the Holy Grail.

"I do have a Bible in German. Do you want to see it?"

The drunkard's eyes widen. "No! Elias, you must watch you say. They'll burn you at the stake!" The drunkard's speech sobers up as he whispers the warning to Elias.

"Some things are worth burning for," Elias says with disappointment. "You should read it."

"I don't know how to read!" the man laughs. "Besides, who'll care for my children if I'm burned at the stake?"

"I suppose you're right," Elias sighs. "But know this... it says in here that it is harder for a rich man to get into heaven than a camel to fit through the eye of a needle."

"What's a camel?"

"It's a beast, about the size of a horse," Elias replies matter-of-factly.

"Oh. So?"

"So? A camel is too big to get through the eye of a needle. The point is that rich men don't easily get into Heaven." Elias sounds exasperated from explaining to his very dim listener. There is a long pause and a frustrated sigh from Elias. "The priests are richer than the richest men in town. They eat, when we starve. While we're dying of fever, they throw feasts and take bribes to perform funerals—"

"Hey, don't bring Ansel into this." The man interrupts. "He did right by his wife. Well, at least he tried to. If I'd had the money to bury my Johanna, I would have. To Johanna!" The drunkard's beer sloshes for a short moment as he raises the mug in toast to his dead wife.

"You misunderstand me, friend. If I were Ansel, I would have done the same. The point is, God would not charge for a funeral or a decent burial. And neither should these so-called men of God!"

"Yeah," the drunkard replies after some time. Is he afraid of what Elias is telling him or just unable to understand it?

"If you ever change your mind…" Elias extends with a hopeless tinge to his voice.

"Sure. Sure." The drunkard feigns appreciation and gives an exaggerated yawn.

"It's too bad a unanimous decision was not reached today."

"Yeah…"

"I believe it best if everyone boycotts the Church. Divided, we are far less strong. What shall happen to those of us who continue the boycott without the support of the rest of Airsbach?" Elias presses.

"It's getting late. I think I'm going to go," he yawns again dramatically.

"Yeah, I should, too. I hope you change your mind."

"If you'd asked me ten years ago, I'd be right there with you, but I have children to care for. I like Ansel's idea. I think we should all just go to the other church," the drunkard says.

"Yeah," Elias sighs. "I cannot help but wonder if they're any better."

"Only one way to find out." The man slaps Elias on the back, picks up his cloak, and leaves.

Ivo walks by me and stops. He kneels down and whispers, "I'm going to get one more drink, and then I'll leave. Wait a few moments and follow me out." He heads to the bar, takes his drink back to the table, finishes it, and walks out the door. I wait a moment and then follow him, heading out into the cold street.

I wrap his cloak around him and shake the dirt from my hair. I quickly braid it back and wipe the dirt from my face. He wraps his arm around my shoulder and briskly rubs my freezing arms as we walk back to his house.

"Did you hear anything about next Sunday?" I ask.

"No. You?"

"Not much." I relay what I heard from Elias's conversation. "It sounds like everyone likes your idea. The people of Airsbach might find another church," I conclude and Ivo nods.

"I'll never go back to St. Laurentius, Ivo… ever. I'll never listen to another word that godless bastard has to say."

Ivo is silent and I am sure we are thinking the same thing. We hope we shan't be forced to.

෧෨෧

The trip back to his house seems too short, and we walk slowly to make it longer, pausing in front of the door. Ivo turns to face me, and I suddenly feel aware of the dirt in my hair and on my face. His arm slides up my shoulder until it embraces the back of my head. His fingers branch through my hair, raising a ticklish shiver down my back. My stomach heats with anticipation. His warm lips press against my forehead, and the tingle lingers. My hands want to dart out and grab the sides of his face so I can kiss him like I should have done a dozen times by now. But I am filthy and this is not how I want our first kiss to be. Instead, I bask in the warm tingle in my stomach and on my forehead. We enter the house quietly, and I lie in his bed with a smile on my face.

∞❧

I drift in and out of sleep, grinning about my kiss. I want the sun to rise so I can see him again, even if it is only to break our fast. Tomorrow is Monday, and, now that it is spring, I shan't see Ivo much at all, for the farmers shall be in the fields from dawn to dusk readying the fields for this year's crops. It makes me sad, for I know I shall be grieved tomorrow without him around. I shall work so I can keep from thinking too much about Mama and too much about missing Ivo. Still, it shall be a long week.

18 March, 1247

"Better wake up, boy," a hoarse voice orders as the breeze of a large object sweeps past my cheek, smacks the wall next to me, and lands with a thud. My hazy eyes flash open, and I shoot up violently from the unfamiliar bed. The room is a blurry brown smudge, and I try to quickly rub the sleep from my eyes.

"I said, get up!" the voice commands, and my vision clears in just enough time to see the second boot fly at me right before it slams into the side of my face. My fingers rush to the furious heat above my cheek.

I narrow my eyes at him, pick up the boot, and throw it at his head, but he dodges it.

"Watch yourself, girl. If you were quicker you'd'a' ducked," Erik scolds with a drunken slur.

"I was sleeping."

"You sleep too long," he growls.

Ivo told me his father woke him in this way. I didn't put much thought to it, but now it all makes sense. The odd bruising on his arm and stomach the day Father disappeared came from his father's hateful hands, not from clumsiness, hard farm labors, or even horseplay like I had thought. Ivo's being beaten. Badly. It makes my hands shake with anger.

I pinch my lips and bite my tongue to hold back any retort. I'd like to tell Erik what I truly think of him. He's a lazy, useless, bitter, old drunkard. The words resonate in my head, dying to be spoken, but the boot that struck my cheek was meant for Ivo, not me. If I upset Erik further, who shall he take it out on? What if it is Ivo?

How could anyone want to hurt Ivo? A boy who helps anyone and everyone naturally. A boy who works all day in the fields and then in an apprenticeship by night without complaint. A boy who has a smile upon his face every day. It is a crime that he must wake to this while his father sits around, spoiled from drink, barking orders. It is only the thought of making life harder for Ivo that keeps my mouth closed.

"Boy!" Erik shouts, and spit flies across the room.

"They've already gone, Erik. It's Monday. They're probably in the fields."

Just as I finish speaking, Ivo skids through the door, his hands caked with mud.

"Yes, Father," he huffs, breathing heavily. Ivo notices my welt, and his eyes dart angrily to his father. He rushes towards me, but before he can reach me, his father grips his arm and whips him around. Ivo is strong, but he is young and lanky, the opposite of his stocky father.

"Where have you been? What's she doing here?" Erik barks, his nose pressing onto Ivo's.

"My father ordered me to sleep here last night while you were at the Gopher," I say.

Erik pauses for a moment, looking into his tarnished memory of the night before. His eyes widen as he remembers, and he releases Ivo's arm from his grip, shoving him backwards. Ivo stands, frozen and red-faced, his eyes cast downwards as Erik stumbles outside and pisses.

Ivo turns toward me, and I look upon him with pity. His angry lips squeeze together. He turns his face, averting his gaze, and I notice the swelling in his jaw

I feel frozen. Do I comfort him? What would I want Ivo to do if I had been the one unjustly embarrassed?

"Your father's a bastard, Ivo."

"And what am I to do about it?" He growls.

"I just meant—"

"Is it not enough that I try to take everyone's beatings? I could fight back, you know."

"I, uh—"

"Wait until I finish my apprenticeship." He hisses, his face darkening with anger. "I'll get us all out of here, and then I can show him what I really think of him."

He storms out the back door, past his father, into the manor yard where beds are being plucked of weeds and fertilized for spring flowers. I follow him, not to say anything, just to offer help. I know it is best for now if I turn his mind from his embarrassment.

I join Ivo and Levi at one of the beds and watch as he furiously tears chunk of weeds out, one after another. I give him a few moments to get over his anger, and I pull weeds as well. Levi giggles as he watches me struggle.

"You have to wiggle the big ones, Addie," Levi says, and I notice a small bruise on his wrist. I recall Ivo having black eyes and split lips at an even younger age than Levi's. Suddenly, it is as though I can feel the pain of the blows myself.

"Why don't you show me?" I say so I can look him over for bruises.

"If you pull too hard the top breaks off, and it all grows back." Levi demonstrates though I'm not listening closely. His neck and arms are free of injury, and I sigh in relief. He stands up and looks into my face, checking to see that I've understood his lesson.

"Oh, uh, like this, you mean." I stammer and bend to wiggle a weed free from the soil. I tear it out, roots and all, and Levi nods his head.

"What happened to your wrist?" I ask him.

"Me and Matthew were playing crusaders." He says, looking at the bruise.

I suddenly feel Greta's eyes on me, so I return her stare coldly. How can I respect a mother who allows a man to beat her children so brutally? I expect her to glare back proudly, but she looks upon me with sad eyes and quickly averts her stare, returning to work. Then I think upon what Ivo had just said. He takes everyone's beatings. Who knows how horribly Erik has beaten Greta? Perhaps, he beats the children worse if she tries to protect them. The thought makes me cringe.

I go back to pulling weeds, and Levi continues his instructions on weed-pulling, though I know what I'm doing now. I look up to see a slight smile touch Ivo's face, so I slowly work my way over and let him instruct me on flower gardening.

His face relaxes a bit and the angry blush caused by his father's scolding fades. I am glad for that. We pull weeds, scrape at the soil, add fertilizer, and scrape some more. Levi is absolutely delighted I am there to help, but I cannot stop myself from looking the little boy over for bruises every chance I get.

❧

We finish for dinner early, and I am glad, for I never had a chance to break my fast. I don't want to take another bite of food that Erik has earned, or rather, forces his family to earn. It wouldn't taste the same, now that I see him for what he really is.

"Can I take Ivo to my house for dinner? You have fed me many times. It seems only fair," I ask.

Erik scowls, but Greta intercepts. "Be back after dinner, Ivo."

"Does he really throw a boot at you every day?" I whisper as we walk up Foller Strasse.

"No. Sometimes he throws mugs. You know, whatever is nearest to him," he says with a painful laugh.

"I think I'm safer at home. Maybe you'd be safer there, as well," I suggest. My father, being good friends with Erik, would never allow Ivo to stay with us and leave his father's home, even if he knew how Ivo was being treated. Erik needs Ivo to help with the work.

Ivo grins halfheartedly and nods. His bright blonde hair falls into his eyes and is promptly swept aside with a toss of his head to reveal the huge bruise of dark purples, blues, and greens that I'd made last night with a cobblestone. I stop to stare piteously at it, and he places his hand gently on the welt on my cheek.

"Does it hurt?" he asks, as he traces the welt lightly.

"A little... it's not too bad."

"He's such a bastard," he sighs, and I nod in agreement. "I'm sorry."

"It's nothing compared to what I did to you last night," I say. But what I do not say is, "It's nothing compared to the beatings you've endured for God knows how long from your father."

A cold mist floats through the streets causing the ground to mirror the milky grey of the sky. If it were not for the row houses, it would be hard to tell where the ground ends and the sky begins. It is still early, well before dinner, which makes me wonder how early Ivo had awoken. Did he get any sleep at all? He never seems to need it. When we'd catch fireflies, even at midnight, he ran with the same speed as he did during the day. My eyelids felt like they were carrying bags of flour by midnight, as did the rest of my body. I doubt we got back to his house before three in the morning. I woke as the bells struck seven, and Ivo was up well before that, probably five o'clock if he'd finished all of his work by now. Normally, he works the fields until sunset, eats supper, and then heads to his apprenticeship with Michael, the armorer. I doubt he ever gets more than five hours of sleep. My stomach twists into knots on fewer than seven hours sleep.

"Aren't you tired?" I ask.

"No," he replies as if it is a peculiar question, as if I am the strange one for needing sleep.

"You only slept two hours."

"So?" He says with a shrug. We walk silently for a few blocks.

"Galadriel should be going home today," I say hopefully. "Perhaps, she's already gone."

"I doubt she'd leave without saying goodbye."

"Do you like her?" I ask.

"I don't know. I don't know her," he shrugs.

"She fancies my father. I know it. Last night, Father placed his hands on her shoulders for a moment, and she blushed! And she beams with delight when he tries to pretend to like her cooking. I wish she'd just go home," I huff.

"I'll race you to the house," Ivo says, changing the subject.

"Do I get a head start?"

"Does it matter?" he replies arrogantly.

"Probably not," I laugh. I pick up a dirt clod and throw it at his stomach, which he successfully dodges. "Depends on how much of a head start you give me."

"To the count of five?"

"Ten," I counter, but rather than reply, he starts counting.

"One... two..." I gather my skirts and bolt through the crowds of Filzengraben. "...three... four... five..." Ivo finishes counting just as I see the door to my house. Just as I feel I might beat him this time, he leaps past me effortlessly and reaches the door first.

I fake a pout and open the door, expecting Father to be working at his bench, but he is not. The house is strangely silent. Ivo and I run up the stairs, and I wonder if Father is quietly dining at the table. He's not. Mugs are strewn about the table, benches, and floor, remnants of the night before. A snore roars through the house, clearly coming from his bedroom. Father has finally slept in his own bed again, I think happily. He must be sleeping off his drinks from last night.

I climb to my room to wash my face and change my chainse. To my surprise, the room is empty. Galadriel has left already. Better yet, I have not been sent away with her! I smile happily. If my welted cheek hurts, I am too numb with glee to feel it. Perhaps Father stayed up all night and escorted her to the gate as early as possible.

I descend the ladder clumsily, racing to Father's bedroom to hug him, for I am so happy he has changed his mind and shall let me stay in Cologne. But just as I enter his room, and the words "good morning" beginning to roll off my tongue, I am halted by a horrific site before me.

My shirtless father cradles a bare-shouldered, sleeping, yet stupidly grinning Galadriel in my mother's bed. My gasp wakes

Father, whose startle shakes Galadriel awake as well. Frozen with shock, I stand as my eyes well with tears, and my cloak slips through my fingers. Galadriel clutches the blankets and tries to hide beneath them as Father squints his eyes, trying to see who is standing before him. Is this why he wanted me to stay at Ivo's? So he could take Galadriel to Mama's bed?

"How could you? In *her* bed!" I scream at them both. I snatch up my cloak, wipe the tears from my cheeks, and run from our house.

"What happened?" Ivo calls and follows me out the door.

The most saddening thing is that the one person I want to run to is the one person that I cannot. I need my mother. I pause halfway down Filzengrabben. Where am I going to go? Should I run out Severin's gate and to the woods to her grave just so I can tell her about her husband's betrayal? And how could I, even if she is dead? My heart jumps hard and fast. I sob, choking for air. The crowd seems to spin around me, and I do not know in which direction I am headed. Two long arms wrap around me, holding me up. Ivo whispers in my ear. "I know where we should go. Come on."

I let him take me across Cologne and out St. Kunibert's gate, half-carrying me as I cry.

There is a huddle of oaks just outside the gate. If you climb them, you can see the beauty of our homeland; boats from different lands floating up and down the Rhine, patches of farm fields filled with workers, the streaks of bright hues in the streams around the city as dyers color their cloth, and the myriad of steeples of Cologne and Neuss.

Ivo finds the thickest tree and raises an eyebrow at me. He wants to climb. I shake my head, knowing very well that I'm not going to be able to stand much longer, much less climb because my hands and legs are trembling so badly from my anger. So he sits with his back to the trunk, and I sit next to him. Over the course of the afternoon, my head transitions from his shoulder to his lap. He plays with my hair as I weep, mumbling curses at my father.

The sun eventually breaks through the clouds, and varying shades of green cascade through the myriad of leaves above us. The combination of warmth, exhaustion, and the hushed sounds of the river lull me into sleep.

My nap is dreamless, the kind that feels like I have closed my eyes for just a moment but have really slept for many hours. It is better than the nightmares I usually have. My head throbs behind my puffy eyes and nose. My stomach knots, and the lump in my throat swells as I miss Mama and pity her at the same time for having such a terrible husband.

I hope she knows nothing of any of this, that Heaven keeps her ignorant of the troubles on Earth. If Heaven is a blissful place, then how could she know of them? How could she enjoy Heaven if she did know of them? My logic brings some peace. If Mama cannot see us, then she cannot see me suffering. She didn't see what happened this morning, or worse what happened last night between Father and Galadriel. Perhaps she does not know. I try desperately to convince myself.

I open my eyes and roll over, looking up at Ivo who has fallen asleep against the tree trunk. The sun, while still high in the sky, is beginning to descend behind us. It shines through a treeless patch of sky, haloing the crown of Ivo's head. So he needs sleep after all. His face is peaceful, but his head rests crookedly on the trunk of the tree. He is heavenly and painfully distorted at the same time, much like Christ on the cross, or so many of the martyrs, whose pain decorates the stained glass windows of the churches in Cologne.

I know Ivo is likely to face punishment for not returning to his parents' house for work, but I cannot bring myself to wake him. Perhaps I can come up with a grand lie to tell Greta and Erik, blaming all of this on me, so he can at least escape one beating. I watch him as clouds roll over us and disappear into the distance.

∞

My neck is sore from lying in Ivo's lap, and I can't stand it another moment. I sit up and Ivo wakes viciously, throwing punches. His eyes are wide open and wild with fright. I shriek and call his name, but even though his eyes are on mine, they look through me. He turns on the tree and punches it until his knuckles bleed. I pounce on his back, shaking him and shouting his name, but nothing helps. He mumbles something and I stop shaking him, desperate to hear the name of the person he is fighting so hard.

"How could you do it?" he shouts so loud it flushes a hundred tiny black birds from their trees. Then, just like that, he stops. Ivo returns, his arms and eyes relaxing again. He must see the terror in my eyes. "What? What's wrong?" he says sleepily.

"You were having some sort of fit or terror," I cry. "Look at your hands. You were punching the tree. I tried to wake you, but I couldn't." I look into his eyes expecting surprise, but there is none. He shrugs like it is nothing new. "What were you dreaming about? What's upset you like this?"

"I cannot remember my dreams," he replies shortly.

"Ever?" I ask. "You look tired still. Put your head on my lap for a while."

"I don't want to sleep anymore," he says, and I pity him more than ever. He doesn't even have solace in his dreams.

"Wouldn't it be nice if we could just run away," I say.

"And how would we live? You are a woman shoemaker with no coin to start her trade, and I am not yet done with my apprenticeship with the armorer."

"We could run away and live in the woods," I suggest.

"You'd not last a day in the woods," he laughs.

"Probably not alone."

"Probably not at all."

"Just because I am clumsy doesn't mean I am useless, you know."

"Fine, how are we going to survive?"

"Well, we could stock up on things for a while so we didn't go into the woods empty-handed. I can cook. You can farm. We can learn how to hunt while we ready ourselves. We'd make a little dwelling at first until we could make a bigger one. I thought we could move close to another city, but not so close that we'd be bothered by the politics of princes and bishops."

"The woods are filled with things much eviler than princes and bishops," Ivo says.

"Like big, fat, old witches that shall fatten us up and turn us into gingerbread?" I laugh.

"I meant thieves and wolves. What do you mean witches?"

"Your mother never told you the story of Hansel and Gretel?" I widen my eyes in surprise.

"My mother's never been much of a storyteller."

"It's a story Mama used to tell me to keep me from wandering off into the woods alone. I don't know why though. We aren't really near the woods."

"It's been a long time since I've heard a good story." Ivo rests his hands behind his head and leans back against the tree trunk.

∽◎∾

Mama had usually told me this story during the day, for she thought it might give me nightmares, but it never scared me. I begged her to tell it to me night after night, curled in a night shift under my blankets, our breaths steaming in the cold of the night. The thought brings me back to another time. A happier time.

∞

"Tell me the one about the children and the witch with the gingerbread house!"

"Again?" She asked, feigning surprise, for every time she told me a new story of hers, I made her tell it over and over until I memorized it completely.

"Please," I whined and pouted my lips as pitifully as possible.

"My little Snow White. Does nothing scare you?" Mama laughed.

"Why do you call me that?" I said with a scowl.

"Why do I call you what?" She replied, smiling.

"Snow White," I humphed.

"Because your skin is as bright and beautiful as freshly fallen snow. Now do you want me to tell you the story or not?"

"Tell me! Tell me!"

"All right, then." She said and scooted her back against the wall. I slid deeper beneath the covers and rested my head on her lap as she played with my hair. She rarely made it to the end of her stories before I'd be fast asleep.

"Once upon a time…." I prompted.

∞

I've had the story memorized for years, but I know I cannot tell it like her. She would do all the characters' voices in just the right way. A lump in my throat swells at the memory, but I cannot let the pain of my grief let me forget her. Mama's stories were a part of her. In a way, telling them brings her back to life.

"Are you going to tell the story or not?" Ivo says.

"Give me a moment. I'm trying to remember how it goes." I lie, swallowing hard and trying not to let the sentiment bring tears to my eyes.

"On the edge of a great forest lived a poor woodcutter with his wife and two children. The boy was called Hansel and the girl Gretel. The woodcutter had little to bite and to break, and once, when great dearth fell on the land, he could no longer procure even daily bread."

"Wait, what's a dearth?" Ivo asks.

"I'm not sure. Perhaps it's an old word for drought or bad soil."

I continue. "Now he, the father I mean, thought over this by night in his bed, and tossed about in his anxiety. He groaned and said to his wife: 'What is to become of us? How are we to feed our poor children when we no longer have anything even for ourselves?'"

I use my most wicked voice for the evil stepmother. "'I'll tell you what, husband,' answered the woman. 'Early tomorrow morning, we shall take the children out into the forest to where it is the thickest. There we will light a fire for them, and give each of them one piece of bread. Then we shall go to our work and leave them alone. They will not find the way home again, and we shall be rid of them.'"

I muster a deep surprised voice for the husband. "'No, wife,' said the man, 'I will not do that. How can I bear to leave my children alone in the forest? The wild animals would soon come and tear them to pieces.'

"'Oh, you fool!' said she. 'Then we must all four die of hunger. You may as well plane the planks for our coffins.' The wretch left him no peace until he consented.

"'But I feel very sorry for the poor children, all the same,' said the man," I say in a deep voice.

"Unable to sleep for hunger, the two children had heard what their stepmother had said. Gretel wept bitter tears, and said to Hansel: 'Now all is over with us,'" I say in a little girl voice.

"'Be quiet, Gretel,' said Hansel. 'Do not distress yourself. I will soon find a way to help us.' And when the parents had fallen asleep, he got up, put on his cloak, opened the door below, and crept outside. The moon shone brightly, and the white pebbles, which lay in front of the house, glittered like silver groschens. Hansel stooped and stuffed the little pocket of his coat with as many as he could fit. Then he went back and said to Gretel: 'Be comforted, dear little sister, and sleep in peace. God will not forsake us,' and he lay down again in his bed.

"Before the sun had risen, the woman came and awoke the two children, saying: 'Get up, you sluggards! We are going into the forest to fetch wood.' She gave each a little piece of bread and said: 'There is something for your dinner, but do not eat it up before then, for you will get nothing else.'

"Gretel took the bread under her apron, as Hansel had the pebbles in his pocket. Then they all set out together on the way to the forest. After they had walked a short time, Hansel stood still and peeped back at the house, and did so again and again.

"His father said, 'Hansel, what are you looking at there and staying behind for? Pay attention, and do not forget how to use your legs.'

"'Ah, father,' said Hansel. 'I am looking at my little white cat, which is sitting up on the roof, and wants to say goodbye to me.'

"The wife said, 'Fool! That is not your little cat,'" I say in the wicked stepmother voice. "That is the morning sun which is shining on the chimneys.' Hansel, however, had not been looking back at the cat, but had been throwing one of the white pebbles from his pocket on the road.

"When they had reached the middle of the forest, the father said, 'Now, children, pile up some wood, and I shall light a fire that you may not be cold.'

"Hansel and Gretel gathered brushwood together, as high as a little hill. The brushwood was lit, and when the flames were burning very high, the woman said, 'Now, children, lay yourselves down by the fire and rest. We will go into the forest and cut some wood. When we have finished, we will come back and fetch you away.'

"Hansel and Gretel sat by the fire, and when noon came, each ate a little piece of bread. They could hear the strokes of an axe, so they believed their father was near. It was not the axe, however, but a branch which he had fastened to a withered tree which the wind was blowing backwards and forwards. They had been sitting such a long time, and their eyes closed with fatigue. They fell fast asleep.

"When at last they awoke, it was already dark. Gretel began to cry and said, 'How are we to get out of the forest now?'

"But Hansel comforted her and said, 'Just wait a little until the moon has risen, and then we will soon find the way.' And when the full moon had risen, Hansel took his little sister by the hand, and followed the pebbles, which shone like newly-coined groschens, showing them the way.

"They walked the whole night long, and, by break of day, had arrived at their father's house. They knocked on the door, and when the woman opened it and saw that it was Hansel and Gretel, she said, 'You naughty children! Why have you slept so long in the forest? We thought you were never coming back at all!' The father, however, rejoiced, for it had cut him to the heart to leave them behind alone.

"Not long afterwards, there was again great dearth, or drought I suppose, throughout the land, and the children heard their mother saying to their father at night, 'Everything is eaten again. We have only half of a loaf left, and that is the end. The children must go. We will take them farther into the wood so that they will not find their way out again. There is no other means of saving ourselves!'"

"He could just take her into the woods and leave her there," Ivo interrupts. "She probably eats as much as two children."

"I suppose, but I think she'd be a bit suspicious. It is her plan after all."

He nods.

"Where was I?" I ask.

"The evil stepmother wants to leave the children in the woods again because they have no food," he replies.

"Oh, right. So the man's heart was heavy, and he thought, 'It would be better for you to share the last mouthful with your children.' The woman, however, would listen to nothing he had to say, and instead scolded and reproached him. He had yielded the first time, so he must yield again.

"But the children were still awake and had heard the conversation. When the parents were asleep, Hansel got up to collect pebbles as he had done before, but the woman had locked the door, and he could not get out. Nevertheless, he comforted his little sister, and said: 'Do not cry, Gretel. Go to sleep quietly. The good Lord will help us.'

"The stepmother woke them early in the morning and forced them from their beds. A piece of bread was given to them, but it was even smaller than the time before. On the way into the forest, Hansel crumbled his in his pocket, and threw a morsel on the ground every now and then.

"'Hansel, why do you stop and look round?' said the father. 'Go on.'

"'I am looking back at my little pigeon which is sitting on the roof, and wants to say goodbye to me,' answered Hansel.

'Fool!' said the woman, 'That is not your little pigeon. That is the morning sun that is shining on the chimney.'

"Little by little, as they headed into the forest, Hansel threw all the crumbs on the path.

"The woman led the children deeper into the forest, where they had never, in their lives, been before. Again, a great fire was made, and the mother said, 'Just sit there, you children, and when you are tired, you may sleep a little. We are going into the forest to cut wood, and in the evening, when we are done, we shall come and fetch you away.'

"When it was noon, Gretel shared her piece of bread with Hansel, who had scattered his by the way. Then, they fell asleep and evening passed, but no one came to the poor children. Again, they did not wake until it was night. Hansel comforted his little sister and said, 'Just wait, Gretel, until the moon rises, and then we shall see the crumbs of bread which I have strewn about. They will show us our way home again.' When the moon came, they set out. But, alas, they found no crumbs, for the many thousands of birds, which flew about in the woods and fields, had picked them all up.

"Hansel said, 'We shall soon find the way,' but they did not find it. They walked the whole night and all the next day from morning till evening, but they did not get out of the forest. They were very hungry, for they had nothing to eat but two or three berries, which grew on the ground. When they were so weary their legs would carry them no longer, they lay down beneath a tree and fell asleep.

"It was, now, three mornings since they had left their father's house. They began to walk again, but only got deeper and deeper into the forest. If help did not come soon, they would die of hunger and weariness.

"It was midday when they saw a beautiful snow white bird sitting on a bough. It sang so delightfully that they stood still and listened to it. And when its song was over, it spread its wings and flew away before them. They followed it until they reached a little house, and the bird alighted on the roof. When they approached the little house, they saw that it was built of bread and covered with cakes, and the windows were made of clear sugar. 'We will set to work on that,' said Hansel, 'and have a good meal. I shall eat a bit of the roof, and you, Gretel, can eat some of the window. It will taste sweet.'"

"You're making me hungry," Ivo interrupts.

"Do you want to hear the story or not?" I reply.

"I have a pfennig. Do you have any coins?" he asks. I dig into the pockets of my cloak. "I have four."

"Let's go into Hay Market before it closes and get some bread or cakes," he says. "Tell me the story as we walk."

I nod. "Where was I?" I ask.

"Hansel is eating the roof and Gretel is eating the window," he replies.

"Oh, right." Ivo stands and reaches a hand to help me up. We walk on toward Kunibert's gate heading back into the city.

"So… Hansel reached up above and broke off a little of the roof to see how it tasted, and Gretel leaned against the window and nibbled at the panes.

"A soft voice cried from the house, 'Nibble, nibble, gnaw. Who is nibbling at my little house?'" I say in a gruff voice.

"The children answered, 'The wind, the wind. The heaven-born wind,' and went on eating without disturbing themselves. Hansel, who liked the taste of the roof, tore down a great piece of it, and Gretel pushed out a whole round windowpane, sat down, and enjoyed it. Suddenly, the door opened, and a woman as old as the hills, who supported herself on crutches, came creeping out.

"Hansel and Gretel were so terribly frightened that they let fall what they had in their hands. The old woman, however, nodded her head, and said 'Oh, you dear children, who has brought you here? Do come in and stay with me. No harm shall happen to you.'

"She took them both by the hand, and led them into her little house. Good food was set before them. Milk and cakes with sugar, apples, and nuts."

Ivo's stomach growls loudly, and it startles me. I laugh, and he shoves me playfully.

"I thought someone had let a bear loose!" I tease and shove him back. "Do you think you shall make it to Hay Market, or will I have to carry you?"

"I'm not the one who swoons in the street." He teases back, and I narrow my eyes at him. "Are you going to finish the story or not?"

"All right. All right." I say with a giggle as I try to remember my place in the story, but I cannot.

"The children were eating at the witch's table." Ivo prompts.

"Afterwards, two pretty little beds were covered with clean white linen. Hansel and Gretel lay down in them and thought they were in Heaven.

"The old woman had only pretended to be so kind. In reality, she was a wicked witch who lay in wait for children. She had only built the little house of bread in order to entice them there. When a child fell into her power, she killed it, cooked and ate it, and that was a feast day for her. Witches have red eyes, and cannot see far, but they have a keen sense of smell, like the beasts, and are aware when human beings draw near.

"When Hansel and Gretel came near to her cottage, she laughed with malice, and said mockingly to herself, 'I'll have them. They shall not escape me!'

"Early in the morning before the children were awake, the witch was already up. And when she saw both of them sleeping and looking so pretty with their plump and rosy cheeks, she muttered to herself, 'That will be a dainty mouthful!' She seized Hansel with her shriveled hand, carried him into a little stable, and locked him behind a grated door. Scream as he might, it would not help him.

"Then she went to Gretel, shook her till she awoke, and cried: 'Get up, lazy thing. Fetch some water, and cook something good for your brother. He is in the stable outside and is to be made fat. When he is fat, I will eat him.' Gretel began to weep bitterly, but it was all in vain, for she was forced to do what the wicked witch commanded.

"Now, the best food was cooked for poor Hansel, but Gretel got nothing but crab shells. Every morning, the witch crept to the little stable and cried, 'Hansel, stretch out your finger that I may feel if you shall soon be fat.'

"Hansel, however, stretched out a little bone to her, and the old woman, who had dim eyes, could not see it, and believed it was Hansel's finger. She was astonished there was no way of fattening him up. Four weeks had gone by, and Hansel still remained thin. She was seized with impatience and would not wait any longer. 'Now then, Gretel,' she cried to the girl. 'Stir yourself, and bring some water. Let Hansel be fat or lean, for tomorrow I will kill him and cook him.'

"Ah, how the poor little sister did lament when she had to fetch the water, and how her tears did flow down her cheeks! 'Dear God, do help us,' she cried. 'If the wild beasts in the forest had but devoured us, we should, at any rate, have died together.'

"'Just keep your noise to yourself,' said the old woman. 'It won't help you at all.'

"Early in the morning, Gretel had to hang the cauldron with the water and light the fire beneath it. 'We shall bake first,' said the old woman. 'I have already heated the oven, and kneaded the dough.' She pushed poor Gretel out to the oven, from which flames of fire were already darting. 'Creep in,' said the witch, 'and see if it is properly heated so that we can put the bread in.'

"Once Gretel was inside, the witch intended to shut the oven and let her bake in it, and then she would eat her, too. But Gretel saw what she had in mind and said, 'I do not know how I am to do it. How do I get in?'

"'Silly goose,' said the old woman. 'The door is big enough. Just look, I can get in myself!' She crept up and thrust her head into the oven. Then Gretel gave her a push that drove her far into the oven, shut the iron door, and fastened the bolt. Oh, how horribly she howled, but Gretel ran away, and the godless witch was miserably burned to death."

Ivo laughs at this, and I smile.

"Gretel ran like lightning to Hansel, opened his little stable and cried, 'Hansel, we are saved! The old witch is dead!'

"Hansel sprang like a bird from its cage when the door opened. How they did rejoice and embrace each other, and dance about and kiss each other! As they no longer had any need to fear her, they went into the witch's house. In every corner stood chests full of pearls and jewels. 'These are far better than pebbles!' said Hansel, and thrust into his pockets whatever he could. And Gretel said, 'I, too, will take something home with me,' and filled her pockets full.

"But now, we must be off,' said Hansel, 'that we may get out of the witch's forest.'"

"I think I would have stayed until I had eaten the entire house," Ivo says. I'd never really thought of that, and I nod, for I would do the same. I like sweet things.

"The forest seemed to become more and more familiar to them, and, at length, they saw from afar their father's house. They ran as fast as they could and rushed into the house, throwing themselves around their father's neck. The man had not known one happy hour since he had left the children in the forest. Their stepmother was dead. Gretel emptied her pockets until pearls and precious stones ran about the room, and Hansel threw one handful after another from his pocket to add to them. Then all anxiety was at an end, and they lived together in perfect happiness."

I finish the story just as we arrive at the market.

"Did your mother make it up?" he asks.

"I'm not sure. I never asked." I wish I could ask her now. I swallow hard. "She always told the story so well. I'd imagine someone else must have told her the same story when she was a little girl."

He nods. "It is a strange tale."

"It makes you wonder how people come up with such things, doesn't it?"

"Yeah, I suppose. Either way, it was a good story, and you're a good storyteller, just like your mother." He says the words honestly, nonchalantly, as if he is commenting on the weather. Little does he know it is one of the greatest compliments I've ever received. He looks at the different bakers' stands for the best price.

"Two cakes and two loaves," Ivo orders. He gives up our pfennigs and hands me a loaf and a cake.

"So what about thieves?" Ivo said.

"What?"

"I doubt we'll have to worry about witches when we live in the woods, but what about thieves."

"Well, you beat that tree half to death today while you were asleep, so you could probably handle a thief or two. Just teach me how to fight, and we'll be fine."

"They travel in troupes. The two of us against eight or so criminals?"

"Well, I don't know these things." I say. "Maybe we'll find a place where no one else can find us."

"That's close to a city?"

"Fine, it's not a great plan, but it's better than the way things are now." We eat one loaf and the cakes. Ivo stops at the front of my house.

"Let me walk you home," I suggest. "I can explain to your parents why we were so late."

"They'll just think we're lying, or they'll get into a fight over it. It'll make things worse."

"There has to be something we can do," I say.

"Addie, he isn't going to kill me," he chortles, and before I can argue, he is walking toward his house. My stomach twists with guilt and worry. I grab his arm.

He turns, and he looks into my eyes. His brow knits, and he sighs. "If Mother thinks he'll beat me too badly, she'll make sure he's too drunk to do it."

I narrow my eyes at him, sure that he lies to make me feel better.

"Let it be, Addie," he says firmly, tugging his arm from my grasp. I bite my lip with worry. His lips fold, and he approaches. He wraps me in his arms. "It's only a few more months," he whispers, and then kisses my forehead. Just as quickly as he's embraced me, he releases me to head home.

In a few more months, he'll be an armorer. He'll have his own house and never suffer a beating at his father's hands again. The thought offers me little solace. If it weren't for me, he wouldn't get the beating he's going to get tonight, and there is nothing I can do about it now.

I look to the door of my home, not wanting to go inside. It feels like the very walls were violated last night. Still, it is the place that smells of Mama. The place where she cooked our meals. The place where she told her stories as she tucked me in at night. My stomach twists, and a knot rises in my throat. I grab the knob, and my hand shakes. I release it, and take a step backwards. I will myself to enter, so Father and Galadriel can suffer my judgmental glare, but I find myself staring at the door, unable to enter my own house.

22 March, 1247

The week passes dreadfully slowly. Galadriel was gone by the time I returned home on Monday. Father buries himself in work, which is just as well, for I cannot stand to look at him. The only time I set foot in his workshop is when he's at market, or when I'm on my way out.

~~Ivo's father has buried his whole family~~ in work since he was "too sick" to work Monday. It seems Ivo wasn't lying when he said that Greta gets Erik drunk to protect her children. Erik had passed out again Monday, and that saved Ivo from punishment for returning home late. By Wednesday evening, I needed to be busy, so I could keep from thinking about how much I missed Mama and how much I hated Father. I needed to escape the walls of this house, so I went to Ivo's and offered to help them work.

I suppose I was less than helpful, for, when I wasn't looking, one of the goats kicked over a nearly full milk pail. Erik screamed something about how his blind grandmother, God rest her soul, could milk a goat better than me and sent me home. So what if I cannot milk a goat? I doubt that drunkard could ever make a turn shoe.

I made shoes yesterday while Father was at the market, but that offered little distraction from my hatred for him and that whore

Galadriel. But I earn a pfennig for each shoe I sell, and, perhaps, if I save enough coin, Ivo and I can share a home of our own.

When Father returned, I went to the market. I talked to Michael as he packed his leather up for the night. He told me that Otto and his wife had taken sick with the fever. Otto's mistress, Ilsa had taken sick as well. For a moment, I felt a little guilty for being so angry with Father, for at least he's still alive, but then I thought of how I found him in my mother's bed with Galadriel, and the sentiment quickly passed.

I haven't spent a single pfennig on cakes since Ivo and I went to the market earlier this week, which is a feat for me. Each time I walk by the confectioners' stands and smell the doughy sweetness, I've had to tell myself that a coin spent on cakes is a moment longer in my father's house. The house where he bedded a woman only a week after Mama's death. The thought turns my stomach enough to keep the coins in my pocket.

Father had been coming home late each night, so I ate every meal alone. But not this evening. This evening, we eat sitting across from each other. It makes it hard to eat at all.

"There's a welt on your face." He says casually.

"Really," I say sarcastically, raising my hand to the mark. "I hardly noticed it."

"How'd you get it?" Father asks through a mouthful of pottage.

"Erik threw a boot at me." I reply.

"What did you do to make him do that?" he asks.

Of course. It must have been my fault Erik threw a boot at me. "Nothing. He mistook me for Ivo. His sight's about as good as his dead grandmother's."

"He managed to hit you with the boot, didn't he?" Father retorts. I roll my eyes.

Father drinks his ale, and there is a long silence between us.

"Do you love her?" I ask. He doesn't answer.

"Do you?" I prod.

"Don't start, Adelaide." He warns.

"I want to know."

He drops his spoon into his bowl. "Do you now?" He says, his eyes narrowing. "You want to know? Here is something you should know. You're a child living under my roof, eating my food, and you will know what I want you to know."

I shove my bowl forward. "I suppose it doesn't matter either way. It doesn't change what you did. You bedded another woman in Mama's bed, and you didn't even have the decency to wait until her body was cold."

His slap falls hard on my already welted cheek and knocks my head back. I rush my hand to the wound and my mouth falls open.

"You struck me!" I say with surprise.

"You gave me cause," he replies gruffly.

"What have I done but defended my own mother? She isn't here to defend herself!"

"Would you like another?" Father asks.

"Another wound for defending my mother?" I spit. "I'll wear it like a badge of honor. Slap away if it makes you feel better," I say through my teeth and look him directly in the face. I won't give him the pleasure of seeing me brace for his strike.

He huffs and rises from the table.

"Are you going to marry her? Is she going to come live with us?" I say quickly. He stops where he stands, and I think maybe I've put the thought in his head. I wish I could take it back.

"You think Galadriel's..." he pauses to laugh, "... going to live with us? I must have hit you harder than I thought."

It is a rather foolish idea once I think about it. Why would Galadriel leave her land and titles to live in a cobbler's house? Perhaps the question I should have asked was, "Are we going to go live with her?"

I do not dare to put any other ideas in Father's head, so I do not ask.

23 March, 1247

As I stir the pottage, I wonder if anyone will go to St. Laurentius tomorrow. Father hasn't said where we shall go, and that worries me. I hope he doesn't think I shall go to St. Laurentius. I'll never go back there, and if he, or anyone else for that matter, tries to make me, I shall walk right up to the altar and spit in Soren's ugly face.

The steps creak as Father stomps up them slowly. He's worked all day in his shop, and we haven't spoken since he struck me yesterday, which is fine, for I do not wish to talk to him either. I do not wish to see his face. I do not wish to hear him speak. I do not wish to smell that mix of leather and ale that announces his presence. My stomach is in knots, for I deeply do not wish to sit at the table with him. I would take my food in my room if it weren't for my wanting to know where we shall go for tomorrow's Mass.

Neither of us speaks, and the entire meal is silent, except for the occasional slurping. I do not dare to ask him my question, for I am sure he's still angry with me. He could make me go to St. Laurentius as punishment for yesterday. He keeps his silence, and I leave the table for bed, not knowing. I am not tired. It isn't even dark. I just want to sleep. I want to do nothing, to be nothing, for just a little while.

∽◎◟

I dream that we don't go to church, but everyone else in the city does. Father keeps to his workshop, filling the nearly dozen orders for shoes we must complete by the end of next week. I work on orders, too, sitting by the hearth so I can easily avoid him. I jump at a sudden pounding on the door. "Who would come to see us?" I wonder. Everyone is at Mass. The pounding thumps louder followed by a splintering crack as the door breaks in. The house shakes as a dozen pairs of feet stampede into Father's workshop. The noise drowns out my own screams, and I rush down the stairs to see a mob of men whose fists rain down upon someone, something in the middle of them. I cannot see who they are beating, but I know it is Father. I scream, but no one looks. I run and slam into the pack, beating on the back of one of the men-at-arms. He turns, backhands me, and I fall to the ground.

Father is dragged, barely conscious, from our house, and, suddenly, I am at the gallows in the middle of Hay Market. Soren declares Father a heretic. Those who do not know him throw garbage in his bruised and swollen face as he is dragged to a cross lying on its side. Rather than hang him or burn him at the stake, he is to be crucified. Not upright like Christ. That is too great an honor. Soren orders for Father to be crucified sideways, hanging from one arm, slowly melting into death.

Blood splatters as Soren's henchman, Johan, hammers foot-long nails through Father's wrists. Soren salivates over his revenge. Johan pounds the nails with a *knock-knock-knock*. The sound continues over and over. *Knock-knock-knock, knock-knock-knock, knock-knock-knock....*

∽ର୧

I thrust upwards with a rush, escaping the nightmare and throwing my sheets several feet into the air. A cold sweat coats my skin, and the cool air chills me to the bone. I hear the knocking again, though I know I am awake.

Father's feet thump across the floor and down the steps. I sit frozen, paralyzed with the still-vivid fear from my nightmare. My mind relaxes enough to run through the people who would visit so late.

"Hello, Ansel," says a calm voice. "May I come in?"

"Did anyone follow you, Elias?" Father asks.

"I don't believe so," Elias replies with an air of feigned puzzlement.

"Good. Now go home."

"Can we at least talk about this?"

"I'm going to the cathedral tomorrow," Father says tersely.

"Your wife—" Elias begins.

"Do not use her as a pawn in your rebellion!" Father bellows, no longer watching his volume. "What happened to her was one man's fault."

"That *one* man represents the Church and all that's wrong with it. They live like princes while the people succumb to the fever. They won't even give our loved ones funerals without bribes."

"I'm going tomorrow."

"But—" Elias interjects, trying desperately to win over a man who is immovable.

"I'm going."

"I understand. The people shall do what you do, Ansel. If you go, Airsbach goes, too," Elias sighs.

"They'll go anyway, Elias, for the safety of their families. Good night."

Elias sighs. "Good night."

I figure Father would slam the door in Elias' face, but he shuts it gently. Does he think I am still asleep? I climb down the ladder into the main room as Father heads back to his bed.

"Don't," he snaps, walking past me.

"What?"

"We're going tomorrow," he orders, turning the corner to his bed.

I do not hate him so much after the dream I just had. I throw myself at him and hug him tightly.

"That won't work." His arms wrap around me slowly, like they'd forgotten how to.

"I'll go to Mass," I say looking into his face. "I want us to go as long as it isn't to St. Laurentius."

"Good. Then go to bed. Mass starts in a few hours." He pats my back, and I ease my vice-like grip on him. Both of us head to bed.

I turn and ask, "What kind of rebellion is Elias starting?"

"Go to bed. And don't ever ask me that question when other people are around. Do not mention Elias at all," Father says in a steady voice, walking toward me. His stare could have frozen boiling oil. It demands immediate compliance.

"Yes, Father."

24 March, 1247

My sleep is riddled with nightmares, so I rise early in the morning to escape them. My stomach is knotted, and my eyes are puffy from exhaustion. I scrub my face with the cold water in my basin, untie my braid, run my fingers loosely through my crinkled hair, and re-braid it. Perhaps we can sit with Ivo's family today at Mass. Surely they'll also go to the cathedral instead of St. Laurentius. The knots in my stomach release at the thought of seeing Ivo. I hope the sun comes out, and we can spend the whole day in the shade of the trees outside Kunibert's gate. The thought warms my stomach in a strangely pleasant way.

I let Father sleep as I sit on my bed and look out the window. The streets are still empty. The morning is cool, so I wrap my cloak around my shoulders and slide my legs beneath the covers. I maintain my vigil over Airsbach, watching for parishioners heading to church.

An unfamiliar crowd of pilgrims approach, probably on their way to the cathedral to see the relics of the Three Magi. Still, there are no townspeople in the street. I haven't heard the bells ring yet and worry for a moment that it is later than I think, yet it can't be since I have been up since dawn.

The pilgrims are always the first to Mass, but perhaps I should wake Father. I shed my nightshift and put on my hose and chainse when I hear faint voices in the distance. I wriggle my head through the neck hole and rush back to my window. A dozen or so guild members and their families are walking west on Filzengraben. Members of the group are almost unrecognizable in the distance, and it takes me a moment to notice the two armed provincial guards among them. "Oh no," I gasp. The guards have been dispatched to escort the people of Airsbach to church, though, to which church, I do not know. I throw on my surcote and rush to Father's room.

"Father, get up. We have to go." I order, rushing to his bed, and tugging his arm.

He opens an eye, and then closes it, surely noticing that the sun hasn't fully risen. "It's too early. Leave me," he grumbles, rolling away from me.

"Get up!" I shout and toss the covers off him. "The guards are escorting people to church. We have to go now."

"What do you mean?" He asks as he plants his feet on the floor and stands in his night shift.

"I saw the guards walking with a group of people down Filzengraben."

"Did you see them enter a church?" He asks, annoyed.

"No."

He groans as he makes his way far too slowly to the window near the hearth.

"We must go now! If the guards get here before we leave, they might make us go to St. Laurentius. I won't go back there! I won't!" I cry. My heart pounds, and the sting of tears is heavy behind my eyes.

Father peers out the window and looks back at me angrily. "There are only a few people in the street."

"Yes, but there are guards with them!" I say, pointing to the two armed men escorting the small group.

"Fine, I'll ready myself," Father sighs. "Now go and—"

He's interrupted by a thunderous pounding below us and a large snap in the workshop. Someone has broken in the door. Father throws a cloak over his shoulders, and we are suddenly, silent. The soft, slow tapping of footsteps echoes from the workshop, followed by the clobbering of a heavier set of feet. I freeze. My heart drums off the bones in my chest.

"Oh, this is the right house, all right. Look at all the shoes," a nasally voice declares.

"Outstanding work," a deep voice groans sarcastically. "Doesn't look like anyone's here. They've probably already left."

"No, I know they're here," says the nasally-voiced man while the other man sighs in annoyance. "I'll check the beds. You check the living quarters."

Father motions for me to turn around so he can quickly change into his chainse and surcote. My stomach twists, and the air feels too thick to swallow.

"Listen, bastard, we were given strict orders." the deep voice warns.

"My name's not bastard! It's Haimo!"

"No matter what your name is, you're still a bastard," the gruff voice quips. "And I don't take orders from the likes of you."

"One day, my Father'll be Archbishop of Cologne and he'll claim me, and you'll be sorry that you ever called me that."

The other man roars with laughter, and their boots pound up the steps. "Your father? Father Soren? Archbishop of Cologne!"

Before they reach the top of the stairs, Father walks out, and I follow him.

"Who's there?" Father calls.

"There they are! I told you they were here," shouts the nasally voice, pointing a thin finger at us from across the room. "Where do you think you're going?"

"To church," Father says matter-of-factly. "Walk with us if you must."

"We have other orders," Haimo says. "You'd better behave yourself, cobbler, or else I'll—"

"Who gives your orders?" I interject, and the large man laughs. He doesn't have to say. I already know this is Soren's doing. I just want to hear him say it. Who else would want to do this?

"Everyone sit down," the large man orders. I recognize his face, his voice, but I cannot pair them with a name.

Father eyes them for a moment, and I know he is wondering if he can fight them both so that we can escape. The large man grabs the hilt of his sword and looks from Father to me, sending us a clear warning. Father huffs and heads to the table. I reluctantly follow.

"Just behave yourselves, and we'll all be all right." The large man says, and then I recognize him. His father was one of the old bakers in the city. His name is Aldo, and he is the youngest of four. The old baker, who's been dead a few years now, had only enough work for two of his sons. The other two were forced to find their own trades. Aldo's younger brother, Adolph, found success as a tanner, but rumor was that Aldo had failed one apprenticeship after another before he was accepted as a guard.

I had seen Haimo many times at St. Laurentius, ogling girls in a most sinister way with his buggy eyes. His gaze doesn't merely pierce, it lances deeply. I feel his eyes on me, looking me up and down. I look out the window to avoid his gaze, to avoid giving him any hint of interest.

"I shall watch her," Haimo says with insinuation. "And you watch him," he says to Aldo.

"No," Aldo retorts, annoyed.

"Why do you always tell me what to do?" Haimo hisses.

"'Cause I outrank you, bastard," barks Aldo.

"Well, my father—"

"My father...my father," Aldo mimics with a whine. "Do you see what I put up with, Lord?" Aldo calls raising his hands to God.

Haimo mumbles something under his breath.

"Now, what do we do?" Haimo asks.

"We sit here until we get orders," Aldo replies, and Haimo sighs. Then, Aldo looks to me. "You be a good girl, and get us a mug of ale."

I look to Father who nods. I do as I am ordered. With full mugs in hand, I walk back to the table, and slam the mugs before Aldo and Haimo, spilling a third of the contents onto their laps.

"God damn wench," Haimo hisses at me, brushing the ale from his hose as I head back to my seat.

∞⟡∞

My fear turns to boredom as time passes painfully slowly. The guards watch us in silence. Haimo sulks, but Aldo seems relatively content with the silence. The bells chime nine, ten, eleven, and it shall soon strike noon. I wonder what will happen then. I notice Aldo's knee pulsing like he is nervous about something.

"You have to piss, don't you? I told you not drink so much ale," Haimo scolds.

Aldo growls at him.

"So go. I can handle these two."

Aldo returns a doubtful glare. Haimo is about Ivo's size, but without the lean strength that comes with hard work. Aldo's knee bounces harder and faster in his discomfort. His brow furrows, and I can guess what he is thinking: *I can't leave her alone with Haimo, and Ansel's strong enough to take him alone.* Father slithers a hand behind me and races his fingers up my back like they are two running legs. I know what this means. When I get the chance, run.

"I'll take the girl with me," concludes Aldo. "I've got my dagger on her, Ansel. Behave yourself."

Father stares, stone-faced, straight into Haimo's eyes. Aldo yanks me up by my arm, and I mimic Father's emotionless face as best I can. He holds me in front of him by the point of his dagger as we descend the stairs and walk out to the front of the house. I am a yard away with my back turned to give him privacy. At the sound of the first trickle, I run. I am a block away before he even notices, and three blocks away before he can finish urinating and is ready to chase me. Father charges out the front door, barrels into Aldo, and knocks him to the ground. By the time I reach the corner, Father is beside me.

"Where are we going?" I pant, trying to keep up my speed.

"I don't know."

"To church? Before it's over?" I suggest.

"Too late," Father replies.

"The Gopher?"

"Not open. Everyone's… at church…. Out Severin's gate…. Then down to the cottages…. Someone shall hide us… for a few coins," he huffs. He grabs me by the arm, and we run toward the gate. It is within our sights, but it is closed. Will Gregor be there? Will he open it for us?

"Stop them!" a voice yells. I look behind me and Haimo is running toward us cradling a bloody nose. The bells echo through the city, and I know it is noon. Mass is over.

Three provincial guards step from the gatehouse to the front of Severin's gate. Father grabs my arm, and we turn toward St. Pantaleon's Church. If we can just make it there and the crowds are let out, perhaps we can hide among them.

The three guards are young men, not lanky boys with bloodied noses, nor fat men who have been knocked over and are covered in their own piss. These men aren't tired from running, and they don't have skirts to carry. They are fast, and they gain on us so quickly, I am afraid to look back. People begin to fill the web of streets around St. Pantaleon. If we can just get there, I know we can lose them. I hear their feet pounding closer, and I push myself harder. Someone grabs the train of my cloak, and I scream. I pull the string that ties it, and I am free again.

One person points to us, then another, and, soon, most of the crowd around St. Pantaleon's looks upon us. And, then, something horribly strange happens. Father stops. He just stops running. Two of the men plow him down.

"Run!" I hear him yell as the men grapple with him.

But I can't run from him. What if I never see him again? I know it is not what he wants me to do, but I run to him. The third man grabs me. My feet fly through the air as I kick and cry for him to let me go, to let Father go.

⁂

Haimo meets us as we get back to Severin's gate. He whispers to one of the guards holding Father, and the men nod emphatically with wide eyes. The gate is opened, and we are walked along the outside of the city, which I find very strange. Why would they walk us along the outside of the city? I suppose they do not wish for anyone to see us. I am glad for it because I am quite embarrassed to be under arrest, especially as I have done nothing wrong.

My stomach falls, and the breath is knocked from my chest when I see my greatest fear rising before me--the infamous North Tower. I open my mouth to scream, but nothing comes out. I swallow the hard lump in my throat and gulp air, trying to catch my breath. Just as we stop before the North Tower, I open my mouth again and scream; hoping someone I know shall hear me and come to our aid. My mouth is silenced by a thickly-gloved hand. I bite as hard as I can, but don't manage to catch flesh. The North Tower is where men are locked away and forgotten about. This is where men are tortured for information or for false confessions. I am not worried for myself. I am a girl, a child, hopefully, in the eyes of the cruel men within these cold stone walls. But what of Father? What shall happen to him? We are rushed up spiraling stone steps and separated. I am thrown into a dark, damp cell where I scream of our innocence until I have no voice left.

∞ఴౖ∞

I do not know how long I am in the dark. Every scream I hear, I fear belongs to Father as he is being tortured. It is the most horrid feeling, even worse than the last moments of Mama's life, for I cannot hold his hand. I can do nothing to help him except pray. And so I do, until my knees are raw from the damp stone floor.

The cell opens, and just outside the frame of the door stands the Archbishop. My mouth drops with shock. It *is* true. He *is* here. I had overheard rumors in the market that the Archbishop had only returned to Cologne to help search for a new man to oppose the rightful King Conrad. Of course, if that is true, than the Archbishop, once again, risks a traitor's death. The Archbishop supported an anti-king by the name of Henry Raspe. Raspe took King Conrad's crown, and then died shortly after. King Conrad was restored and the Archbishop was forced to beg his forgiveness and swear fealty to him or risk losing his head.

He is a slight man with icy, scheming eyes and thin lips. I bow to him, though I have no desire to. "I hear you make trouble in my city," he says with the accent of a man who spends most of his time abroad, probably securing his own interests in Rome. "I am good at dealing with troublemakers."

"Please, I beg you to have mercy." I drop to my knees. "Father and I tried to go to your cathedral, but—"

"I have not asked you to speak," he interrupts. "Ignorant, indeed."

"And feisty, Your Excellency," pipes the guard who caught me. "She kicks like a mule and bites like a dog."

The Archbishop turns on the guard whose face goes white. "Leave us," he snaps. The guards bow and race from the room. The door to my cell closes behind them.

"Do you know what happens in this tower?" he asks.

"Yes, Your Excellency," I reply thickly, feeling my tears well.

"Do you love your father?"

"Yes, Your Excellency!"

"Then you would save him, if you could?"

"Yes, Your Excellency!"

"Does your Father urge rebellion upon the Church?"

"Your Excellency, if I may explain—"

"Yes or no," he prompts.

"No, Your Excellency, he tries to stop them."

"So you know of plots?" he replies with a raised eyebrow, and I know I have said too much.

"I have overheard a stranger's whispers, but also overheard my father tell this man that he shall go to church, and he has no desire to see a rebellion."

"Of course you would defend your father. I shall have to find ways to get the truth from him, if I cannot get it from you." He turns to leave and I grab his robe.

"I swear it on my mother's soul, Your Excellency!" I cry. "He is innocent!"

He turns and I can tell he almost believes me. "Perhaps you tell the truth about your father's innocence, but I know you lie of something else. You know who incites the rebellion, and yet you keep it from me. For this, you and your father shall be punished. But I can be merciful. If you tell me who incites the rebellion, then your punishments shall be light."

I stall as long as I can, but the Archbishop grows impatient. I hope a brilliant lie shall come to me. A lie that he shan't see through. A lie that can save us all. But nothing comes.

"His name is Elias, Excellency," I mumble quickly, looking away, wishing I had never mentioned this stranger at all, wishing I had never overheard his conversation, and hoping the Archbishop doesn't ask for more. But more than anything, I hope I have saved my father.

"You shall confess that your father ordered you to abandon the Church, and tell no one of any other story, or I shall have to change my mind about your father's punishment."

I wonder if he is seeking a confession in order to punish us as heretics and that all of his other promises are lies.

"But that is not the truth, Excellency. It was—"

"Ah, but, stupid, stupid girl, I do not care. And those are the kinds of words that might make my men want to drive a hot poker up your father's rectum and burn you both as heretics," he smiles.

"Then I shall say whatever pleases you, Excellency," I say, swallowing hard. I feel powerless, and that the best I can do to save Father from torture, and us from death, is to do what the Archbishop wants.

"Perhaps you aren't so stupid after all," he says.

He turns and leaves without another word. I want to ask what our merciful punishment shall be, but I don't want to try his patience and make things worse. I start to kneel again for prayer, but guards enter my cell and yank me up by the arms.

"Where are you taking me?" I ask in terror.

"If you are a good girl and stay silent, you are to go to the stocks for missing Mass," a guard answers. I want to cry out that we didn't miss Mass and that we didn't get a hearing, that only one man decided our fate before the eyes of no one else. But I'm too afraid to say it. If the Archbishop can put us in the stocks without a hearing, what else can he do to us? I think back to the tormented screams from my cell in the North Tower, and it makes me cringe.

"And what of my father?" I ask.

"How should I know?"

త్ఁౖ

I am marched through Hay Market, though it is empty. I notice the stocks hold a handful of villagers, one of them being Elias. I don't even look him in the eyes, for I am so ashamed of what I've done to him, but at least he is in the stocks and not dead. Two stocks are empty, and I realize they are for Father and me. I sigh with relief. We shall both live through this.

A guard unlocks my stocks and flips it open. He drags me over, and I obediently place my head and hands in position. Father is brought out a few moments later, and I haven't felt such relief since the day I found him at the Gilded Gopher after he buried Mother. I told God in my prayers that if He delivered us from this, I would never mention Father's affair again, I would forgive him, and that I would be a good girl. Father doesn't fight the guards either, and I am glad that, besides a bloodied lip, he looks to be all right. The sun begins to descend, and the air grows cool as the wind blows. My cloak has been left behind, and I know I am in for a long, cold night.

⚬⊙⚬

"What happened?" Ivo says as he kneels before me so he can look me in the face. "Who did this to you?" His eyes dart back and forth, looking into mine.

"Do not ask," I say through chattering teeth. "If I say, we'll be killed." He looks at me with such pity for just a moment, and then his jaw locks. His brow furrows, and he punches the base of the stock with a *thwap* that echoes through the frigid, night air. He rises and shakes his hand, muttering curses.

"Was there a hearing?" he asks, but I don't answer out of fear for all our well-being. "It's Soren, isn't it? He did this," he says heatedly.

"*Sssssshhhh*," I plead. "Stop, Ivo. You'll get us all killed," I whisper through chattering teeth. "Ivo, I am so cold," I say, shivering. He whips off his cloak, ties it around my neck, and rubs his hands against mine to warm them.

"Do you have gloves at your house? Does your father? I'll fetch his cloak and yours."

"We don't have gloves. Besides, the guards would notice them. They probably won't notice the cloaks, though...but my cloak fell off, into the street, during the chase."

"Where?"

"Don't bother looking for it. Someone has surely taken it by now."

"You keep mine then." He says. I want to argue. I know the mornings shall be cold for him without it, but I don't know how I'll make it through the night without a cloak.

"Thank you," I say.

"I'll fetch your father's cloak and bring some mulled wine. Does your father have any coin?"

"Yes, at the house. They are in a purse somewhere near his bed. Why?" I ask.

"I'd use my own coins if I had them."

"No, I don't care about the coins. What do you need them for?"

"So I can stay at the Giggling Pig." He points down the market to a tavern frequented by the Butchers' Guild. "Just in case." He shrugs and whips the hair from his eyes. I give him a worried look. "Don't worry. My parents know. It was my father's idea that I stay here and watch over you both. Besides them, no one else knows.... I'll make sure no one else knows. I'll make sure nothing else happens to you."

"What about your apprenticeship? Does the armorer know? Will he let you take leave?"

"He knows I need a leave, but he's been told that it is best that he doesn't know why." He puts his hand against my face, knits his brow, and pouts pitifully at me. "Don't let such things worry you." I let my neck release and rest my head in his hands. He kisses me on the forehead and is gone.

25 March, 1248

I have never been so cold. My teeth chatter, and I shake violently even though Ivo has placed a second cloak over me. I try to keep my feet moving to stay warm. This has been the longest night of my entire life.

People file to Mass for Annunciation Day, but pay little attention to us. It is not until noon, when Mass has let out, that we are addressed. The Archbishop parades through Hay Market just as the bells toll. A procession of parishioners, provincial guards, and clergymen from the many churches in Cologne follows him. The councilmen from the wealthiest patrician families of Cologne follow as well, whispering to each other and looking upon the Archbishop with suspicious eyes. I wonder if they are angered that the Archbishop has sentenced us without a hearing by them. I hope they see that their power is being taken, for I don't doubt the ambitions of Konrad von Hochstaden, nor should anyone else.

The people in the market part for the parade like the Red Sea parted for Moses. The faces in the crowd show a mixture of confusion, fear, contempt, and surprise. We have all wondered if the Archbishop was really here since his warnings were nailed to our doors only eight days ago. I, of course, had learned of his return last night in the North Tower, but it is news to them.

A few of the provincial guards give alms to the poor and crippled as a few others hand out pfennigs. A woman crosses herself and gets two pfennigs for it. Suddenly, everyone is crossing themselves, cheering, or kneeling to see if they can get two pfennigs, too. It seems the price of adoration, the price of abandoning reason is low in Cologne; it only costs two pfennigs. Two pfennigs buys smiles, bows, hurrahs, and holy gestures for the Archbishop who abandoned us for Rome during the Great Fever, a man who is about as holy as Judas.

Soren saunters at the right side of the Archbishop, which is just where he belongs, at the right hand of Judas. Soren's nose is in the air haughtily. His lips squeeze into a pursed smirk, which pushes his fat cheeks into his baggy eyelids, causing him to squint.

The Archbishop raises his hand, and the crowd grows silent. "These heretics confessed to me a grievous sin."

The crowd collectively gasps, and a few shout curses at us. The Archbishop raises his hands again, and they hush. Many stand on their toes and lean closer to listen. They are anxious to hear the details of our sin, the more horrendous the better. Punishment for us means entertainment for them.

"They have abandoned the Church!" he proclaims. The market is silent. There are no gasps, no hisses, no curses. The Archbishop's face sags in disappointment. I'm sure he wonders why there are no cheers for our punishment. Soren's proud smirk falls away, and he catches my stare as I smile impishly at him.

Who cares if we have abandoned the Church? Not the people of the market, or so it appears, unless, of course, there are more coins in it for them. If I weren't so miserable or scared of further punishment, I think I'd laugh out loud.

This isn't a terribly interesting scandal. Perhaps if he'd said we'd abandoned God or had become witches, the people might be a little more interested in our crime. It also may have helped if he'd had us dragged out as prisoners, but we are in the stocks already. Our sentence has already been issued. The people know there isn't to be a hanging, or a burning, or a cutting off of limbs.

Besides that, the Church has lost favor with the people since its priests have stopped giving last rites and funerals. Since its clergymen have grown fat from our tithes, Since the Archbishop had parchments nailed to the doors of every house in the city, ordering people to attend Mass or face punishment.

The people who were given pfennigs for crossing and kneeling at the sight of our Archbishop now turn from him and make their way back into the market. His eyebrow raises, and he snaps his fingers at the guard. A half-dozen of the men-at-arms toss pfennigs into the air to lure the crowd back to him, and most of them return.

The Archbishop raises his arms to the sky. A holy gesture from an unholy man. "Today is the first day of the New Year! Today is the day of the Annunciation! Today is the day that God graced us by announcing to the ever-blessed virgin that he would put our savior in her belly that He might save us. We are all sinners and deserve God's wrath, but on this day so very long ago, our Heavenly Father showed us His everlasting grace and mercy. We, too, can be merciful, and, in honor of the Annunciation, I have decided not to burn these heretics at the stake, but guide them back into the good graces of the Lord."

There is applause from the crowd and the guards shower the crowd with coins again.

"But they must serve a penance to rectify their sin!" The crowd applauds and cheers louder. Their enthusiasm is rewarded with another showering of coins. "They have spent one night in the stocks and must spend another two." The crowd boos and hisses us.

Two more nights, I think. I ache from head to foot already. I nearly froze last night. How am I to make it through two more nights?

"Good people of Cologne, let them suffer as they should to be absolved from their sins. Let us pray they reform so we shan't have to burn them on the pyre. And let it be known that the next heretics I find shall be burned so all can see the horrors of an eternity of hellfire!" The crowd cheers its loudest.

The throng dissolves into the market for Annunciation celebrations as dozens of others rush at the Archbishop to make requests of him. Soren saunters toward me, smirking proudly.

"You thought you were pretty smart, didn't you? You didn't think I would find out about your little plan, did you? Oh, but I did. You'd be surprised at how little I had to pay for that information, and now look at where you and your father are." He cocks his head to the side. "I bet you'd like to throw another stone at me now, wouldn't you? But you can't with those pretty little hands bound, can you? No, no, no…" he goads.

"You've become a thorn in my side, girl, and I think you'll find that I can become a spear in yours." He pulls a cloth from his robes, and I recognize it immediately. "This was your mother's, was it not?" He places it beneath his nostrils and breathes in deeply. "She smells lovely, nothing like that day we burned her."

I'll claw out his eyes, I think as I shove my hands through the holes as far as they can go.

"You are a feisty little witch!" he laughs. "This is the last of your mother's things. I am having the rest of them burned in the streets right now. I am having *all* of your things burned in the streets."

I pull backward, slamming the base of my head hard against the wood. My neck burns from the pain, but I try again desperately to break through the stocks so I can get Mama's clothes, her lavender satchels, anything that smells like her, anything that reminds me of her. Soren laughs.

"Do you want this back?" he asks smugly, and I narrow my eyes at him. Of course I want it back. He knows I want it back. "Swear to me, on your mother's soul, that you shall sit in my church every Mass for the rest of my days. I shall save you a seat in the first pew so I can look upon your angry, defeated face."

I collect all the saliva in my mouth and spit, hitting him on the side of his nose. "Keep it," I hiss.

He wipes my spit from his face with the cloth. "Very well, then. I think I shall use this to wipe my arse." He rises and walks away.

The tears are heavy behind my eyes. I shall not let him see me cry. I shan't even hang my head so he can think that I am defeated. I huff angrily, desperate not to let the sobs or the tears surface. After a few moments, he disappears into the market, and I put my head down and sob quietly.

❧

As sunset turns to twilight, I hear a familiar set of footsteps, and a tall, thin waist pauses in front of me. Ivo. He kneels, and looks into my eyes sadly.

"I heard you're going to be in there for two more nights," he says with pity.

"Yeah," I reply hoarsely.

"I brought you something." He reaches into a satchel and pulls out a chainse that belonged to Mama.

"How did you get this?" I gasp. All our things were burned." He places the garment in my hand. Had they not been pinned, I would have cradled it to my face.

"I saw the guards putting all of your things into a pile, so I grabbed this before they set it on fire. Here, give it back so no one realizes it's yours." He pulls the chainse back and stuffs it in the bag. "Are you hungry?"

"No."

"Are you sure?"

"Yes, Father might be." Ivo checks on him, but he won't eat either. Truth be told, hunger pains me, but none of us have the luxury of privacy or chamber pots, and I refuse to defecate outside like a dog. It also doesn't seem quite fair to eat when Elias and the others have nothing.

"I'll be in the Giggling Pig again. Whistle three times if you need me, or scream if you're in danger. I'll be keeping watch." I nod before he heads to the tavern.

"Wait," I say, and he turns. "Can you bring me some warm wine? I am so thirsty."

If I am to bear another frigid night, I'll need wine to warm my stomach and soothe my rigid muscles. Perhaps I might even find a way to sleep, though I don't know how.

This night is just as cold as the last, and I find no comfort in telling myself that, after tonight, there is only one more to go. My teeth chatter, and my body shivers. I must tense my stomach and run in place to stay warm, though I am beyond tired. I see and hear things I know are not there. I am stiff all over, and I stretch as much as I can to keep the pain bearable. I try to roll my neck and wrists about to ease the stiffness in my arms and shoulders, but, eventually, I give in to the cold, the pain, and the exhaustion and try to rest. Unfortunately, sleeping means hanging by my throat, knees dangling, so rest is impossible. I am frustrated into tears.

A whistle trills through the icy nighttime air as a pair of boots shuffle in the distance. The sounds come from behind me, making it impossible to see who makes them. It is a hallucination from being overtired, I tell myself. Pay it no mind. Father, who is nearly a foot taller than me, rests his knees on the ground without strangling himself. Motionless, he appears to sleep.

The scuff of the boots grows louder and closer by the moment. My chest constricts as I debate whether or not I should scream for Ivo's help.

The whistling pierces the air from directly behind me. I hold my breath. The warm breeze of a body passes me.

The scuffling grows quieter as the body veers off to my left. It is probably some drunkard making his way home after a long night of indulgence. I look over to see who the stranger is. A dark-haired, lanky figure stands before to Father, drawing back his fist.

Just as I am about to scream for Ivo, I see him run past me. The dark-haired man lands a punch on Father's jaw and Ivo crashes into the man whose feet fly into the air as he lands on the hardened ground with a thud. The man gasps for air as Ivo rolls him over and starts punching. Father shakes the stock, trying to free himself and cheers on Ivo at the same time. The dark-haired man whimpers, curls into a ball, and cowers behind his arms, but Ivo doesn't stop, landing blows on his sides and his back.

Ivo pauses for a moment, exhales a few hard breaths into the cold night air, and punches a few more times before he stands. The man rises to his hands and knees, coughing and spitting blood from his mouth. Ivo circles, ready to go at him again. The man stands, and the moonlight shines upon his swelling face. I recognize him immediately. It's the priest's bastard, Haimo.

"What's wrong, Haimo? Can't land a punch unless a man is in chains?" Ivo says to Haimo who stumbles with his fists drawn shakily. A red trail trickles down his nose and stains his surcote.

He stumbles some more, and a smirk spreads across his face, still smug despite his beating. "There is, still, one more night for them, and I think I should like to keep that pretty little girlfriend of yours warm."

Ivo's eyes narrow when the word "pretty" passes Haimo's lips, and he charges again, barreling him to the ground once more. He punches his face then focuses his blows on Haimo's stomach. Father rattles the stocks as he fights to free himself, shouting curses at Haimo. Ivo stands and spits on his face as he groans in pain. He pulls back his foot and kicks Haimo as hard as he can between the legs. Haimo howls, rolls to his side, and retches.

"That was a low blow!" Haimo whimpers.

"So is forcing yourself upon a girl in the stocks."

Ivo approaches Father. "You all right, Ansel?" He asks.

Father nods. "He landed a weak punch, worthless whoreson," Father says, looking upon Haimo, who stills rolls about groaning in pain. "Looks like you've got a little of your father in you, after all."

Ivo nods his head, but I know he doesn't see any comparison with his father as a compliment. He walks toward me.

"Are you all right?" He asks. I nod.

"Are you?" I reply.

Ivo nods. His knuckles are bloodied, but, other than that, he hasn't a scratch on him.

"How'd you know he'd come after us?"

"I knew someone would. Remember Anna Metzger?"

"Yes." I pause as I remember her. Her father was one of the butchers, but three years ago he got sick and died. The family had no coin, and she'd been caught stealing from a baker who turned her in immediately. They sentenced her to two days in the stocks at only thirteen years old. She had a baby less than a year later. It was a real scandal in the borough. People thought she had turned to selling herself to get enough coin to feed her family.

"She wasn't a harlot like people thought," Ivo sighs. "She entered the stocks a maid, but she didn't leave one."

"No!" I gasp, not wanting to believe it. Poor Anna. Ivo shakes his head, stands, and walks back to Haimo.

"If you speak of this to anyone, you shall lose your tongue and your testicles," he says.

"I don't know that I have any testicles left," Haimo groans.

"I don't think you ever had them to begin with, but my threat stands. If I am arrested, or if they are harmed, I know people, many people, who shall see you tortured in ways you can't imagine. Things shall be done to you that would make the executioner blush." I am shocked to hear Ivo sound so much like his father.

Haimo looks up with terrified eyes and nods. He stands and limps away. Ivo returns to me.

"You sure you're alright?" He asks, kneeling to look into my face.

I nod. "Well enough for someone in the stocks," I say and wave my hands to illustrate my confines. "Thank you." I look at his face carefully and suddenly notice how much he has changed. The childish softness of his face has hardened. He is quiet, contemplative, and threatening men with torture. I am grateful for what he has done for me, but feel guilty that he has had to. These are hard times, indeed. I wonder if I shall ever again see his wide grin and the tiny lines that used to fan out on the sides of his eyelids.

"You should go back so no one can accuse you of helping us. Get some sleep. I'll yell if we need you."

He nods and begins to walk back to the tavern.

"But before you go, could you scratch my nose?" I ask.

His shoulders droop, and he sighs. He turns around and saunters back.

"Higher... lower... left... more left. It's between my cheek and my nose...." He gets the spot, and it feels absolutely heavenly.

"Anything else before I go?" he asks, pretending to be annoyed.

"No. Thank you, though," I say, trying to smile.

26 March, 1248

I am more vigilant now. Every snap of a twig, howl of the wind, and hoot of an owl makes my heart pound with fear. I am beyond fatigued, and, surely, half the noises I hear aren't real. I debate crying for Ivo a dozen times, but I don't. I know he must be tired, but I doubt he's as tired as me, for I haven't slept in two nights.

Each time I get into a comfortable position, my eyelids fail me. As soon as I fall asleep, my legs collapse, forcing me to fall back. My head smacks painfully against the back of the stocks, wrenching my neck. I stumble back to my feet as the muscles in my neck twist into knots. I bite my lip to stifle whimpers of pain.

Eventually, the tension dulls, and I am left with a burning throb from head to hip. My feet shuffle as cramps shoot through my legs and back. I drift briefly into sleep over and over, and I fall back again and again.

"One more night," I chant through chattering teeth. "One more night."

The sky lightens and the artisans come to set up their stands. A dense fog seeps through the market, and I can't tell whether the day shall be sunny or cloudy. I lean into the stocks and stretch my neck in small circles. The block chafes my neck terribly, but my head is too heavy for it to carry any longer, so I reluctantly rest on the rough wood. The fog clears, and the sun peaks through thick clouds, warming my back. Perhaps, if I just close one eye, I won't fall asleep, but soon the other eye is heavy, and I fight to keep it open. I can close my eyes for a moment, I think, just for a moment.

※

Thwap! The stocks shake, and I awaken in just enough time to turn my face from the projectile. A rotten apple smashes against my cheek, spraying its putrid flesh across my nose and lips. I spit the slimly pieces from my mouth, but a few pieces stick to my tongue. I gag.

"I got her!" a filthy red-headed boy cries. His friends cheer and pat him on the back. A shorter urchin steps forward, aims, and throws his apple at me. This time, I bow my head so the rotten fruit can land in my hair rather than near my nose or mouth, but his apple doesn't even hit the stock. His friends laugh at him, and the boy sulks.

I narrow my eyes and shout, "Hey!" But before I can threaten them, they run off and disappear into the horde, squealing with laughter.

Once they are gone, I realize that I had been sleeping before they'd started throwing spoiled fruit at me. I sigh pleasantly, grateful to have finally learned how to sleep in this thing. If I lean into the stock, my legs don't give when I fall asleep. I fall asleep again and hope, vainly, that I don't rise until tomorrow when we shall be freed.

∽◎∾

"Adelaide!" someone calls, and I groan. "Adelaide!" It is Father's voice. I open my eyes, but my vision is cloudy. The market is quieter than normal. My vision clears as I pull back on the stocks to give my legs and back a stretch.

I can hardly believe what I see. The Archbishop and his guard parade into the market again, to the awe of the small crowd, who, again, receive pfennigs for their reverence. Did I sleep through the day and the night, I wonder optimistically. Is it time to be set free?

Then, I realize, it can't be morning. The sun is too far in the west, and the crowd in the market is too small. It must be late in the afternoon, which means it is not Wednesday morning, and I have another night in these bloody stocks. I dully wonder why the Archbishop is here. I hope he's here to set us free early, but I doubt he would ever be merciful. Perhaps he's here to make further examples of us.

If that was it, surely Soren would be in the front row to watch, but I don't see him. I search through the crowd for his smug face, and then I see *her*. I am dreaming, I think, but my body hurts, and I am terribly hungry, so I must be awake. I'd rub my eyes or pinch myself to check, but my hands are bound by the stocks.

Galadriel steps forward in a fine velvet dress. What is she doing here? She left days ago. How could she even be here? How would she even know to be here?

Her face is as regal as a stone sculpture. She looks at the Archbishop like she's waiting for him to speak. Today, she plays the role of a countess, just as she did when we went to St. Pantaleon's to guarantee Peter's safety and freedom from his captors. The

Archbishop raises his hands in the air, and the people of the market hush immediately.

"People of Cologne," he says loudly. "There has been a great injustice done to two of our own!"

The crowd gasps with disbelief, and I can see their eagerness to hear the news. I shake my head, for I'm sure the Archbishop has known of this injustice for two days now, but his threats against Father are still fresh in my mind, so I won't dare tempt him.

"Ansel Schumacher and his poor daughter Adelaide are victims of a terrible plot," he says woefully, feigning pity for us.

The crowd edges closer to him, to us. The children stand on tiptoe as they wait to hear.

"Two of our own forced Ansel and Adelaide to miss Sunday Mass. The plot was confessed to me just this morning! God forgive me for not knowing and for punishing the innocent! But how, oh Lord, was I supposed to know of such wickedness among my own guards!" He places his head in his hands dramatically as the crowd looks upon him with pity and bewilderment.

I am sure the people wonder who among the Archbishop's servants has betrayed him. I know, and he does, too. I am sure he has known since Father and I were brought to the North Tower, but he didn't care. I hope he intends to punish the real criminals now and not another pair of innocents like Father and me.

"Father Soren of St. Laurentius Church, Haimo Fitzoda, and Aldo Becker plotted to keep Ansel and his daughter, Adelaide, from Mass to settle personal scores! They were held prisoner in their own home!" The crowd boos and hisses as Haimo and Soren are pushed through the crowd by the guards with bound hands and gagged mouths. Haimo still limps from the beating he received last night. Soren is bruised and bloodied, too. "These men led me to believe that you good people of Cologne planned a most heinous and wicked revolt against your Holy Mother Church, led by this humble shoemaker!

"Is Soren right, people of Cologne? Do you intend to turn against God, against the Church?" he cries out.

The crowd cries "No!" emphatically, and some of the women even weep. Aldo is pushed through the crowd and stands, his head bowed in shame, next to the Archbishop. His wife follows, holding their little girl Leah who is the same age as Levi. Worry weighs heavily on her face, making her look older than she is.

"Here stands the man who confessed to this horrible plot," the Archbishop says, a stern finger pointed at Aldo. "He won't be punished as harshly as the others, but he shall be punished for his part in the crime. Aldo, you are hereby released from service to the provincial guard and banished from Cologne. Release the innocent and string up the guilty."

The crowd roars for justice. Nooses are tossed across poles that have been used for hasty hangings before. Just as Soren and Haimo are about to be sent to their deaths, the Archbishop whispers something to Soren, whose eyes narrow in anger. He screams through his gag. A horrified shriek pierces the roars of the crowd, and Oda, Haimo's mother, runs to the Archbishop, kneeling at his feet and begging him to have mercy on her son. She claws at his robes, but he pushes her away with his feet. When he refuses her, she doesn't run to her son, but to Soren, beating him with her fists until the guards drag her away.

The last time I see Soren and Haimo is with a rope around each of their necks. I have wanted this since the day of Mama's funeral, but it doesn't make me as happy, as I imagined it would. There is a reason the Archbishop has changed his mind about our sentence and Soren's guilt, but I doubt it has anything to do with justice.

Two guards come to my stocks with keys in hand. The lock releases with a click. It is the most beautiful sound I have ever heard. The men open the stocks, and I try to stand as soon as the log is lifted over my head. It is a stupid thing to do. A horrible pain stabs me in the back, and I fall backwards. I feel the breeze of someone running toward me, and someone catches me by the pits of my arms before I hit the ground. Ivo.

My joints are locked, and I imagine I look like a hunchback. He lays me gently on my side, but I wince as my arm touches the ground, thinking my shoulder shall snap before it can hold weight. He turns me onto my back and cradles my head. My neck slowly releases. The column of my back cracks pleasantly, and the warmth of blood flows into my joints, allowing them a little movement.

I turn my head and watch as the guards toss the wood of the stocks over Father's head. He does exactly as I. He tries to stand and then falls back, but no one is there to catch him, so he hits the ground hard. The velvet of Galadriel's dress rustles as she rushes to his aid. I look away and shake my head sadly, for she plays the role of his wife again, and I can hardly bear it. If only I wasn't too stiff to stand, I could have been the one to him help him.

I lie still as the market fills in response to the deafening cheers and jeers of the crowd, always hungry for blood in this large, unforgiving city I call home. Above the riotous shouts and cries, I hear Oda's shrieks. I cover my ears, but cannot drown them out.

It seems forever before the cries of the crowd die down, and I realize Soren and his son are dead. The mob grows bored, and they dissolve into the alleys around the market back to their homes or the taverns just as quickly as they had come.

I can see the corpses swinging from the ropes. Oda holds Haimo's feet and desperately tries to lift him, wailing in grief. His eyes are closed, and his face has the same lifeless, grey tint that Mama had at her funeral. Soren's buggy eyes and mouth gape open, his purple tongue visible. It is so ghastly a sight, I look away for a moment, and, then, I remember how long I've waited for this. I think of how he defiled Mama and burned every reminder I'd had of her. This is just how I want to remember Soren. I look and hope the memory lasts.

26 March, 1248, Evening

Ivo places my arm over his shoulder and lifts me. My shoulder pulls painfully at first, but then my arm and back warm from the stretch as I straighten my right leg to stand. He wraps an arm around my waist, and I step on my left leg, which gives way beneath my weight. He catches me quickly, and I shift back to the stronger leg.

Oda weeps at Haimo's feet now. She has abandoned her desperate hopes of saving her son, and I feel sorry for her. She suffers greatly, yet she's committed no crime besides being Soren's mistress for a time. Still, she didn't deserve to watch her only child hang. I can't imagine having to watch such a thing. I think, if I were her, I'd rather myself hang instead.

No one mourns for Soren. How horrible it must have been for him to die alone without comfort, without knowing he'd be missed. I smirk with satisfaction at the thought, finally getting a taste of justice, but I am unable to enjoy it fully. His punishment was just, but he wasn't hanged for the right reasons. He wasn't hanged for defiling Mama's corpse, for taking bribes, or for abandoning his congregation when they needed Sacrament. The Archbishop had Soren executed for another reason, yet I do not know what it is. His hanging had nothing to do with framing Father and me. I want to know the real reason, but I fear the more I know, the more vengeance I shall seek.

Finally, more feeling and strength returns to both legs, though I must still lean on Ivo for support. I take one last look at Soren, and we leave Hay Market, heading towards our homes.

"Where are we going?" I ask, swallowing hard, for I know we cannot go to my home.

"I don't know. To the gopher?" He suggests.

"Do you think they'll let me in?"

Ivo appraises me with a pitiful look. "They'd better."

I look at Father as Galadriel helps him follow us. His limp is bad. Cuts and bruises cover his face. Vengeance has cost me more than I bargained for. Our possessions have been burned. Father and I've spent two days in the stocks. The Archbishop could have had us tortured and killed. And now, Father cleaves to Galadriel. Even Soren paid for revenge, it cost him his life and that of his son's. Vengeance comes at a price to us all, but we never seem to know the charge until the deal is done.

Galadriel's arrival and our early release are no coincidence. She must have had something to do with this. If so, God charges for answering my prayers, and the cost is too steep for my taste. Vengeance against Soren has brought Father closer to Galadriel, and, in her eyes, balanced the scales between us.

Galadriel and Father stop to talk to Gregor and Ivan as we go on without them. Ivan's eyes are red and puffy. He buries his head in his hands, and Father pats him on the back. Gregor stands close by, looking upon his friend with great pity. I remember, now, that Ivan's sister had taken sick a week ago.

I look to Ivo to ask about Ilsa, but I already know the answer. He just shakes his head.

"What of Otto and his wife?" I ask, and he shakes his head again. "Did they take them on the cart?"

"No, they were buried in the night, outside the city walls."

My breath catches for a moment. I haven't seen Erik or Greta or Levi in days. They haven't come to see us once since we were placed in the stocks.

"What of your mother, your father, Levi? I haven't seen them in days. Are they—"

"They're all right." He interrupts. "Busy in the fields. It's spring."

I sigh with relief. "It's just that I hadn't seen them. I worried."

"That's like you, isn't it? Stuck in the stocks and worried for everyone who is not. My father visited yours earlier today. You were asleep so he let you be."

I look back at Father who's talking seriously as Galadriel stands beside him, waiting to catch him if he falls. I would stay back to give my condolences and keep an eye on Galadriel, but I don't think I'd know what to say. I don't know Ivan well, and my presence might make him uncomfortable. Besides, I feel a thirst, a hunger, an exhaustion that I've never felt before. The promise of ale and bread from the Gilded Gopher is too tempting to pass up.

It seems like a long way to the tavern as my limp slows us down, but I have a new appreciation for walking and feel great pity for those who cannot. It helps to walk even though I ache all over. Blood warms parts of my body that have been cold and stiff for far too long. Feeling rushes into my left leg, and it tingles unbearably. I shall be glad when I can put my weight on it again, for my shoulder aches from hanging onto Ivo.

I look up and see the sky. Brilliant oranges line the clouds as the sun sets, and I have to avert my eyes, for the brightness is blinding. The firmament darkens from pink to lavender to shadowy blue, and a few stars glow softly, even though it is still light. The trees, rooftops, and church spires darken before the luster of the setting sun. I haven't seen the sky in days. I don't know that I'd ever appreciated it as I do today.

Smoke billows out of the many chimneys of the hundreds of row houses surrounding us in all directions, and I find the aroma of smoldering wood on the crisp evening air strangely comforting. I breathe it in. I let it fill my lungs.

I let my fingers slide against the cool bricks of our great city wall, which have smoothed with age. The coolness seeps into my fingers.

Cologne looks, smells, and feels as it always has, but it is not the same. I cannot help but despair at what our city has become as I look upon the city wall and the people who amble down the street in the setting sun. Any one of them could catch the fever tomorrow, be dead by Friday, and be dumped in the pits by Saturday. They could be sent to the tower without knowing why and hanged without a hearing. Two men died today without a hearing. A few days ago, Father and I were threatened with torture and placed in the stocks for no reason. It could happen to any of us, all of us. There is no promise of tomorrow, and though there never really has been, the odds of a happy tomorrow used to be better in Cologne. How things have changed. It is scary the amount of power one man can hold and the toll one illness can take.

Ivo knocks on the door to the Gilded Gopher, and a woman opens it cautiously. She has skeptical eyes, but takes one look at me and lets us in. Ivo helps me down the stairs, though I can walk on my own if I place a hand on the wall.

"Can you sit?" he asks.

I nod, and he helps me into a chair. I put my head down on the table and stretch, groaning with pleasure as Ivo walks behind the bar. I sit up in anticipation of what he will bring. My stomach roars. He turns the corner of the bar with two mugs in his hands and two loaves of bread beneath his arm. I reach for the mug and drink ferociously. Ale trickles down the sides of my mouth. My tongue is as dry as saw dust and soaks up every drop that isn't swallowed. I pant for breath once I empty the mug, moan in delight, and reach for the bread. The sweet scent of the loaf fills my nostrils, and I can taste it before even placing the crust to my lips. My stomach howls, commanding me to eat. I thought I'd known what hunger was, but I'd never gone without food for two whole days. I devour the loaf in four bites.

"Thank you so much," I groan, and he smiles. I put my head back down on the table and he places his hand on my back, rubbing up and down along my spine.

"I love you," I groan with a laugh, and he stops rubbing. I feel the weight of what I'd just said. I turn my head to look at his face, resting my cheek on my forearm.

"You love me?" he asks.

I look up and think for a moment. "Yes. I do." He looks down and smiles, but he doesn't say he loves me, too. He doesn't say anything. An embarrassed blush rushes to my cheeks, and I want to pull the hood of the cloak I am wearing up over my face to hide. I swallow hard, and I wish I could take it back.

"Do you love me?" I ask weakly.

"More than you know, I guess," he says with a laugh. "How did you not know?" He brushes a tangle of hair behind my ear. I smile.

"You never said so."

"Many men say they love a woman, but don't. It's what a man does that shows a woman he loves her, not what he says."

"A brilliant excuse." I tease, shaking my head. "You were just afraid I wouldn't say it back."

He smiles. "As you were a moment ago."

I shrug my shoulders. "I still said it."

"Not intentionally," he scoffs.

"It is a good thing that I did or else it might never have been said."

There is a knock on the door upstairs followed by the sound of limping down the stairs. The door to the tavern swings open, smacking the wall hard enough to make the room shake, and Father limps in with Galadriel in tow. He heads toward the barrels behind the bar, fills two mugs with ale, and limps to our table. Large waves of ale spill over the sides of the mugs, and Ivo rushes to help him. Father and Galadriel sit across from us, and I look into my half-full mug.

"We live another day." Father says as he plops heavily into a chair, raising his mug.

We all raise our mugs in toast. "To another day," we say, inharmoniously and drink our ale. Father empties his mug in a matter of large gulps. Ivo rises and fetches him a second.

"Was it your doing?" I say to Galadriel. "Did you get us set free early?"

"No, I was on my way to beg for your release, but the Archbishop was already on his way to set you free."

"I'm confused," Ivo says as he takes his seat.

I had forgotten that Ivo only knows what the Archbishop revealed at the market. I had to keep the truth from him before. The Archbishop said that he'd stick a hot poker in Father's rectum if I told anyone the truth, but we are free now. Besides, the tavern is empty, and no one but us shall know the truth.

I relay how Haimo and Aldo held us captive, and that we escaped only to be recaptured. I reveal how the Archbishop threatened and interrogated me. Worst of all, I confess my betrayal of Elias. I expect to be called a Brutus, a Judas, but Father and Ivo look on me with pity instead of anger and shame.

"Then most of what the Archbishop said was true," Ivo confirms. "It was Soren's plot."

"The Archbishop has known that for two days," Father adds. "I told him when we were in the tower."

"Perhaps he thought you were lying, Ansel." Galadriel adds. "Criminals always defend themselves with lies."

"We're not criminals." I snap.

"I know that. But how was the Archbishop to know?"

"I tried to tell the Archbishop what really happened." I explain. "He told me he didn't care. He said if I said anything else about it, he'd have us burned as heretics."

"No!" Galadriel gasps.

"He kept asking me if Father planned a revolt. It was all that interested him. I told him 'no,' but he didn't believe me until I swore on Mother's soul. Then, he told me that if I said we missed Mass on purpose and stayed silent about the rest, Father wouldn't be tortured."

"He forced the same confession from me." Father admits.

"Then he told me that we were being punished because I lied and said I didn't know who incited the rebellion when I knew it was Elias all along," I go on. "But the guard who took me to the stocks said I was being punished for missing Mass."

"So the Archbishop was protecting the hog-shivver," Ivo says through his teeth. "Why would he do that just to hang him in the end? It makes no sense."

Galadriel gasps and places her hands to her lips. "I know why Soren was hanged! I overheard the Archbishop say something to Soren just before the hanging." I suddenly remember the moment just before Soren's hanging when I saw the Archbishop whisper something in his ear, and Soren's eyes widened with rage. "He told Soren he'd never be able to blackmail him again."

No one speaks for a moment. "So Soren was blackmailing the Archbishop?" I say.

Galadriel nods.

"Do you know what Soren had on him?"

"No," she replies. "He didn't say."

"Well, we'll never know now," I huff.

We drink our ale, and I almost choke on a gulp as it comes to me.

"So the Archbishop did believe us when we told him what Soren had done! I bet he had Aldo interrogated just after you told him what really happened, and Aldo confessed. That's why we were in the North Tower so late.

"The Archbishop probably would have arrested Soren for leading him on some wild goose chase, but he realized he could kill his blackmailer instead. He even used me to get to Elias." I shake my head, for I'm angry at my own stupidity.

"He had us put in the stocks so the people of the market would feel sorry for us when he was ready to set us free. Then, he knew the crowd would turn on Soren and Haimo for framing us. No one would care that Soren and Haimo didn't get a hearing. The people would want to see them strung up on the spot, and they were. If there was a hearing, Soren could have exposed the Archbishop's secret, and the Archbishop didn't want that to happen."

"He planned to let us go today. He needed the market to be full so his plan would work," Father adds.

"Right. If he'd let us go at sunrise tomorrow, the market would have been empty. He let us go today so he could have the large, bloodthirsty audience of the market -- a crowd to support the hanging of Soren and Haimo without a hearing."

"So you were pawns," Ivo says. "We have to tell the guilds. This is wrong!"

"No." Father says. "We're not telling anyone."

"You were unjustly sentenced! Everything you own is gone!"

"And what do you think the guilds will do?" Father asks with a raised eyebrow.

Ivo pauses. "Make complaint. When the patricians find out--"

"He'd kill us first."

Father is right. The Archbishop isn't afraid to spill blood in order to protect his own interests. Ivo grows silent.

"I'm done risking my family, Ivo."

Ivo nods.

"Does anyone else know that you overheard the Archbishop, Galadriel?" Father asks.

"No," she says. "Why?"

"If he thinks we know about the blackmail, we could still be in danger."

"Don't you think people might get suspicious of him if we were to disappear?" I ask.

"Maybe, but it's best if he doesn't have reason to kill us." He sighs.

"But you both told the Archbishop what Soren did the night you were arrested. What if the Archbishop thinks you'll tell others that he knew of Soren's guilt two nights before he let you go?" Ivo reasons.

"The Archbishop could just say he didn't believe us. Who would take the word of a pair of cobblers over that of a priest? Besides, we were caught running away from the guards in the middle of the street," I say. "And, like I said before, people shall grow suspicious of him if we disappear. I'm sure we're safe now."

I may say we're safe, but I don't know that I believe it. I fear that if Father worries for my safety, he'll send me away, especially now that Galadriel has returned.

"Aldo's a dead man," Father says. "He knows too much, and the Archbishop won't risk him talking, even if he is banished. The Archbishop needed a witness against Soren and Haimo today. That is the only reason he needed Aldo alive. He has served his purpose. He'll be dead before the week is through."

"Piss on Aldo," Ivo says heatedly. "He didn't care when you and Addie were taken to the stocks. You know what could have happened to her." I know he's talking about what happened to Anna, what Haimo threatened to do to me.

Father scowls. "Let the devil have them."

"What made you come back? How did you know?" I ask Galadriel, though, as soon as I say the words, I wish I could take them back. I have just given her the opportunity to paint herself in a saintly hue.

Father looks to Galadriel, and she stares down at her own mug, running her fingers up and down the sides nervously like a love-struck fool. She's been naked before my father, and yet she pretends she cannot even look him in the eye, playing coy like some French slut. I want to slap the look from her face.

"When I arrived on my estate, I had this horrid feeling," she starts. "And it grew worse. I couldn't sleep. I couldn't eat, so I left for Cologne Saturday morning.

"Gregor was manning the gate when I arrived. He told me what happened, so I went straight to the Archbishop as quickly as I could, but he was already on his way to free you."

"Thank you for what you did today," Father says, squeezing her arm and Galadriel blushes. "It was very brave." He rises with his mug in hand.

I say nothing, for I'm fuming. Really, I have nothing to thank her for. Father gives me a look of warning.

"Thank you for trying to help." I start, and Father heads to the bar for more ale. I lower my voice to a whisper. "You and my Father seem to have a powerful connection, don't you, for you to have had such a strong feeling that he was in danger when you were so very far away. It must be love, and so soon after my mother's death...." Galadriel's face pales, and she looks to Father who continues to fill his mug, not having heard a word of what I'd just said to her. "What a miracle," I hiss sarcastically.

Father returns, siting heavily in the chair, placing the mug to his lips. I really should have stopped there, but I don't.

"I wonder if she knows what you both did." I say, crossing my arms. Ivo nudges me in the ribs, cuing me to stop, but the rage takes me over, and my lips are possessed. "I pray she doesn't know that her own cousin bedded her husband not even ten days after she died."

Father slams down his mug and the ale splashes over its brim. He swallows hard.

"I pray that every night. Do you Galadriel? How can she enjoy Heaven after witnessing such a betrayal?"

"Adelaide!" Father growls in warning, but I do not waver.

I push back my chair and stand before them. "If it was me, I think I would haunt you both for the rest of my days."

Galadriel's eyes fill with tears, and I am glad to see them. For every tear she sheds in guilt, I'm sure I've shed a dozen more in my grief at what she's done. I avenge my mother with every tear she spills, but I don't care to look upon her anymore, so I turn on my heel and head toward the stairs.

"Adelaide!" Father shouts, and I turn defiantly to stare him down. He rises from his chair and marches toward me. We are nose to nose, and I no longer feel so brave. He grabs my arms. The ale on his breath burns my eyes.

"I've warned you not to mention that," he says through his teeth.

"Are you going to hit me again?" It is more of an accusation than a question. The anger falls away from his face, and he pulls me by the arm toward the bar, out of Galadriel's ear shot.

"Three days ago, I thought I might never see you again." He says, his eyes darting back and forth as they look into mine. "We have nothing but each other now. I hope to not have to strike you for the rest of my days, but it is a father's duty to make his daughter mind. I'll do my duty by you. I promised your mother that, but I beg you. Don't make me strike you, Adelaide."

I sigh, and my shoulders fall. I think back to the prayers I said in the North Tower, in which I promised never to mention their affair again. God answered my prayers, but I broke my promise. I nod. Perhaps, if I humble myself before Galadriel, God will forgive me. I turn, and walk toward her.

"I think you'll find I have a bit of a temper," I say evenly. "I apologize." I don't apologize for hurting her feelings, and I don't apologize for defending my mother's honor. I'll never apologize for that. "May I go now, Father?"

"Not yet," he says and then sighs. "You and I leave tomorrow. Galadriel has offered to house us, and we shall be gracious guests," he says, and limps back to the table to sit beside her.

"What? I don't want to leave!" I cry, and he shoots me a look of daggers.

"You'll do as you're told," he replies. "Galadriel has a room for you at the White Stag tonight. Be in it by the time I get there. I wish to have words with you alone."

26 March, 1248, Night

I walk away as my anger toward Father, my hatred of Galadriel, and plans of revenge against the Archbishop spiral through my thoughts.

How could Father want to leave Cologne and move in with that harlot? If his affair with Galadriel was like stabbing Mama in the chest, going to live with her is like twisting the knife. How can he not be burdened by that? It makes no sense to me. Surely Haimo must have hit Father harder than I thought last night, for he doesn't think clearly at all. All I can do now is hope that once he is rested and fed, he'll come back to his senses, and the seed of guilt I've planted shall grow quickly within his thoughts.

If the guilt of his affair doesn't shake him from his decisions, I shall have to remind him of what we'd be leaving behind. Cobbling in Cologne is our legacy. There are too many generations of us Schumachers to recall. Cobbling has always been what I've expected to do with my life and pass on to my children. Besides that, if we leave, we'd abandon our friends while Cologne faces a crisis far worse than any of them realize. Our friends stood by us when we gave Mama's second funeral and boycotted the church even though it endangered them. How could we just leave them behind to bear the fever and a tyrant alone?

I know Cologne has become a dangerous place, and, in the last fortnight, I've thought to leave many times. But this is my home. This is all of our homes. We can't surrender it to an old, power-hungry man who shall be gone in a month or less, or shall be dead in a decade or sooner. We have to stay and try to make this the Cologne it once was. If we don't, the council and the people lose their voice. We could be condemned without hearings. Our dead shall be dumped in the pits without the Sacraments they are owed, the Sacraments we pay for with our tithes.

If Father stands by his decision to make us go, and he is more stubborn than I, so he just may do that, I shall make sure we return to Cologne within a fortnight. I shall make Galadriel hate me more than I hate her. I'll be rightfully cruel to her when Father can't see; but, when we are in front of him, I shall be sickeningly sweet to her. I'll make false complaints against her. If she doesn't force us out, he shall want to leave. I'll have to be quick about it though, before they do something hasty, like wed. But I have done all I can do tonight, and Father is too angry with me to hear anything else I have to say.

For now, I have other scores to settle. I have more seeds to plant so I may someday see the Archbishop fall. Vengeance has cost us, I know it. I feel the pain of it in my aching joints with every step I take. I feel it in my stomach as I watch Father and Galadriel grow closer, but I tire of being the pawn in someone else's game of chess. I am the player now. I shall always be the player, I promise myself.

"Where are you going?" Ivo asks, as I pass his house and head toward the cathedral. I pull the cloak over my head and hide my face.

"To find Aldo," I say.

"Why?"

"I have to tell him something."

"You're not going to warn him, are you? He deserves what he gets, Addie."

"It's not to protect him. He has a wife and a daughter to provide for. What shall happen to them if he dies? What if little Leah is put to the stocks for stealing bread to keep from starving. What if she is wronged like Anna Metzger and ends up with child, a child she can't provide for? What if she or her mother become so desperate that they end up at the Gilded Gopher just so they can provide for themselves? They didn't do anything wrong. Why should they suffer for Aldo's mistakes? Besides, he may be of use to me one day, so I need him to live." I continue toward the Archbishop's palace. "Hide your face beneath your cloak so no one recognizes you."

I walk up to a guard and ask where Aldo lives. He points me in the right direction. Aldo's home isn't far from the palace. I compose myself before I knock as I need to look strong and unafraid. I breathe deeply and knock on the door. Aldo answers with sword in hand.

"I suppose you're here to gloat," he says.

"No."

"What is it then?" he asks impatiently.

"If you don't leave tonight, you'll be face down in the Rhine within the week. Take your family and go, and don't let anyone know where."

"What do you care if I'm killed?" he asks.

"I don't, but I should like to see the Archbishop squirm a little when he realizes you aren't dead. Perhaps you could have a little revenge of your own on him in time. You could have a few letters written to the patrician families of the Cologne council about what really happened today. I doubt they are very happy right now that the Archbishop killed two men without their say. The council is very powerful, and I think they would like to see Cologne without an Archbishop to compete with for power. Or, if you don't care for revenge, then I should like to know that your daughter, Leah, has a father to provide for her so she doesn't turn to thievery or harlotry in order to survive, even if that Father is as despicable as you."

I turn and leave without parting words. Ivo looks at me with shock, as if he no longer recognizes me.

Anger stays with me as I head back toward Filzengraben, not caring where that road shall take me. My vision haloes as I walk, though my legs have a mind of their own. I don't feel them at all. It surprises me that I am still standing, for I have slept and eaten so little these past three days, but I don't feel tired at all, and even Ivo struggles to keep up with me. My mind is full of hatred, anger, and revenge. It fuels me. I won't accept the unfairness of the world. The world is only fair if we fight to makes it so, and, even then, there is no promise of justice.

I stop before a charred circle of ashes in the road. I am jolted back to the present, the breath knocked from my chest. This marks the spot where all of our belongings had been burned; the blankets that smelled like the lavender of Mama, all of her clothing, her dried flowers, the spoon she'd used to stir the porridge that I couldn't seem to make quite right.

I am so engrossed in my daze that I forget what I would come home to. I feel as though I look upon the world from afar, like I am here, but I am not. I look to the right and see the door to our house hanging crookedly on its hinges. Beyond that, leather scrap, an awl, lasts, and flax thread are strewn about the floor of Father's disheveled workshop. My knees unhinge, and I fold to the ground.

The darkness tries to take me, but I fight it. I hear the light pounding of feet and the echoing shouts of my name. Ivo grabs me under the arms, and my head falls onto his tunic. I breathe in the fresh grass, clean wind, and sweaty scent of him as I try to catch air, as I try to stay awake. He tries to force me up, but my legs refuse to hold me. I fold again, and the darkness wins as I slip into dreams.

∽ꙮꙅ

Snow sprinkles down, dusting the tents and pathways into the Christmas market. The bushes and trees are already coated from several days of light snow. Every year, Mama takes one night off from her normal chores right before twilight to take me to the market while Father works. We rarely buy anything, but it is nice to smell the different foods and spices so beautifully-prepared in time for Christmas, and to see the people come out in their brightly-colored cloaks. The lanterns at each tent glow, making the city a reflection of a clear night filled with stars. It is magical.

We don our best cloaks, our only cloaks, and shuffle through the snow, trying not to slip. Our breath clouds in the air, and my fingers and toes quickly grow cold from the chilly night air. The music of the many performers and glow from the thousands of candles flickering off the fresh snow and cream-colored tents lure us. We can see it, hear it, though we are blocks away. Each tent serves something different: dried fruits, intricately twisted breads, spices I'd never heard of, cakes and breads, wines, silks, furs, and so much more. Most of the vendors ignore us. We don't look like we have many coins, so why waste the time?

But one of the spice men isn't busy and smiles at me the way a father smiles at a girl who reminds him of a daughter he misses.

"You-a like-a thee spices?"

I nod quickly. I smile the way only a six year old can, widely, curiously, and innocently.

"You-a smell, eh?"

The man has leathery skin, like the color Father uses to make most of his boots.

I walk into the tent and peer into the myriad of barrels filled with spices as brightly-colored as the forest in fall: maple reds, burnt oranges, golden yellows, and warm browns. The smells are even richer and more varied. First, I smell the sweet, earthiness of cinnamon and then the sweet, woodsy heat of nutmeg. Next are the tiny black balls of cloves; so strong, spicy, and syrupy. The large white bulbs of garlic smell bitter and buttery. It is a feast for the senses.

"Can we get some, Mama?" I beg, tugging her cloak. "Pleeeeaaaasse."

A round woman covered in a scarlet red cloak edged with furs enters the tent, several small pages following her. Her chubby, bejeweled fingers dart back and forth between the barrels as she barks her order.

"No! No! No! I said ten pounds of sugar! That's not even five!" the woman grunts in frustration. The spice trader rushes back and forth trying to keep up, filling sack after sack with her order. "Surely, there's another spice man in the market. If you can't keep up, I'll take my coins elsewhere!"

"No! No! Don' go! I give-a you-a free pound, eh?"

Mama says a quick "Thank you" to the spice man and hurries me out of the tent.

"How come that lady gets to have lots of spices and we don't even get any?" I pout.

"Here," Mama says, and she places one of her three pfennigs in my hand. "You can get something you want with this."

"How many spices can I get with it?" I ask.

"None," Mama replies.

"How come?" I cross my arms and pout.

"Because you would need many, many more than that to buy spices. To buy one pound of spices, you would have to have one pfennig for each of your fingers and toes, that's twenty. There are things in this market you will like more than those spices that will only cost you the one pfennig. "

"Well, don't you want some spices? They make your pottage taste really good." I try to convince her so I can use my pfennig for something else.

"I suppose so."

"Then, why don't you get some?"

"Because I have two pfennigs, and that's not quite enough."

"Let's go home and get some more, and, when we come back, we'll get even more spices than that lady!" I throw my arms out to show Mama how many bags of spices we shall bring home. "Father would love that."

Mama laughs, "We don't have enough pfennigs at home either."

"Yes we do. Father has a jar. We can use those!" My excitement turns to a whine.

"We need to use those coins to pay for other things like food, rent, tithing, and taxes. And even if we didn't, we still wouldn't have enough coins to buy as many spices as that woman." Mama speaks slowly and sweetly, trying to help me understand, but I don't.

"Well, how come that lady has so many coins and we don't?" I ask. "Does she work harder than Father?"

"No," Mama replies.

"Then, why does she have so many coins?"

"Well… sometimes it's not about how hard you work, but who you are."

"Who is she?"

"She is kin of the Archbishop."

"So she gets more coins because God likes her better?"

"No!" Mama laughs.

"But we're good people. We deserve lots of coins too."

"You're right. We are good people, but that's not the way things work, my little Snow White."

"It's not fair," I pout.

"I know," she sighs.

We walk for a while. The shouts of vendors and the crunch of our boots in the snow being the only sound. I feel very sad that it doesn't matter if one works hard or prays hard, or even does right. Some people shall do the opposite and have more for it. I know Mama sees the sadness on my face.

"But you know what? There are some monks on the corner who have the best gingerbread in the whole world."

"Really?" I cry.

"And they are only a pfennig," she whispers, as though she shares some grand secret with me.

I run ahead of her in search of the gingerbread. I hold my pfennig in an iron grip, though I shall give it away as soon as I get my hands on their confections.

27 March, 1248

My eyes flutter at the cerulean glow of the sky before dawn brightens the room. Dawn? Had I slept through the evening and the night? My stomach burns, begging for food, but the heaviness of sleep wins as I sink back into the mat. I sleep until the radiance of the afternoon sun sneaks into the house and burns the backs of my eyelids. I roll onto my stomach and cover my face with my arm. Sleep again. Familiar voices sneak into my slumber and weave themselves into my countless, forgotten dreams. It isn't the rusty orange blush of sunset that wakes me, but an argument I pretend to sleep through.

"Ivo, we hardly have food for us," Greta says.

"They have no food now. God would want us to be charitable," Ivo reasons. Greta is devout, and she sighs, knowing he is right, but he continues anyway. "She can have my food."

"You are not giving up your food. You'll eat what the Lord has provided for you," Greta huffs. "She doesn't eat much, and she'll probably sleep through another night anyway," she sighs.

I pretend to sleep a while longer so they don't suspect I've heard their discussion, not that Greta would feel bad about it. She would tell me plainly she didn't want to feed me without any guilt for hurting my feelings, but she would never let on that it was because they didn't have enough food. She is too proud for that, and I don't want her to know I've overheard her admit it to her son.

I fake a yawn to warn them I am waking. I stretch, and a warm, heavenly burn flows from my arms into my shoulder blades. My back arches instead of hunching forward like it had been for two days in the stocks. I lay still for a moment, enjoying the feeling of being straight.

"So, you're finally awake?" Greta says as I sit up and brush the tangles of hair from my face.

"Just in time for supper!" Levi yells gleefully.

"Just in time for supper," Greta's repeats with less enthusiasm.

"Oh!" I cry out as I realize I was supposed to be at the White Stag last night. I leap up. "Father's going to have my hide for this."

"I'm sure he's too drunk for that," Greta grumbles. "Erik went and fetched him last night. I haven't seen either of them since."

I twist my back, and it cracks all the way down. Levi's eyes widen in amazement at the sound. I sigh with relief, stretch once more, and sit next to him at the table, across from Ivo.

"You don't have to worry, Addie," Levi says and pats my arm. "You're not in any trouble. My father told your father that you fainted and that we had to watch you, but I didn't think you were ever going to wake up."

I feel stung that Father left me here, though, truthfully, I'd rather be here with Ivo than at The White Stag with him and Galadriel.

"I doubt your father's missed you. He and Father'd been at the Gopher and the Stag all night," Ivo says. His foot nudges mine softly, and I give him a knowing smile as I slide my toe up his ankle.

"And they had lots of drinks, and Father had himself a good time with those damn wanting harlox, and —"

"Levi!" Greta yells, and the little boy jumps, having no idea what he's done wrong.

"They're called wanton harlots, Levi, not wanting harlox," Ivo huffs.

"Ivo!" Greta barks.

"What are wanton harlots?" Levi asks, careful to say the words correctly.

"They're —" Ivo starts.

"They are wicked beings! It is a sin to even say those words," Greta interrupts quickly.

"But you said them to Mary this morning. Remember when Mary asked you why father wasn't in the fields, and you told her to promise not to tell, and you said he was with —"

"Don't say it, Levi. God hears everything," she says, pointing up.

"But you said it, and Ivo said it, and Father plays with the... them," Levi whines in his confusion.

"Then, we shall have to pray very hard tonight so that God forgives us all," Greta says.

Levi pouts and nods his head.

How can Erik allow his wife and children to worry that they might not have enough food while he spends his coins on ale and harlots? I pity Greta for having such a selfish husband. I pity Ivo and Levi, too.

Greta slops a small ladle of pottage into each bowl and gives the blessing. It could have been Galadriel's cooking for all I care, for I am so hungry. My bowl is empty before anyone else's. Greta looks at me with pity and serves me another ladleful.

"Thank you," I say, for it is a lot for her to give. Tears sting the backs of my eyes, and it feels silly to be sentimental over pottage. But it's Greta's generosity that makes me so happy, and, yet, so sad at the same time. This may be the last time I eat at this table, I think, swallowing hard on a mouthful of porridge. I shake the thought from my head.

This is probably my last night in Cologne for a few weeks, I convince myself. But if my plans don't go the way I hope, it could be so much longer. I remove any plans and plots from my mind. If this is my last night in Cologne for a while, then I shall enjoy each and every moment of it.

I taste each bite of pottage now, even though my stomach howls for me to devour it. I watch Levi chew with his mouth open, mashing the food between his gums and teeth. He smiles so widely with all of his boyish innocence, and I try not to think that this might be the last time I see him looking so childlike.

But more than anyone, I watch Ivo. I study his face carefully and try to force each and every feature into my memory. I notice things I've never noticed before. He looks down into his bowl as he eats, scooping large spoonfuls of porridge into his mouth. The left side of his jaw tenses as he chews slowly. His hair falls into his face, and I fight the urge to reach out and brush it from his eyes. I rest my leg against his beneath the table to satisfy the urge to touch him, and he smiles, though his eyes are still on his porridge. He tosses the hair across his forehead and looks up so our eyes can meet. Greta coughs, and we break our gaze. I stare into my porridge for a moment and look up beneath my eyelashes to see the look on her face. I'm surprised to see her smiling. I wonder if she thinks back to when she was fifteen winters. Perhaps she had a suitor before marrying Erik. Perhaps he was the kind of man who would have never lain with harlots, never hit his children, and provided for her.

I had never really liked Greta much until she sent Brother John to give Mama a proper funeral. She has always been harsh like Erik, but, now, as I see her smiling lightly, I think that she probably wasn't always that way. I can see life has hardened her. Her life would harden any woman. She catches me staring and looks angry that I have caught her in a moment of sentiment, so I avert my eyes quickly.

"You should be heading to the White Stag after dinner," Greta says coolly. "Ivo, you walk her and bring your father back with you."

"Can I go?" Levi says.

"No," Ivo and Greta say at the same time.

ဝသ၆

My stomach settles not long after I finish the second bowl of pottage. Everyone except for Levi is finished with supper. Ivo stands, and I rise to follow him out. Greta isn't the kind of person I would expect a hug from, but she embraces me tightly and puts on a brave face. "You be a good girl for your father," she says, and I nod.

I kiss Levi on the top of his head. He hugs me tightly and sniffles. It breaks my heart to see him cry, and it makes me wish even more that I didn't have to leave, even for a day. "I won't be gone that long," I say, and brush my fingers roughly through his hair. I hope it's true.

The sun is setting as Ivo and I walk closely together up the Witschen Alley. Our hands brush only once before he gently wraps his fingers around my palm. Tonight is a night of no regrets, for tomorrow I won't be here. And really, what is the worst that can happen tonight? Ivo winds his fingers in between mine and smiles the way I love with tiny lines reaching out in little arcs around his eyes. It feels like forever since I have seen him smile like this. I stare at his face and try to memorize it. The thought of not seeing it brings a sting to my eyes, so I take a deep breath and push the tears back. I can't cry now. That's not how I want to spend my last night in Cologne.

We pause before the door of the White Stag. "I doubt Father shall drink tonight. I shall see him to bed and sneak out. Will the armorer let you out early?"

"I doubt it. We'll have to meet after midnight," he says. "Besides, I have something to take care of."

"Me too. Meet me here then. Half past midnight?"

"I can't wait," he smiles.

27 March, 1248, Night

I knock softly on the door to Father's room. I hope he sleeps, but the doorknob twists, and I curse my terrible luck. Of course he's awake. The door opens a crack, but it isn't Father peering at me, it is Galadriel. So they share a room and bed again. My lip curls into a grimace at the thought. I am a dog about to bite the mistress of my master, but then I notice the look in her eyes.

At first, her irritated gaze and pursed lips ask: *What do* you *want?* She is displeased, perhaps still angry with me for calling her a harlot yesterday. I glance past her to Father who lies sprawled out and face down on the bed. His mouth gapes open, and his head rests in a puddle of his own drool.

"It looks as though my presence wasn't too sorely missed," I say, past Galadriel to Father.

Galadriel follows my gaze and, then, looks down. The harshness of her face gives way to a soft, childlike pout. She's having second thoughts about us, I assume with satisfaction. Father's indulgences displease her already.

She isn't half the woman my mother was. Mama would have never shared a bed with Father after he'd worried her all night. She would have never sat by and sulked, hoping that her pout might somehow make Father change. But still, I am happy to see Galadriel's disappointment. Perhaps she shall change her mind and leave for Bitsch without us tomorrow.

"If Father wakes, let him know I'm here," I tell her. "But I'm unwell and plan to sleep for the rest of the night to regain my strength for our travels." I hope this deters anyone from checking on me until morning, though I doubt Father shall wake for a long time. "My room is cold. Would you hand me Father's cloak?" I ask.

Galadriel raises a suspicious eyebrow. She looks to Father. "Well, I doubt he shall need it," she sighs. Father's cloak hangs over the edge of a chair. She slowly fetches it and hands it to me.

"Thank you," I say, though I hate speaking the words.

Galadriel nods her head and closes the door. I stick the key to my room in the lock and twist until the door pops open. It is a small dreary room with one candle on a small table, a little fireplace, and a small, dingy bed. I sit and look upon the vacant market. The sunset has darkened to dusk, but I need the cover of night, an empty market, and a bolt cutter to do what I must. For now, at least I can fetch the bolt cutter.

I climb out the window, down the ivy vines, and drop to the ground. I pull the hood of my cloak over my head and walk to Severin's gate. Just as I am about to turn the corner onto Severin's Strasse, I stop myself.

I don't know if I can do this, I think, swallowing hard. What if I get caught? What if Gregor gets caught?

I feel flushed, and my palms grow sweaty. I can't see Gregor sent to the stocks for me, and I can't go back to them myself. I peer around the corner and see Gregor and Ivan talking in the distance. I press myself against the row house on the corner.

I must do this, I think. I will never be able to live with myself if I don't fix this, and there is no other way for me to get a bolt cutter. I'll just have to be very careful. I take a few deep breaths for courage, compose an innocent look upon my face, and push myself from the wall of the row house.

Ivan and Gregor stop their discussion before I get to them, looking at me strangely. They must think I am going to ask them to open the gate so I can leave the city. They must think I'm crazy to want to do such a thing, for it is almost dark, and no woman would want to be on the outside of the city walls at night.

"Do you have a pair of bolt cutters, Herr?" I ask Gregor, smiling sweetly.

"Whatcha be needin' those fer?" he grumbles and raises the eyebrow above his one good eye.

"I don't know. They aren't for me. They're for my father."

"He sent ya out alone, at night? Don't seem like Ansel."

I shrug my shoulders. "He's not well enough to make the trip himself."

Gregor nods knowingly. "They're in the shed over there," he says and points. "Make sure ya bring 'em back...in the morning. A young girl shouldn't be roamin' the city alone at night."

"Yes, Herr." I grab them quickly before I can change my mind or they ask any more questions.

I carry the cutters beneath my cloak as I walk quickly back to Hay Market. I hate being on the streets alone at night. I've heard enough tales of ravaged girls and slit throats in the back alleys to be fearful, and there are fewer night watchmen than ever because of the fever, but that may be a good thing for me tonight. I am back at the White Stag before the bells strike eight, and I know I shall have to wait a long time before the market is empty for the night.

I almost head to the stocks a dozen or so times, but am so frightened that I shall be caught. Two and a half very long hours pass before I feel sure enough that the market shall stay empty. I step lightly and remember to continually scan the area as I approach, but luckily, no one comes. Before I know it, I am standing before him with bolt cutters in hand.

"What do you want?" Elias says hoarsely, not lifting his head.

"To set you free," I say, and he looks up.

"Adelaide?" he says, and I nod. "But why?"

Perhaps I should tell him it's my fault he's here, sentenced to die of thirst in the stocks, but I don't. I have to get him out and quickly at that. I have one chance to set him free. I look both ways to make sure no one is around and lift the bolt cutters to the lock. I squeeze, but the iron is thick. I use the muscles in my shoulder and then in my chest, but I'm too weak. Frustrated tears sting my eyes as I realize it won't work. I'm too weak. Elias shall die here, and it shall be my fault.

I wonder if I can somehow use my weight to break the lock. I step back and look at the stocks, thinking for a moment. I try leaning one bar of the cutter against the stocks and push all my weight onto the other. The iron starts to give. I pry the cutter open and try again, bouncing on the bar until finally the lock snaps. I almost cry out in triumph, but this is only the first of many steps it shall take to make sure Elias is safe and that I am not sent to the stocks for freeing him.

I carefully place the cutter and lock on the ground so as not to make a noise. I push the heavy wood of the stock up as high as I can, and Elias falls back. I wince as he hits the ground hard, knowing well how much it must hurt. I grab the cutter and run around the stocks to where he lies in the dirt. I grab his arms and drag him toward the alley by the White Stag. He clenches his teeth in agony, and I look away from his face, for it is a stark reminder of the pain I felt yesterday morning. I pity him, but if I slow down, now, someone could see us, and then we'll both be placed in the stocks.

Elias is very heavy, and I rest for a moment to catch my breath and look around to ensure we aren't being watched. Night watchmen cross an alley in the distance. I gasp and pull again for all I am worth until we are hidden in the shadows of the alley next to the White Stag.

"Why did you do this?" Elias asks with a groan, but I still don't have the courage to tell him the truth.

I prop him up against the building. "Do you think you can stand yet? We have to get you inside before someone sees you are gone." I pull him up by the arms, and he groans as he tries to stand. He leans over me, and the stench makes me gag. I look down and see that urine and feces stain his tunic. The foul odor of putrid fruit wafts around his face, and I see pieces of rotten apple in his hair. He leans against the wall, but needs me to hold him for support.

A few drunken men stumble from the White Stag, and so I pull Elias farther into the shadows of the alley.

"They let that heretic go?" a heavyset man asks his friend with a slur. The three of them meander toward the stocks, and one relieves himself on the wood.

"I don't know," his short, stocky friend says with a stumble. He looks down and pauses for a moment before bending over to lift the broken lock from the ground.

I curse at my own stupidity. Why did I leave the lock on the ground?

"We have to go now, Elias!" I whisper.

I wrap my cloak around his shoulders and dishevel my hair to hide my face. Elias shifts his weight to my shoulders, and I hold my breath as much as I can. I cannot bear his weight, and we fall. The three men stand up straight, and I know they've heard us. The heavyset man turns his head, and, for a moment, I fear he looks me straight in the eyes. My heart pounds against the bones in my chest until his gaze shifts, and I know he hasn't found us out. We are hidden well enough by the shadows.

Elias tries to rise again and groans.

"Wait," I hiss, afraid that if the men hear us again, they may check to see what caused the noise.

The man finishes his piss and turns to his friends. "You think there'll be a reward for the man who finds the heretic?"

The heavyset man rubs his chin in contemplation, and my heart pounds anxiously again. "He's probably long gone by now," he says, belches, and rubs his stomach with a groan.

"Eh, you're probably right," his friend replies. The moment the sigh of relief seeps through my lips, I hear footsteps behind us, less than a block away. It's a night watchman heading straight for us.

"Hide your face, Elias," I command and pull the hood over him. "And don't say a word." I smear some dirt on my face and surcote and dishevel my hair a little more.

I cross my arms and pretend to shiver as I walk slowly toward the guard.

"What do you want?" the watchman asks gruffly. I grab his arm.

"Please, Herr, you must help us," I say with a cough. "Father has the fever. I fear he'll die in the streets." I point to Elias who is slouched on the ground, hiding beneath his cloak.

The watchman's eyes widen as he snaps his arm from my grasp. "Go on with you," he says, shooing me away. I shiver again.

"Please, Herr. I am so very cold." He turns and quickly walks away without another word, and I return to Elias.

"What did you say to him?" he whispers.

"I told him you had the fever, and we needed help." Elias shakes his head at the irony. I look to the stocks and see the drunkards have moved on, but it shall not be long until someone else heads toward the market. It shall not be long until people are looking for Elias. "We must go now."

I pull him up by the arms, and he leans against the wall once more, but, this time, when he leans over me, he carries more of his own weight. Between the stench and his girth, I can still hardly bear him, but we make it into the White Stag. I take him up the stairs and unlock the door to my room. We limp to the bed, and he falls upon it. I drop to the ground, gasping for clean air, but Elias' stench lingers in my nostrils. I head to the window, sticking my head out in the hope that the cool night air shall free me of his putrid smell. It takes a few moments, but it works.

I sigh with relief. It is done. I've freed Elias, and he is hidden in my room. I run to the bar to fetch him bread and ale. The air comes easily to my chest now as the guilt of betraying Elias leaves me. I couldn't have left Cologne without righting this wrong. The burden would have been too heavy to bear forever.

I twist the door knob quietly just in case Father sleeps lightly next door. Elias looks upon me with tears in his eyes.

"Why did you save me?" he groans, hoarsely.

I set the loaf of bread down on a small table and rush toward him with the mug of ale. "Drink." I put the mug to his lips, careful to breathe through my mouth so I do not gag at the smell of him.

I lift his head, and he sips. "Why?"

"Because I want you to live," I say, and it is as much of the truth as he'll ever get out of me.

The church bells strike twelve, and I curse. "I have to go, but you can stay here for the night. Quick, hand me my cloak.

I'm supposed to be outside the tavern waiting for Ivo in half an hour, but I must return the bolt cutters before the guards go about looking for them. If Gregor is asked where his cutters are, and he says he has given them to my father, then we could be sent back to the stocks or worse, and Elias shall surely be killed too.

I look out the window once more to see a night watchman and two guards standing by Elias's stocks. I sneak out the back door of the tavern and head down the alley behind the White Stag. It'll take me longer to get to Severin's gate, but at least the guards won't notice me.

The narrow alleys are darker than the main streets, and my heart pounds with fear. At least I have the bolt cutter, I think. I could use that as a weapon if someone were to try to attack me.

I peer around the corner of Filzengraben and squint my eyes as I look down Severin Strasse. The gate is vacant except for Gregor and Ivan, so I rush toward them.

"What'd I tell ya 'bout walkin' the streets at night?" Gregor scolds.

"I'm sorry, Gregor. I had to do this. No one must know I had this," I say as I put the cutter back.

"Ah, I knew I shouldn' a let ya use it," Gregor gripes. "What'd ya go an' do now, girl?"

"If I tell you, you'll be in as much danger as I am now." His eye widens. "If anyone asks you about the bolt cutter, act as though you're confused. Or else I'll be killed."

"All righ', all righ'," he says, looking at me strangely, and I turn to make my way back to the White Stag.

I know I shall be at least a quarter hour late, but I don't run, for I know the watchmen and the guards are on alert for any strange behavior. I hope Ivo's waiting for me. I know I am late, but once he hears what I've done, I know he'll understand. On second thought, he'll probably be angry with me for doing something so dangerous.

I turn the corner, and Ivo isn't there. I hope he is running late, too. I fear he'd been waiting for me, grew frustrated, and then headed home for the night. If he isn't here soon, I shall go there to look for him, though I'd like to be done roaming the city alone at night.

I toss my arms about as I wait to ease the strain in my shoulders and chest from trying to break the lock. Smoke fumes fester densely in the air, heavier than usual, but before I can ponder why, Ivo runs up behind me in a panic.

"We have to go," he says breathlessly.

"What happened?" I lift his cloak. His chainse is covered in black dust. "You're all sooty. Are you all right?" I grab him and feel for injury.

"We have to go." He pulls me, but I stand firm.

"Was there an accident at the armorer's?" I ask.

"No. We have to go now," he orders with a cough.

"But—" He grabs me by the arm and starts pulling me through back alleys toward Severin's gate. "What's happened? Are you in trouble?"

"Give me your cloak," he orders. "I'll give it back once we're out of the gate."

I untie it and hand it to him. He whips it around his shoulders, covering his own cloak. "We can't go out Severin's gate, but the Weier gate is usually manned. Are you all right?"

He starts coughing. "I'm fine."

"You're not. What happened?"

He stops and swings me around. "For our safety, you must stop asking me that. I'll tell you everything when we are out of the city. But for now, I need you to act as though nothing is wrong."

I nod fearfully. The sky grows brighter, and I wonder if the moon rises behind us, but we are racing through narrow streets, and I can't see much of the sky beyond the rooftops. Ivo wipes the soot from his hands on my cloak and pauses to wipe his face as well. It doesn't make a great difference. It is dark, though, and the soot that covers him could easily be mistaken for dirt.

We reach the Weier gate, and the guard is asleep. I cough to wake him without startle. He opens the gate without paying us much attention, heads back to his booth, and closes the gate behind us. We continue toward the creek.

"Can you smell the smoke on me?" Ivo asks. I don't even have to stop to check, for he reeks of smoke.

"Yes, it's awful. What's happening?"

"Turn around and see for yourself," he replies.

I turn quickly and gasp. Flames, taller than any church spire in the city, lap at the night sky.

"Did you—" He nods before I can finish.

"The cathedral," he says. "It'll be nothing but cinders by morning."

Ivo has set the greatest church in Cologne ablaze, and with the fire raging as it is now, it shall surely burn to the ground. I am frozen from the shock.

He throws my cloak to me and jumps into the creek. "Turn around." But I am still frozen. "Turn around, Addie," he orders, and I do, though I am dumfounded in my surprise at what he has done. His chainse, surcote, and cloak land beside me. Still, it takes me a moment to realize that he is now naked in the creek. My stomach tenses. I find myself no longer thinking of the fire. I keep reminding myself not to turn around.

"Scrub my clothes in the creek," Ivo says, his teeth chattering. We need to hurry. Soon it'll be like daylight, and people'll come out of their huts to see the fire."

What if he is caught? I rush to the creek bed keeping my back to him and scrub his clothes as fast as I can between two cobblestones, trying to remove the soot and the strong smell of smoke. No one can ever know he did this. He shall be hanged, or burned at the stake, or worse. I've heard of some German cities adopting English forms of torture. The English are the worst. They'll half hang a man, stretch him, and then cut him from navel to nose. They'll rip out his innards and burn them before his very eyes as he bleeds to death. It is the epitome of barbarism. I try not to think of it and scrub Ivo's clothes harder and faster.

The soot appears to fade, but it is so dark, and I cannot see all that well. He is a farmer's son, and his clothes should look a little ragged and dirty. It would probably be more suspicious if his clothes were too clean. I wring them out as best I can and smell them for heavy smoke. They smell no smokier than they would have had he slept beside a hearth, so I hang them on a branch to dry. I shake the soot out of his cloak, and a pile of sealed parchments fall out.

"What are these?" I ask, turning around to show Ivo what I've found.

"Addie!" He yells and sinks into the water to hide his nakedness. I whip back around the other way, my cheeks burning with embarrassment.

"Sorry," I utter.

"Don't get those wet." He orders.

"What are they?"

"I'm not sure. I found a pile of them inside a chamber in the cathedral. They all have the Archbishop's seal." Ivo says, shivering. "Are you almost finished?"

"I just need to rinse your cloak."

The dark color shall hide any smoke stain, and if I let it soak, it shall take more than a day to dry. I dampen it slightly and shake it once more before hanging it on a branch in the hope that the cool night air shall remove the odor.

"Toss your surcote behind you," Ivo says. His teeth chatter harder. He shall need to wear something when we return to the city, and it is smart of him to think to wear my surcote. I unfasten my belt quickly, nervously, and toss my surcote as far behind me as I can. Ivo swishes through the water and I hear his wet feet sink into the mud beside the creek.

I have never listened so closely to Ivo's footsteps before, but they seem loud and slow to me now. Every footstep, every drop of water that falls from him echoes in the night. My belly tightens, and I realize I'm holding my breath.

Fabric shuffles as Ivo dresses. I am just about to ask him if I can turn when his hand touches my shoulder, and I am startled. I turn to face him. I have never seen so much of his skin before. He has the pale skin and slight muscular curvature of the marble statues that adorn our churches. He shivers pitifully, and I rush to wrap my cloak around his shoulders. My fingers find themselves running through his wet hair.

"Why?" I ask, looking into his eyes. Why would he burn down the cathedral?

He looks away. "That man doesn't deserve a cathedral. I would have burned his palace if I could have gotten into it," he chokes and shivers.

I peel open the cloak upon his shoulder and slide slowly into it. He looks down into my eyes as I press against him and run my hands up and down his arms and back trying to warm him.

Ivo sighs, and his chattering slows. He wraps his arms around me tightly, and I feel I should never need anything else in my life as long as I can feel this way forever. He releases me with a disappointed sigh.

"It will be good for the gatekeeper to see us entering the city. Then we can't be suspected of burning the cathedral, for he can say he saw us outside the walls. Hand me my wet clothes. We'll say I fell into the creek if anyone asks."

"You'll freeze if you put them back on!"

"I won't wear them for long. Your house is abandoned now. We can go there and start a fire. I'll change back into your surcote. It's only for a short time."

"Very well," I say and fetch his clothes in a hurry so we can get to my house and warm ourselves by the fire.

❦

The flames are so wide and high now that Cologne is lit like the daytime, and the streets are crowded as though it is the Christmas market. A madman runs through the streets claiming it is the Rapture. Women and their frightened children cry. Villagers kneel in prayer as others look upon the flames with great awe.

Ivo and I aren't even noticed. I could probably run through the streets naked, and no one would give me a second look. I doubt I shall live to see a day like this again, a day when a city as grand as

Cologne sinks into the scorching circles of Hell. Everyone shall remember what they were doing this day. It shall be the talk of taverns and in the tales we tell our grandchildren.

∽ℰ

The door to my house is still ajar from a few days ago when Aldo broke it in. Ivo goes in first to make sure no vagabonds have taken it over. It is empty. Father's desk is there, but all his leather and tools are gone. We climb the stairs, and the kitchen is empty with the exception of the table. I don't dare enter my parent's bedroom or climb the ladder to mine. I try to pretend that this is a stranger's house and not the only home I have ever known, and that, after this day, I may never see again. It brings the burning of tears to my eyes, but I have sworn to enjoy this last day in Cologne. Ivo has worked so hard to make it memorable, even in burning down the cathedral. If he isn't caught, it shall be the greatest gift I ever received. I can only imagine how the Archbishop squirms now. Wait until he realizes Aldo has disappeared. The patricians shall see the Archbishop as weak for sure. Perhaps, they shall strike like wolves on an injured stag. I cannot wait to hear of his disgrace.

"We will hang your clothes by the fire, and you can have my surcote again," I suggest. Ivo's lips are blue from the cold. He nods, shivering. I stand and turn my back again. I remove my surcote and toss it behind me, closer than before. I kneel to start a fire in the hearth. He peels off his wet clothes, and they drop heavily. I can feel the weight of his steps coming toward me. He is close enough that I could turn and touch him. I could.

The fire kindles, embers glowing. I rise brushing the soot from my hands. Ivo places a hand on my shoulder and brushes the hair from my neck. It tickles a little, and I turn, grinning widely, almost giggling at the sensation. His boyish expression fades. His face is so serious now.

"My God, you're beautiful," he says, looking down at me. I realize that the light of the fire behind me makes my tunic slightly translucent, and he can see my silhouette, the subtle curves of my body through the fabric. I swallow hard, and my stomach tightens with a mix of exhilaration and anxiety. His hand stays at my neck while the other finds its way to my hip and slides to the small of my back. He pulls me to him, and I close my eyes.

His lips brush mine as my hands slide up his back to his shoulder blades. I slip my fingers beneath the surcote so I can feel the warmth of him. My fingers melt into his skin as I pull him closer, pressing my lips gently against his. His lips press harder, parting mine, as he pulls me closer with a firm arm and weaves his fingers into my hair.

I turn and back up until I am sitting on the edge of the table. I try to look at him in an alluring way. I do not know if I even know how to look alluring, but he rushes toward me, and we are kissing again. I lie back on the table, as he continues to kiss me. A moan slips from my lips, and he jumps back.

"What? What's wrong?" I cry, sitting up.

"I must to stop. We must to stop," he pants.

"No... Why?" I know these are wanton words, but I do not care anymore.

"We are not married yet."

"Oh." I feel myself flush with embarrassment at his denying me. Then the weight of his words hit me, and I smile. He said "we are not married *yet*." We are practically betrothed now, for I know he intends for us to marry soon.

I want to say that we could be married. I want to beg him to let me stay with him, to live with his family as his wife. I can sell my shoes in the market while he finishes his apprenticeship. Then we can find a home of our own.

"I cannot marry you. Not until I'm an armorer and have my own shop," he declares.

"But why?"

"Because I don't want you to be a poor farmer's wife," he says.

"There's no worry of that. You're nearly finished with your apprenticeship, and I'm nearly my father's equal at cobbling. I'm ready for a stand of my own. All I need are the tools." I reason.

"And how will we purchase the tools? We haven't the coin to pay for them." He says and then sighs.

I pout, for he is right.

"Sit with me for a little while before we have to go back," he says.

I walk toward the hearth and feel his clothes for dampness. They are warm and nearly dry. "You can put your clothes back on," I say and toss him his chainse and surcote. "But that means I shall need my surcote back," I tease. I approach him and pull at the surcote, playing as though I shall peel it off him.

"Adelaide, turn around," he laughs.

"Are you sure?" I add, in jest.

"Adelaide!" he laughs. A few times I pretend I shall turn around and peak at his nakedness just to make him laugh. He warns and scolds me. As soon as he is dressed, he pounces upon me, tickling my neck. I laugh and wriggle until we end up on the floor, kissing again until he makes me stop. For the rest of the night, I sit between his legs and lie with my back on his chest, telling him stories as he runs his fingers through my hair.

My last night in Cologne is almost perfect. Many who live long enough shall tell their children and grandchildren of this night, 27th of March, 1248, the night our great cathedral was burned to the ground. But the story of my night with Ivo, that is one story I shall keep for myself.

28 March, 1248

A strong grip on my arm pulls me from slumber and yanks me straight to my feet.

The sleep clears from my eyes just as a harsh slap hits my face. "I've been looking for you all night!" Father shouts.

I cry out and fall heavily to the floor. My head smacks the wood. My ears ring, and the room seems to tilt for a moment. Ivo's eyes are wild, and I realize he is trapped in another night terror. Father looks at him strangely for a moment. Then he looks back at me. His face droops sadly for a moment, before he snarls at Ivo. I know what Father thinks. He thinks I've given myself to Ivo. Anger hardens his face as he heads toward Ivo, but I lunge between them.

"No!" I cry, and throw myself over Ivo in case Father decides to strike him.

Father pulls me back by my hair, and I squeal. "Do you think of no one but yourself! Do you realize I have looked for you all night? That Erik has looked for Ivo? That we thought you both were dead?"

"I… I'm sorry," I cry. He pulls my hair so hard that I must stand on my toes.

"What would your mother think?" he hisses before releasing my hair. I drop to my hands and knees. He means to hurt me with these words, and his cruelty shocks me.

"What would she think of *me*? What would she think of *you*? You're the one who's betrayed her!"

"I've warned you never to speak of that!" he roars. I try to get to my feet, but slip, only managing to clumsily stumble a few feet away. I brace for a strike that does not come. Ivo has woken and stands between us with a poker in his hand.

"Do not touch her," he growls, and holds his hand out to me. I take it, and he pulls me up so that I stand beside him.

Father narrows his eyes at Ivo for a moment. "Did you lie with her?" he asks angrily with glassy eyes.

"No."

"Do not lie to me, boy," he growls.

"He tells the truth," I say, and Father looks to me with disbelief. "He has a conviction that I do not. That *you* do not. He will not have me, not until we are married, not until his apprenticeship is finished."

Father's eyes widen from the sting. His scowled lips and narrowed eyes melt into a devastated pout. I expect him to scream at me, to disown me, but he just shakes his head and walks down the stairs with slumped shoulders. I hear him pull the chair out from his desk and sit down.

"Are you all right?" Ivo asks and examines the rapidly swelling bump on my head.

"I'll be fine," I say, though it smarts at his touch. "What about you? Your father must be furious." I say, worried at the punishment he shall receive at his father's hands.

He shrugs. "It was worth it."

I anxiously bite my lip at the thought of the beating he'll receive. He reaches for my hand and squeezes it gently.

"Don't worry." He smiles. "Between the last few days in the fields and the nights in the taverns, I doubt he has it in him to give me a proper beating."

I sigh. "Can't I just smuggle you away in the carriage and take you off to Galadriel's castle." I say with a smile.

He laughs. "I think we're in enough trouble as it is." He replies.

I look down the stairs into Father's workshop. "He'll never forgive me for this," I sigh.

"He will," Ivo says. "At least, I hope so. I'd like a nice dowry for marrying you." He smiles, and I punch him playfully in the arm.

"I hope you like shoes." I quip.

He shrugs. I know this is the last time I shall see him for a while. "I wish you could stay," he says, stroking my cheek.

"Me too." I sigh as I reach for his hand and rest my cheek on his palm. "You could marry me now and keep me here." I say, half jesting. He smiles, but does not answer. I swallow the rejection hard and change the subject. "Elias is going to visit you in the night and teach you to read," I say. "Then we can at least write each other."

"Elias?" He replies, giving me a strange look. "He's sentenced to die in the stocks for heresy."

"I set him free a few hours ago. He's resting in my room at the White Stag."

"Does your father know about that?" he whispers. I shake my head and smile devilishly.

He laughs and shakes his head. "Let me walk you to The Stag," he offers. I am very tempted, but I shake my head.

"I should wait for him," I say and look upon Father, sitting sadly in his workshop. "Besides, your family is worried for you."

I place my other hand in his, and tears pool upon my eyelids. I smile through my sadness, and, with a single blink, the tears stream down my face. Ivo leans down, and we linger in our last kiss. I walk him down the stairs and watch as he walks out the door down Filzengraben until I can no longer make out his shape through the smoke.

I turn to check on Father, intending to give a half-hearted apology. I feel badly for hurting him, for worrying him, but, if given the chance, I would live this night again in exactly the same way.

"Father," I utter, "I'm—"

"Leave me," his voice cracks. "Go back to the room. We leave at the strike of seven." I think I'd rather have him yell at me than look so terribly disappointed.

⊷⊶

It is the dawn that lights the sky now, for the cathedral fire has been quenched. Clouds of smoke hang heavily over the city and float through the streets. I hold my cloak to my nose so I can breathe easier. I think of Ivo as I head back to the White Stag, careful not to get lost in the dense fog. I hope he isn't caught, though who would suspect him of burning the cathedral? As long as no one saw him light the fire, he should be safe. I shall pray for it every day until I can return to Cologne, and we can be married.

I walk into the White Stag, which is empty, and up the stairs to my room. Elias sleeps on the bed. I sit on its edge and look over the city of Cologne. Artisans and merchants make their way through the cloudy market to set up their stands. Their faces are soulless masks. Unlike me, they aren't happy to see our cathedral burned down. But they do not know the Archbishop for the scoundrel he is, that he doesn't deserve a cathedral and the tithes that come with it. A cool breeze blows through the open window, and I put my hands into the pockets of my cloak for warmth. My hand brushes the many parchments that I had hidden in them, just as Ivo had asked me. I rip them out, tearing them open one by one, looking for something, anything that might be of use against the Archbishop.

There is nothing of use within them. Most of them are minor business matters, and a few are marriage contracts. I toss each one into the fire. There is one letter left, addressed to Count William of Holland. I have little hope for it, but I break the seal anyway.

⇛⇚

Dear Count William,

As is widely known, our Holy Roman Emperor is not as holy as he might think himself. His excommunication has been, yet again, issued by His Holiness, Pope Innocent IV, nullifying his claim to the Empire, and more importantly for you, his son's claim to the German throne. I, and a great many of the Church's allies, have secured your title as King of the Romans. Gather your armies. Raspe needed them, and so shall you. Do not forget that it is holy men and God who raise you to king, and if you disappoint Him and his servants, we can easily put someone else in your place.

Konrad von Hochstaden, Archbishop of Cologne

⇛⇚

I read the letter three times and sit back heavily with disbelief. Is this what Soren knew about the Archbishop? Did Soren somehow intercept this letter or one from the Count of Holland and hold it over the Archbishop? If so, Soren must have threatened to bring it to the attention of the people of Cologne, causing the Archbishop to worry about revolt. Or Soren threatened to inform Emperor Frederick or his son, King Conrad, of the treason.

But what if his plans were grander than that? I think back to the day when Father and I were held captive by Haimo and Aldo. Haimo said his father would be Archbishop of Cologne one day. Aldo laughed at the preposterousness. Forwarding a letter like this to the king may have caused Konrad von Hochstaden to lose his head, especially since he's betrayed the king before. Soren's loyalty to our true king could have been rewarded with a grand promotion, say as the new Archbishop of Cologne. I guess I'll never know for sure what Soren knew about our Archbishop. Dead men don't talk, but this seems to make sense. I wonder if Soren never intended to blackmail the Archbishop at all. What if Soren truly meant to frame us by allowing Haimo and Aldo to hold us captive? Maybe the Archbishop realized all this talk about rebellion was a web of lies spun by Soren to seek revenge on us for embarrassing him, except it backfired. When the Archbishop realized that the only man in Cologne against the entire Church was Elias, he knew Soren had lied in order to settle personal scores. When the Archbishop confronted Soren, he pulled out the letter and blackmailed him to keep himself from punishment, but he never intended to keep the Archbishop's secret. He intended to use it to usurp his position. How else could Haimo have assumed his lowly father would ascend so high? Konrad von Hochstaden would have felt like a cornered dog, and so he bit.

After the realization, I am frozen. What can I do with this? How can I use it? Anyone caught with it could be accused of burning the cathedral. I can't do anything with it, and I cannot allow Ivo to either. It puts us all in danger.

Then, an idea comes. I rush to the fireplace and pull out a charred piece of wood, put the parchment on the desk, and write on the back side. My penmanship is horrid, but the message I write is legible.

Herr Aduct, I found this letter in the cathedral ashes. God wills you to read it.

I tuck the parchment in the pocket of my cloak and rush to the Aducht manor in New Market, taking back alleys so I do not accidentally run into Father. I hide my face in the shadow of my cloak's hood and the thick, agitated strands of my disheveled hair, hoping not to be recognized. The narrower the alley, the thicker the smoke. I can hardly see a yard in front of me and must breathe through the fabric of my sleeve. Because I can barely see where I am going and because I am in such a hurry, the walk seems terribly long, but I arrive, unperturbed at the block in New Market that makes up the Aducht estate. I muster a deep breath as I approach the door, pulling my hood a little further out to make sure my face is well hidden. I avert my gaze and knock on the heavy wooden doors. The door opens, and I mask my voice.

"A letter to Herr Aducht from His Excellency," I say, deepening my voice. I hold out the letter and the servant takes it.

"Thank you," the maid replies. "I shall see that he gets it right away." I turn on my heel before the door closes and rush back to The White Stag, hoping that Father does not get there before me. Let the patricians handle this. People like Father, Ivo, and I would just end up like Soren and Haimo if we tried to use this information against someone like Konrad von Hochstaden, trampled like flies under the hooves of a great war horse.

❧

It is half past six when I tiptoe up the stairs and enter my room at The White Stag. Elias still sleeps, and I assume that means Father hasn't come here to look for me. Moments later Elias stirs, which is a good thing, for I was just about to wake him.

"Is this a dream? Am I dead?" he asks, and I shake my head.

"You're free. Remember last night?" I say, and see the recollection in his face. He nods, and I smile at him. He sighs.

I kneel beside him. "Elias, do you remember how I said that I needed you to live?"

"Yes," he replies, though he looks a little afraid of what I am about to say next.

"I need you to do something for me," I say, and he nods. "There is a boy, named Ivo, son of Erik Bauer."

"Yes, I know of him," Elias says.

"I need you to teach him to read."

"I cannot stay in Cologne. I'll be killed!" Elias argues.

"There must be someone on the outside of the city who would house you."

He shakes his head.

I pull out my purse and place it in his hand. It holds all the coins that I'd been saving so Ivo and I could run away together. "Here. Pay someone to take you in. The people on the outside of the city do not know you're an outlaw."

He nods reluctantly. I take a few coins from the purse before he can change his mind and go down to the tavern. I purchase enough bread and ale to last him two days and another night in his room. I head back to the room and set the food on a small table.

"Once you are safe, find Ivo and figure something out," I say. "Be careful, Elias. The cathedral was burned to the ground last night. Cologne is a dangerous place now."

I turn the door knob and step outside.

"Addie!" he calls and I turn.

"Thank you," he says. Little does he know, he owes me nothing. What I have done for him, I have done for myself. I nod and close the door behind me.

⌙⌒

The brown carriage horse paws at the ground, ready to head into the fields. I pet him on the nose, and he snorts. I step into the carriage without bothering to hide my tears.

"Addie," a voice calls, and I see Levi running toward me carrying my mother's tunic. "You almost forgot this." I step out of the carriage and take the tunic. I place it to my nose and breathe in Mama's lavender scent. Praise God, the smoke has not ruined the fragrance.

"Thank you," I say, and he wraps his arms around me, squeezing me tightly.

"Oh, and Ivo wanted me to tell you something."

"Is he all right?" I ask.

"Papa was going to beat him, but when he found out that Ivo was with you all night, he patted him on the back and said, 'That's my boy.'"

I roll my eyes. "So what did Ivo say?"

"He says that he loves you," Levi sneers.

"Why is it that your brother can never manage to utters these words himself? What's the matter with him?" I ask in jest.

"A great many things, if you ask Father." Levi replies. "Ivo says he'll come for you next year, if you'll still have him."

I laugh. "God willing, I will return before next year."

I grab Levi by the arm and pull him close, disheveling his hair with my fingers. Then I kneel down, looking into his cavernous eyes. A figure approaches through a passing cloud of smoke. It is Father. I swallow hard.

"Well, little messenger, tell your brother that I love him, too."

Levi groans. "All right. I'll tell him." He hugs me one more time, says goodbye, and runs home. I rise and try to gauge Father's expression. He flashes me a severe look.

"Get in." He orders, pointing to the door of the carriage as he heads into the White Stag. I immediately obey, climbing back into the carriage. I sit upon the hard wooden bench, rest my head on the sill of the window, and let the tears spill down my cheeks.

We will depart Cologne before the sun has fully risen with Galadriel and only the clothes on our backs. We say no departing words to our many friends.

I look out the window to the city that has been the only home I have ever known. I can feel Mama die again. I shall never walk the Christmas market with her. I shall never run into the house caked in mud, have her clean me up, and hear her call me "her little Snow White." The only item I have of hers is the tunic Ivo had rescued from our house before all of our things were destroyed. I hold it in my arms, wishing with all my heart that I had her comfort at this moment. But if I had her, none of this would be happening at all.

I place Mama's tunic to my nose, closing my eyes. It takes me far, far away to a time that seems so long ago. I am in my bedroom as the cold wind seeps through the slits in the shutters. I press close to Mama for warmth as she tells me the beginning of my story, the story of Snow White. My life was perfect then, and, I suppose, when a life is perfect there is little to tell. Perhaps, that is why Mama never added to my story. Or perhaps she truly wanted me compose it myself. She gave my story a beautiful beginning though. I picture Mama as the queen sitting regally at the window sill sewing. She wasn't much older than I am now. The beginning of my tale was the ending of hers. Now, I come to the middle of my own, and it is always the middles of stories that are best to tell, but the hardest to live.

The middle of my tale shall not be long, I tell myself. Galadriel and Father's affair has begun to unravel already, and I shall pull the strings until there is nothing between them but animosity. We shall be home in a month. Then, Ivo and I shall be married. I will have my happily ever after, and no one shall ever take me away from the people I love ever again.

It shall not be long.

COMING EARLY 2014

ੴ ੴ

THE FAIREST OF ALL

ੴ ੴ

BOOK TWO IN *THE FAIRYTALE KEEPER* SERIES

To get sneak peeks into the next installments of *The Fairytale Keeper* series and receive up-to-date information, please follow author Andrea Cefalo at:

The Official Website:	www.thefairytalekeeper.com
Facebook:	www.facebook.com/AndreaCefalo
Twitter:	www.twitter.com/AndreaCefalo
Pinterest:	www.pinterest.com/andreacefalo
Goodreads:	www.goodreads.com/andreacefalo

Author's Note

Many people ask how I came up with the idea for *The Fairytale Keeper* series. The idea came to me during a children's literature class. We were comparing fairy tales across cultures, and the professor said that nearly all cultures had a Cinderella story. If that's true, then either the real Cinderella lived hundreds, or thousands, of years ago, or there is just something so compelling about such a story that most cultures created their own. What my story presupposes is maybe all of Grimm's fairy tales are based on a real person, and I posit that that person is the real Snow White.

All of the characters in this first installment of *The Fairytale Keeper* series are fictional with the exception of the archbishop. Konrad von Hochstaden served as Archbishop of Cologne from 1238 to 1261. Out of all of the archbishops of Cologne, Konrad is one of the most famous. He was an imposing political figure during his time and a dangerous man to cross, though that didn't keep the people of Cologne from refusing to recognize his authority as sovereign over their city.

Though I've found no evidence of a great fever in Cologne during this time, terrible illnesses ravaged many other cities during the Middle Ages. Bubonic plague hit Europe twice, once in the sixth century and again in the fourteenth. There is some debate about whether or not influenza existed before the sixteenth century, but illnesses called "fevers" afflicted European cities throughout history, killing many people.

The Cologne Cathedral was, in fact, burned to the ground in the thirteenth century, though my date is off by a few days for plot purposes. In the year 1200, the Sarcophagi of the Three Magi were brought there, and these relics made Cologne an important stop for pilgrims.

When I first started *The Fairytale Keeper* series, I envisioned Cologne as a small town with lots of farm land and a small market, but thirteenth century Cologne was a commercial city. Its location on the Rhine, and its position between well-traveled land routes, made it a prime location for trading. Flemish cloth, wine from the Moselle region, furs, leather, gold and copper works, armor, and weapons are just a few examples of goods exported from Cologne.

Reader's Guide Questions

1. Why do you think the author chose Snow White to be the voice of *The Fairytale Keeper*?

2. How do Grimm's' fairy tales differ from the fairy tales you were exposed to as a child? Do you think Grimm's fairy tales should be told to children? Why or why not?

3. Adelaide and Ansel paid a high price for Katrina's funeral and their revenge against Father Soren? What, if anything, do you think they would have done differently if given the chance? What would you have done in their situation?

4. Some characters in *The Fairytale Keeper* play different Grimm character roles. For example, Ansel is the father in the "Snow White" story, but also the shoemaker in "The Elves and The Shoemaker." What roles do you think the main characters may play in the upcoming installments in this series? Do you think Ivo will get cast in a role? Who do you think he will be?

5. Ivo says that it is sometimes our weaknesses that make us strong. What do you think he means by that? Can you find an example of a character with a weakness that brings them strength?

6. In what ways were people suffering from mental illnesses especially vulnerable during this tumultuous time? How does treatment of those with mental illness differ today than during the Middle Ages?

7. Archbishop Konrad Von Hochstaden was a real person living during this time period. Do you think it is fair for authors to fictionalize real people? Why or why not?

8. Adelaide seems to dislike Galadriel from the very beginning of the story. Why do you think this is? Do you think Galadriel deserves Adelaide's judgment or should Adelaide be more understanding?

9. Adelaide makes some questionable choices, such as sneaking into The Gilded Gopher and giving up Elias to the Archbishop. Are her actions justifiable or not? How do you think she feels about the choices she made?

10. Do you think Adelaide changed after being in the stocks? Why or why not?

11. The story ends with Adelaide, Ansel, and Galadriel boarding a carriage to leave Cologne, but that leaves major characters, like Ivo behind. Do you think they will really leave? Why or why not?

12. How does *The Fairytale Keeper* compare to historical fiction novels you have read? The novel has somewhat of a cliffhanger ending. Are you interested in reading the next book in the series? Why or why not?

Acknowledgements

- My amazing husband, Ken, who supports me as I follow my dreams and believes in them whole-heartedly even when I don't
- My mother, Nancy, for being my first reader, my best friend, giver of amazing advice, and provider of great books
- My father, Greg, for fostering and expecting greatness from his children
- My sister, Katie, for being the first person interested in this story
- Nana, Papaw, Meme, Aunt Donna, and Grampy for too many good things to list
- Ken, Lisa, Curt, and Katelyn for their interest, enthusiasm, and for being the world's greatest in-laws
- Matt B., Linda D., Gail S., Martha G., Mark C., Corrye V., Tammy S., Lindsay T., Stephen N., Jeff N., Shelleen T., Sherry S., Addie M., and Andrew B. for offering their generous time and support
- My niece Lydia, for thinking that I'm famous and trying to get every adult she knows to buy my books
- Selena, Nic, Xander, Kaydra, and Lydia for helping me be a kid again when I really need it
- Leslie W., Jeanne M., Bailey M., and Robin M., for giving me a sense of peace
- Quigley and Pretty Girl for their wagging tails, sloppy kisses, and hours of sitting by me as I typed away
- Aunt Karen who I know is with me and has something to do with these stories I write
- My Lord and Savior for giving me hope and solace when I need it

Made in the USA
Charleston, SC
21 June 2013